A Plain-Dealing Villain

Daniel Faust, Book Four

by Craig Schaefer

Craig Schaefer / Demimonde Books
2328 E. Lincoln Hwy, #238
New Lenox, IL 60451-9533
www.craigschaeferbooks.com

Cover Design by James T. Egan of Bookfly Design LLC.
Author Photo ©2014 by Karen Forsythe Photography
Craig Schaefer / A Plain-Dealing Villain — 1st ed.
ISBN 978-0-9903393-8-0

Prologue

The smiling man walked briskly along beds of golden dirt, past row after row of archaeologists working on hands and knees in the Bolivian heat. Twine roped off the dig site into a grid of dusty numbered squares where the researchers gently parted the earth with trowels, mesh screens, and camel-hair brushes. If anyone had glanced up as the man passed, they might have gotten a quick impression: white, early thirties, sandy hair, and stonewashed jeans.

Or, he knew, they might see a black man in his fifties, wearing faded overalls. Or an older Latina woman with her greying hair in braids. Either way, he'd just slide right off the skin of their minds. If anyone on the dig team was capable of looking at him—*really* looking at him—they'd think he was a cousin to the Cheshire Cat.

All they'd see was nothing but a smile and a shadow.

The Smile let himself into the dig foreman's tent, ducking under a heavy canvas flap. The tent sweltered under the midday sun, trapping the brutal heat inside and turning the stagnant air into a gluey haze. He sat down at a folding table and powered up his laptop. It was a bulky Toughbook, a brick of rugged black plastic built for harsh environments, with a satellite modem. A sloppy pile of worn-out tarot cards sat off to one side.

The Smile held out his shadowy hand and the cards leaped through the air, riffling into his palm. He shuffled overhand, slow and lazy, while he waited for the computer to connect.

The screen flickered into focus, giving him a panoramic view of a brightly lit boardroom. Eight men and women sat along a table made of rock, one slab of obsidian with its surface polished to a mirror sheen.

"—given the Dakota oil boom," a woman in a pinstripe suit was saying, "Operation Black Seed should move the entire region's index into the desired range while yielding at least fifteen million—"

She saw the others' heads turn and fell silent. Every face stared into the camera. A few looked guilty, like they'd gotten a bad report card and were just waiting for their parents to come home.

"Sir," a man toward the front of the table said. He tugged at the knot in his tie, eyes downcast. "There's been an incident. In Nevada."

The Smile said nothing.

"One of the Keepers," the woman said. "It's dead."

A man in the back of the room leaned forward. "We're still piecing everything together from the chatter out of Washington. Vigilant Lock has an asset on the ground in Nevada, an FBI agent named Harmony Black, and we're tapped into their communications. She's been spearheading a disinformation campaign, covering up the shitstorm that went down at the Enclave Resort."

"I heard about that on the radio," the Smile said. "What do we know?"

The man up front tugged on his tie like it was a noose around his throat. "I've emailed you a full write-up, but to make a long story short, the Keepers latched onto the CEO of the Carmichael-Sterling Group. She discovered an Eden Tendril in Nepal, twenty years ago. Most recently she joined forces with a remnant of Ausar Biomedical to try to...attune herself to the tendril."

"Perhaps I'm misremembering," the Smile said. "Didn't you assure me that Ausar Biomedical was, for all intents and purposes, obliterated? Did we not spend several million dollars currying government influence just to pull their teeth? Am I misremembering *any* of this, Mr. Brown?"

"That—that was a long time ago, sir. We can't be held accountable for—"

"Choose your next words *very* carefully."

Brown opted for silence instead. He sank down in his chair, still squeezing his tie knot.

"There's a bright side," the woman in the pinstripes said quickly. "These new developments uncovered a small treasure trove of data on Ausar's last activities, before they went into receivership twenty years ago. Now we know exactly where the other two tendrils are: Mexico and the Swiss Alps. We have latitude/longitude and satellite surveillance photos."

The Smile remained silent.

"The other Keeper is in Detroit," the man in the back said, "with two of the original Ausar scientists. We've got a kill team on the ground, and they're ready to move in as soon as you give the word—"

"No. Keep them under surveillance, but let it play out. Let's see what happens." The Smile slowly shuffled his tarot cards. "So. Someone did our work for us, taking down a Keeper. Excuse me—they did *your* work for *you*. Who and how?"

A pudgy man with a comb-over and a nervous twitch in one eyebrow raised his hand. "I—I have that, sir. Um, street mage named Daniel Faust. Small time con artist and thief. He's a nobody."

The Smile idly tossed a trio of cards down on the table. The Fool. The Magician. The Tower. He scooped them up and shuffled them back into the deck.

"Las Vegas has a sizable occult footprint," the man in the back said. "Insular community, mostly petty criminals. They've got a détente with the corporate powers that be: they don't mess with the casinos, and in return, the casinos don't red-book them."

"Red book?" the woman in pinstripes asked.

"The black book is for cheats and hustlers. Means you don't get to play in Vegas anymore. The red book's the one the public doesn't know about. That's for cheats and hustlers who use magic. Penalty's a little higher. I hear they're fond of psychic lobotomies."

"So," the woman said, "minimal blowback if we have Faust eliminated. This entire situation is a deviation from the script. I think we should terminate everyone who was involved to tie up any loose ends."

The Smile tossed down another three cards. The Fool. The Magician. The Tower. This time, the image on the third card didn't depict a crumbling medieval spire; now it was a sleek monolith of black glass and chrome rising over a sea of neon lights.

"I have a better idea," he told them. "We still have our eyes on the Knife?"

The man with the comb-over nodded quickly. "Y-yes, sir. It's in Chicago. We can send a retrieval team—"

"Lure Faust to it," the Smile said. "Let's pull a few strings and push him into the path of the Year King. I think the two of them should meet. Worst-case scenario? Daniel Faust dies. Best-case scenario? He serves us, and then he dies. Either way...well, we'll have a little fun, won't we? Also, dispatch teams to permanently seal the Eden Tendrils in Nepal and the Swiss Alps."

"And the one in Mexico?" the woman in pinstripes asked.

"I might want it later. Buy up the land it's on and the twenty acres around it in every direction. Post a permanent guard."

"Satellite scans show a small village within that radius."

"Shame," the Smile said. "The drug cartels are just getting bolder and bolder these days, aren't they, Ms. Green? I hear they've been known to massacre entire villages as reprisal for some imagined slight."

Green nodded sharply. "Understood, sir. We'll deploy our usual fixers."

"Very good. Dismissed. And someone please send me a complete dossier on this Daniel Faust person. I think we might be able to find him a part in our little drama."

1.

A pale yellow moon hung over East Las Vegas. I slouched in the passenger seat of a stolen bakery van. The light from a Chinese restaurant sign washed the empty street in yellow neon. We'd grabbed the van right out of the bakery lot, five blocks away. We'd have it back before morning, and the owners would never know it was gone.

That assumed, of course, that the job went according to plan. I'd had a bad feeling all night, closing on my shoulder like a bouncer's hand telling me it was time to go home. The kid drumming his fingers on the steering wheel to the beat in his head wasn't helping. He was nineteen going on twelve, too damn eager and too damn green.

"Hey," he said, looking my way. "You got a piece, man?"

I arched an eyebrow at him.

"'Cause I don't," he said, "and one of us oughta be strapped. You know, in case of trouble."

I leaned my head back against the cheap vinyl headrest and called out, "Coop?"

I heard rummaging sounds. From the back of the van, a willowy southerner with a bleach-blond goatee poked his head up.

"Yeah, Dan?"

"Tell your nephew why we don't carry guns on a B&E."

Coop sighed and dusted off his hands on his faded jeans. "Burglary gets you one to ten, and they go easy if it's your first ride. If you're carrying a piece? Then it's two to fifteen years and no leniency. Don't matter if you use it or not."

Coop was going to owe me for this. I'd brought him in for a cut of the action because I needed a safe cracked, and he was the best boxman on the West Coast. He'd never met a slab of steel he couldn't punch, burn, or melt his way through. Then he asked me to bring his dipshit nephew Augie along as a wheelman.

"He's looking to get into the game," Coop had told me over a couple of Jack and Cokes. "His old man's bunking up at the Ely State pen for the foreseeable future, so he's no use, and the kid's just gonna end up sharing a cell with him if he goes it alone. He needs to learn how to do things the right way."

I didn't like it. Then he told me the kid would only take a five percent cut of the score. Apprentice wages. I still didn't like it, but I could only handle so much of Coop's puppy-dog eyes. Besides, I owed a wad of cash to Winslow, a gunrunner friend of a friend who helped me out of a jam a little while back. It's never good to owe money to a guy with a cellar full of military hardware. Especially not when he rides with an outlaw biker gang.

I took a deep breath and tried to sound more patient than I felt as I explained Crime 101 to the kid. "Guns escalate things. They're only good for crowd control. We're going in after closing hours, so we don't *need* crowd control."

"Yeah," Augie said, "but what about security? What if they start bustin' caps?"

Bustin' caps. I wondered how many hip-hop posters he had on his bedroom wall.

"Site's handled by Gold Star Security Northwest," I explained. "They don't carry guns, just Tasers and pepper spray. They also make thirteen bucks an hour, and heroics are highly discouraged in their training manual. Their standing orders in case of a burglary are to retreat to safe ground and call the real cops. That gives us plenty of time to bug out if we get spotted and blow it."

"Cool," Augie said. Then he scrunched up his face like he

was doing calculus in his head. "Wait. How do you know all that stuff?"

"It's called research. What I've been doing every single night for the last week like it's my full-time job. I know shift schedules, head counts, and guard timing. The manager, he works late two nights out of five, but there's no way to predict which ones. What I do know is his home address, the names of his wife and their two little girls, and what their bedroom windows look like. If he's there, he'll cooperate, and we won't need a gun to make him do it. Just words."

"Cool," Augie said, his head bobbing like a puppet. I stared out at the street. We had five minutes until the shift change opened our window of opportunity.

I was rusty. I didn't like being rusty. I'd been a little busy these last couple of months, dealing with a mad sorceress and her scheme to take over the world.

I had a strange life.

Bottom line: Lauren Carmichael and all her followers were six feet underground, and that whole ugly mess was in the rearview mirror. The wounds still felt fresh, especially in the still hours of the night, but that just meant it was time to get my life back on track. Nothing in my wallet but a Canadian penny and a couple of moths. This job was supposed to turn things around for me.

Supposed to.

I dug into the pocket of my slacks and fished out my lockpicks, nestled in a forest green oilskin case.

"Here." I handed the case to Augie. "Hold on to these for me."

"What's up?"

The empty street was trying to tell me something. I needed to listen.

"Just stay here," I said. "I want to check something out. I'll be right back."

The target was one block over and one block up. The corrugated plastic sign for the Laramie Brothers Tool & Die Company hung on a wire fence that ringed a small parking lot. The building had seen better days; cracks ran through the frosted glass windows and chips marred the red brick façade, worn down by time and neglect.

I strolled down the sidewalk on the other side of the street, hands in my pockets, keeping it casual. That was what it looked like, anyway. I didn't spend years working for Nicky Agnelli's gang, earning my place at the right hand of Vegas's biggest racket boss, just because I knew how to pick a lock.

I brought a little something extra to the table.

I took a deep breath and stretched out my senses, far beyond the confines of my flesh. Tendrils of psychic energy, luminous purple in my second sight, snaked out and licked the night air. I felt for dissonant rhythms, stray thoughts, dark intentions. I got nothing but empty cars and boarded-up buildings. A stray wind kicked a crumpled hamburger wrapper down the street.

Spend enough time living on the wrong side of the law, magic powers or not, you grow a sixth sense for when things are about to go sideways. Think of it as Darwinism for criminals. You learn when to walk away, you stay in the game for another night. You don't, well...the prisons are filled with guys who didn't spot a setup until they were being hauled off in handcuffs.

I couldn't find anything wrong, but that didn't mean nothing *was* wrong. I'd only ignored that bad feeling in the back of my brain a couple of times before, and I'd always paid a price for it. I walked across the street, toward the company parking lot.

The cars parked along the curb were as low-rent as the neighborhood. Used, rusted, dents patched with Bondo. The van at the end of the block almost fit in. Almost. Tires were brand new, high-end Pirellis with sturdy treads. Then there was the problem with the lights inside the building: I didn't see any. I'd run surveillance for the last five nights, and I could always catch the swing of a watchman's flashlight on the opposite side of the frosted glass, but not tonight.

I stood at the lip of the parking lot and glanced over my shoulder, just in time to see a curtain flutter behind a second-floor window in the apartment building across the street.

I pulled out my burner, a cheap Nokia flip phone with an hour of prepaid time. I'd only need five seconds. Coop picked up on the first ring.

"I'm calling it." I strode away from the fence, heading back across the street. "Scrub everything and get out."

Sometimes I hate being right. The sudden glare of high beams blinded me as a sedan screeched around the corner and slammed to a stop, pinning me in its headlights. Another car, a Metro cruiser with its light bar strobing, pincered in from the other side and painted me in blue and red.

"Leave the van. Get out. *Go*," I hissed. I dropped the phone to the pavement and stomped on it as I raised my open hands and offered up a big, cheerful smile. Car doors swung open and suits jumped out, their guns hard shadows in the piercing light.

"Step back," a woman's familiar voice barked. "Step back and away from the phone. Hands where we can see them."

Harmony Black. I should have known. She was a full-figured blonde, a little on the short side, wearing an eggplant-purple necktie, wire-rimmed glasses, and a silver bracelet that dripped with magical energy. A small retinue of feds followed her into the headlights, and she snapped her fingers at one of them, pointing to the pavement.

"Bag that. See if you can get anything off the SIM card."

Good luck. We'd bought the burners just for this job and paid in cash. If my shoe hadn't cracked the card, all they'd get from it were the numbers of two other anonymous phones. Phones that, right about now, would be wiped for prints and finding their new home at the bottom of a trash can. I didn't break the phone to cover my tracks; I broke it to make it look like there were tracks to find.

"Well hello, Officer," I said. "Lovely evening, isn't it?"

"Special Agent," she corrected me. Then she gestured to somebody standing at my shoulder. "Cuff him."

Rough hands grabbed my arms and wrenched them behind my back. The steel bracelets clicked tight around my wrists, cool and hard. A cop from Metro patted me down. He gave Harmony a shrug when he came up empty.

"You know," I said, "if you wanted to see me, you didn't have to go to all this trouble. We could have a couple of drinks, get to know each other better..."

She got up close and personal. Her stare could have burned a hole right through me.

"Meadow Brand. Where is she?"

I blinked. "I thought she was with you. You mean she didn't show up for her hearing? Wow, that's really surprising. She seemed so trustworthy."

"I have *had* it with you, Faust. You blew it tonight. And now you're going down."

"Sorry," I said, "never on the first date, not unless you pay for dinner. And you have to take me someplace real nice."

Harmony took a step back and looked at me like I was something she'd found stuck to the bottom of her shoe. She turned to the cop at my shoulder.

"Get him out of my sight. The rest of you, listen up! He wasn't working alone. I want you to canvass three blocks in every direction. If someone looks the slightest bit wrong, run them in and—"

The cop shoved me into the back of his cruiser and slammed the door. I wasn't worried about my partners. I knew Coop was busy teaching his nephew one of the most important survival skills in the book: how to make a clean getaway.

As for me, I'd have to find my own way home.

2.

Harmony let me stew for a while, leaving me alone in an interrogation room. The walls were cinder blocks painted pea-soup green. Bolts held a dented steel table firmly to the floor, and a big one-way mirror showed off the bored look on my face. I got up and paced for a while. Then I jogged little laps around the table. I was checking my teeth in the mirror when the door finally rattled open and Harmony walked in.

"Sit," she said.

I sat. Harmony strolled over to the security camera in the corner of the room, reached up, and unplugged it from the wall. Then she took the chair across from me and slapped a thick folder on the table.

"You used me," she said.

"Perish the thought."

"That whole act. Getting Meadow Brand in here, her confession, the whole thing was a con, wasn't it?"

I leaned back. "Hardly. You saved about a hundred hostages, didn't you? I don't see what you've got to complain about."

"I told you, Faust. I told you I wanted Lauren Carmichael. She should have gone on trial for what she did."

"And I'm telling *you*," I said, "you never would have taken her alive."

The last time Harmony had seen Lauren, she was a refined and graying captain of industry. The last time I saw Lauren, she was a twisted monster on the verge of becoming a goddess, mainlining drugs from another dimension and sprouting alien plants from her skin. Not the sort of thing you can explain down in central booking.

"So you murdered her," Harmony said flatly.

"I didn't say that. I wasn't even there. If you could prove I was, you'd have arrested me for it already."

"Right," she said slowly, opening her folder and leafing through a stack of photographs. "Witnesses did see a yellow Bell 407 taking off from the roof of the Enclave. A Bell 407 like the one at Sapphire Skytours. A business owned—and I'm sure this is a sheer coincidence—by Nicky Agnelli."

"Because there's only *one* helicopter-tour company in Las Vegas, right? And Bells are such rare models. Now, I'm going to go out on a limb here and bet that his flight logs are spotless. But you already know that, because you already checked."

"You're still working for him." The way she said it, it wasn't a question.

I slapped my hand on the metal table. "Will you let that go? Damn it, I *do not work for Nicky Agnelli*. We went our separate ways, and that's that."

"All right. Let's try a different name. Meadow Brand."

"Your guess is as good as mine."

Harmony took a deep breath. She raised her hand and pointed at the dead camera in the corner, the plug dangling from its gray plastic shell. The bracelet on her wrist sparkled in my second sight, reminding me that she knew exactly what I was and what kind of world we both lived in.

"Faust. It's just us here. No recordings, no witnesses. Right now I've got agents hunting Meadow Brand from here to Miami since she dropped off the radar. You asked me to trust you when you brought her in. I did. Now I'm asking you for one honest answer. Just one. Are my men wasting their time?"

I looked her in the eye and thought about Meadow's vulture-picked bones, bleaching out in the desert sun.

"Bring 'em home," I said.

Harmony shook her head slowly. "You son of a bitch. That whole charade. I never had a *chance* of closing the Carmichael case."

"You want me to say it?" I asked her, heating up. "I used you, yeah. There were hostages in that building with mercenaries pointing guns to their heads. *You* wouldn't have been able to capture Lauren, and *I* couldn't save those people myself. So yes. I lied to you. I lied to you so that a hundred people could survive the night. Are you really gonna tell me you're *mad* about that?"

Harmony slumped in her chair. She looked tired. The harsh fluorescent light over our heads showed the tiny crow's-feet at the corners of her eyes.

"So you used my raid as cover, you murdered Carmichael, and then you murdered Brand."

"You said that, not me. But let's say somebody did happen to put Meadow down like the rabid dog she was. So. Fucking. What?"

"My job is to uphold the law—"

"Which is why you need people like me," I said, "because the law isn't equipped to *deal* with people like her. I am. You know what the world is like. You've touched magic. You've seen a demon in the flesh. When you fight, though, that badge means you've gotta keep your gloves on. I don't. I use brass knuckles."

Harmony stood up. She turned her back to me, taking a long look into the mirror. I could see her weariness in the reflection of her eyes.

"The magic," she said, "runs in my family's blood. I learned from my mother. She learned from hers. I was a little girl when the spark woke up inside me. I remember...five years old, standing on a stool at the counter next to my mom, learning how to bundle herbs and make a healing poppet. Kitchen witchcraft. Kid stuff. Even then, I knew one thing."

She turned to face me. The tired look was gone, replaced by icy steel.

"My family calls it 'the gift,' but it's not a gift at all. It's a responsibility. The world is full of monsters, and most of them hide behind human faces. Monsters who prey on the weak and the innocent. I wear a badge because that's the best way to use what I've been given, to shine a little light and send the roaches scurrying."

I tried to look nonchalant, but I couldn't shake the tension in my chest, the fight-or-fight reflex poking its head up. I felt like I'd walked into a lioness's den and I was the only food for miles.

"Then I see someone like you," she said. "You've got the gift, just like me, but what do you do with it? You steal. You swindle. You kill. You know what I think, Faust? You're *worse* than Meadow Brand. She was a psychopath. You *could* be a better man. You just *aren't*."

I rested my palms flat against the cold steel table and leaned forward. The tension faded fast, and anger flooded in to fill the empty spaces in my heart. Just like it always did. My faithful companion.

"We're just going to pretend I didn't help save people's lives, is that it? Is that how we're playing this?"

"Right," she said. "Daniel Faust, the knight in tarnished armor. Is that the lie you tell yourself, so you can sleep at night? Pretending you're not a selfish, hungry void of *nothing* that corrupts everything he touches. Everything you did was a means to an end: murdering Lauren Carmichael, so you could satisfy your little vendetta. Look me in the eye. Look me in the eye and tell me I'm wrong. You wouldn't have given two shits about those people if helping them hadn't gotten you closer to killing Lauren, and you know it."

I slammed my fist on the table and shot to my feet, knocking my chair back. It clattered to the concrete floor as I roared, "*She needed killing!*"

I froze. My fingernails dug into my palms. Harmony just stood there. She looked anything but impressed.

"We're done," she said softly. "This little song and dance is over. I can't hang anything on you *yet*, but I can keep you off the street while I look for evidence. Tonight made sure of that."

"You can't be serious," I said. "You've got nothing."

"I've got you attempting a burglary at the Laramie Brothers Tool and Die Company. I've also got a judge who owes me a favor, and he'll make damn sure you're treated as a high flight risk. You're headed for a cell, and by the time you get out I'll have a laundry list of *serious* charges waiting for you. Daniel Faust, you are under—"

The door swung open, and a man wearing a sharkskin suit and a thousand-dollar smile swept into the interrogation room.

"I wouldn't do that," he said, wagging his finger at her. "Finishing that sentence could be hazardous to your career's health. You're in enough trouble as it is."

When Harmony Black and her task force came to town, my girlfriend promised she'd find the best lawyer around. That was Perkins. He was so slick he didn't have fingerprints—literally—and I'd gotten the impression he'd been practicing law for a very long time. As in centuries.

"And you are?" Harmony said.

He snapped his fingers, producing a crisp white business card out of nowhere.

"Perkins, J.T. Perkins, and I'm here to represent the man *you* have been busy persecuting. Tell me, is it routine FBI procedure to interrogate a suspect without his lawyer present?"

"He consented." She narrowed her eyes.

"Let's see if I have this straight. You initially targeted Mr. Faust under the mistaken and entirely unfounded belief that he's a member of the Agnelli crime syndicate. A belief you have yet to provide a shred of proof for. Now you've brought him in for a burglary that, unless I'm mistaken, didn't actually take place."

"He was in the process of breaking into the building," she said. "We caught him in the act."

Somehow, his smile grew even broader.

"Really? He was in the building? Was he even in the *parking lot*? One of your colleagues says he wasn't."

"How did you—"

"Did my client have any burglary tools in his possession? Lockpicks? A crowbar hidden up his sleeve, perhaps?"

"No, but—"

"So he had no way of accessing the property he was supposedly there to burglarize, and he wasn't even apprehended on said property. Very disappointing, Agent Black. A rookie police officer on his first beat wouldn't make that arrest, and you know it. Your zeal to imprison my client speaks to the prejudicial nature of your so-called 'task force.' This isn't a lawful inquiry; it's a witch hunt."

I could almost hear Harmony's teeth grating.

"You have two choices." Perkins ticked them off on his fingers. "One, release my client at once, and we can pretend this never happened. Two, you can proceed with this travesty, I'll have the case dismissed before you can say 'wrongful arrest,' and my next call will be to your deputy assistant director to discuss a lawsuit against you, her, and the entire Federal Bureau of Investigation."

Harmony leaned against the table with one hand. Her shoulders sagged.

"You want him?" she said. "Fine. Take him and leave."

Perkins opened the door, ushering me toward it with a grand sweep of his arm like he was rolling out a red carpet.

"Faust," she said, "one last thing."

I stopped and looked back at Harmony. Her body language said defeat, but the fire in her eyes told a whole different story. The lioness was still in there. Hungry. Pacing. Ready to break loose.

"Tonight was just an appetizer," she said. "If you even think about pulling another heist, I'll be there. If you rob a bank, I'll be in the vault waiting for you. If you so much as shoplift a candy bar, I'll be standing right behind you in the convenience store. Remember this room, because you *will* be back here. Soon."

“Admission of the intent to harass my client,” Perkins said archly.

“Go fuck yourself,” Harmony told him. Then she swung her gaze back my way. “You want to fight with brass knuckles, Faust? Fine. I’ve got a pair of my own. I’ve seen all your little tricks, all your fancy moves. You’ve got nothing left. But as for me? I haven’t even broken a sweat.”

Perkins steered me out of the room, double-time, but I couldn’t shake the fear that turned my palms clammy.

I was afraid she might be right.

3.

Perkins had a present for me: my keys, my wallet and my personal phone, all the things I'd left in his hands for safe keeping while I tried – and failed – to make a little cash that night. He's a full-service lawyer. I had a text waiting on my phone. *Meet me at the usual place*, it read. *Have something for you.*

Perkins leaned over my shoulder, not bothering to be subtle as he read the screen. A cool night wind ruffled my hair. He clicked his tongue and shook his head.

"Communications from Nicky Agnelli? As your attorney, I advise keeping your distance. Why, unlike yourself, that man's a notorious criminal. Allegedly, of course."

More than a criminal, Nicky was the biggest racket boss in Las Vegas. The feds and the corporate-owned casinos might have chased the old mob out of town decades ago, but there was still plenty of crime to go around, and Nicky had his claws in almost all of it.

I used to work for Nicky as his "hired wand," greasing the wheels and helping his crews out with a little black magic. Then things went south in the worst way, and I cut ties. Later he tried to hire me back. When I said no, he tossed me to a pack of feral halfblood demons. Not long after that, he helped take down Lauren Carmichael, saving the world in the process.

What I'm saying is Nicky and I had a complicated relationship.

"Whatever he's got for me," I told Perkins, "I'm pretty sure I don't want it. Just like I'm pretty sure I'd better go find out what it is."

"Have it your way, but remember: the attorney-client bond is a partnership. *I* can't help you if *you* don't help you."

"Thanks. Any other advice?"

Perkins looked up at the sky and took a deep breath. The air glowed from the lights of the Strip, and a great white beam shot straight up over the city to brush its finger against the face of the moon.

"Yes," he said. "Leave town. Mr. Agnelli is the target Agent Black's task force is here to snare. You're the target she *wants*. It's personal now. May I suggest Bora Bora? It's quite nice this time of year. Waterfront cabanas, coconut drinks..."

Sure, I thought. *I can just blow town and fly overseas with all the money I don't have.*

Winslow and his biker buddies weren't going to let me skate on my debt much longer. Didn't help that a run-in with a pack of fanatics called the Redemption Choir had left me homeless, with my best gear, my occult textbooks, and a cash-stuffed mattress all gone in the flash of a Molotov cocktail.

Perkins was right. Any thief worthy of the name knew when it was time to lie low and let the heat simmer down. Before I could do that, though, I needed operating capital.

Like it or not, I needed a fast score. And I was going to have to pull it off right under Agent Black's nose.

* * *

The Gentlemen's Bet was a dive strip club in a part of town where the tourists didn't go. Not the smart ones, anyway. They were closing up by the time a taxi dropped me off in the parking lot, pushing out the last drunken stragglers as dawn lurked at the edge of the city.

I'm getting too old to pull an all-nighter, I thought, rubbing my eyes and handing the cabbie a folded twenty. Working past three in the morning was fine when I had a heist and an interrogation to keep my adrenaline pumping, but the slow ride across the city gave my body plenty of time to realize how long I'd been running without a break. I trudged up the "red carpet"—a runner of Astroturf spray-painted scarlet—and the bald, burly bouncer out front gave me a nod before pushing open the door. Closing time or not, I was always on the list here.

The mirrored stage stood empty, the speakers dead quiet, with only the hum of a vacuum cleaner pushed by a bored-looking janitor to break the silence. I made my way over to the bar, where Nicky's bartender—a frizzy-haired woman in her late forties with hard eyes and stale cigarettes on her breath—was going through the motions of wiping everything down. She looked as tired as I felt.

"Nicky free?" I asked, jerking a thumb toward the back hallway.

"Not yet. He's got another guest. Said I should have you wait here. Want a drink?"

I shrugged. "Don't want to put you out. Looks like you're ready to head home."

"You sure?" Something glinted behind her eyes, a little spark of mischief. "Nicky's buying."

Nicky's people were loyal—they were too scared not to be—but that didn't mean they wouldn't tweak his nose if they got the chance. I knew the feeling.

"In that case, Crown and Coke. Pour one for yourself, too."

"Now you're talking," she said. She didn't get a chance to serve it up, though; the door at the end of the hall rattled and swung open. Out came Nicky Agnelli, hair greased back, dressed in a Hugo Boss suit and rimless Porsche Design titanium glasses, looking like a Hollywood producer. I didn't recognize the man with him, but that didn't stop the back of my neck from prickling.

He was unassuming, a short Indian man in a black suit and blood-red tie, but a vortex of power that shone like emeralds in my second sight swirled around him. He wasn't a demon or a half-blood cambion like Nicky for that matter. Demons felt like barbed wire and black diamonds when my psychic tendrils brushed past them. His essence was all jungles, fertile black peat, and charred meat roasting on an open fire. Symbols and textures and emotions rushed through my mind like I was riffling through a deck of cards, taking his measure.

He wasn't human, I knew that for certain, and I'd only sensed a creature like this once before.

Naavarasi.

At first I thought it *was* her. The rakshasi hunger spirit was an adept shape-shifter, as she'd been all too happy to demonstrate in the past. Then I realized the man's aura was subtly different, like a set of fingerprints that didn't quite match.

So, I thought, *she isn't the last of her kind after all. Great. One was bad enough.*

Juliette and Justine, Nicky's twin bodyguards and personal mayhem squad, filed out behind them. Their usual relentless bubbly glee was gone, replaced by grave silence and unblinking stares. They were scary when they were manic. This was worse.

"So please, give Mr. Mancuso my regards and my thanks," Nicky told the man, "but we're doing just fine out here. You let him know I said that, okay?"

He held out his hand. The Indian just gave him a stone-eyed glare. "A pleasure meeting you," he replied, but his tone made it sound like a death threat.

He walked past me, trailing power in his wake. For a moment, our eyes met. I could feel him reading me, brushing up against my psychic walls like I'd done to him, but his face was a blank slate. He left without another word.

"Follow his ass," Nicky snapped at Juliette and Justine, his voice low and hard. "Don't let him out of your sight for a second, and make sure he gets on the next plane out of town. If he tries anything funny, leave him dead in a fucking ditch."

The twins stalked off, silent. Nicky turned to me and put on a big, friendly smile. I almost believed it.

"New friend?" I asked.

He waved his hand, playing it off. "Liquor distributor. Club business, no big deal. C'mon in back."

I followed him into his office. Between the cigarette-burned carpet, the cheap wood paneling, and the car calendar two years out of date, you'd never guess half the dirty business in Vegas was cooked up in that very room. Nicky dropped into the tall-backed chair behind his desk and gestured for me to take a seat.

"Club business, huh?" I said.

"Forget about it." His gaze flicked away for one guilty second. "So how's tricks? Hey, how's Jennifer doing?"

I sat down and tried not to roll my eyes at him.

"Really? That's your lead-in? Real subtle, Nicky."

"Then you know why I'm asking."

"Maybe yes, maybe no." I shrugged. "Why don't you tell me?"

"The envelope was light this month, Dan."

Jennifer was family. Not blood, but blood didn't matter to people like us. She was my sister where it counted. She was also one of the last members of Vegas's occult underground still doing business with Nicky Agnelli. She didn't have much of a choice, given that she was running her little narcotics empire on his turf.

I figured he was going to ask me about her new deal with the Cinco Calles gang or the tenement by the airport she'd turned into an urban fortress. Apparently he didn't know about that. Small favors.

"The envelope," I repeated flatly, playing dumb.

"Look." He rested his palms flat on his desk. "She knows the deal. She operates in my city, I get to dip my beak. Just a little. You know me, I'm not a demanding guy, but I do insist on dipping my beak. That's not unreasonable."

"She pays you for protection, Nicky. Given Harmony Black is doing her best Elliot Ness impression and rattling cages all over town, I'm thinking Jennifer doesn't feel too safe right now."

"I'm *handling* it."

"Says you." I crossed my arms. "But seeing as Black just busted up my score and hauled me into an interrogation room, call me a skeptic."

"Hey, you're the one who pissed her off, not me. I'm her job. You're her hobby. Know what the difference is? People *care* about their hobbies."

I hated to admit it, but he had a point.

"Was the envelope light?" I asked. "Or was it empty?"

"Light. By one G."

"You have to try and see it her way. As far as you're concerned, your cut is something you're entitled to. As far as she's concerned, she's paying you for a service you aren't rendering. She's making a point. If the envelope was empty, that'd be a whole different deal."

"I can't let anyone short me, Dan. I can't have it. You know how many people in this town pay out to me? You know what would happen if they found out I let Jennifer get away with this?"

"Which is why," I said, unfolding my arms, "I guarantee she hasn't said a word to anyone about it. You need to make things right with her. That's what she's telling you."

Nicky scowled. The whites of his eyes swirled behind his glasses, turning runny-egg yellow as the stress brought his demon blood to the surface. Faint red veins like bloody spiderwebs pulsed under his temples.

"*She* needs to get right with *me*. I'm the general. She's a goddamn soldier."

"She's more than that, and you know it." I leaned forward and rapped my index finger on his desk. "Meet her halfway, Nicky, that's all I'm saying. You want my advice, there it is. Don't get pissed if it isn't what you wanted to hear. You want a yes-man, go hire one."

He leaned back and pressed the heels of his hands to his eyes, taking a deep breath. His thin lips twitched, silently counting to ten. When he lowered his hands, his face was back to normal, human disguise firmly in place.

"Yeah. Yeah, okay. See, that's why I like you, Danny. You never bullshit me."

Wish I could say the same about you, I thought, but I kept my poker face on.

"That why you called me out here?" I asked.

"Nah, that's side business. I hear you're looking for a job."

I tried to unclench my jaw. Nicky knew exactly how hard up for cash I was, and he loved nothing more than bending me over a barrel.

"I'm freelancing now, Nicky. You and me, we've got a truce, but that's all we've got. Especially while Agent Black is dogging both our footsteps. I shouldn't even be in the same area code as you until this all blows over."

He waved his hand like he was shooing away a fly. "I'm strictly a middleman on this. Nothing that'll connect you to me or give the feds anything to chew on. You think I *want* them to get any dirt on you? We know each other's secrets, Danny. I need you quiet, just like you need me quiet."

"I'm listening."

He smiled like he had me right where he wanted me. I suppose he did.

"Forget this nickel-and-dime stuff. I've got a line on a score that requires a man of your talents. A *real* score."

4.

Nicky got up and wandered over to his wet bar. He held up a bottle of Canadian Club and a glass, giving me a questioning look. I nodded.

"The name Cameron Drake ring a bell?" he asked.

"Don't know him."

He poured three fingers of whiskey and slid the glass across the desk to me. "Guy was a nobody, a roofing contractor or something. Then about a year ago, he bought a lottery ticket on his way home from work. Won the Powerball. Forty million bucks, and he took it all in a lump sum instead of spreading it out. Paid out the ass in taxes, but he just couldn't wait to get his shopping spree underway."

"Fool and his money. Drake's the mark?"

"Drake's the client," Nicky said, pouring himself a glass and sitting back down. "He's got a taste for more than Italian cars and fifty-foot yachts. He's a collector. And the stuff he's been collecting lately, well, it's the sort of thing your crowd is into."

I sipped from my glass. The whiskey burned its way down my throat, just like it should, and spread a little cloud of warmth in my stomach.

"And how do you come into the picture?"

"He came out to Vegas a few months back, looking to party like a rock star. I hooked him up with some grade-A blow and a couple of former Penthouse pets. I've been on his speed dial ever since, whenever he needs something...exotic."

I turned my hand slowly, watching the amber liquor roll against the sides of the glass.

"How exotic are we talking?"

"I don't know." Nicky shrugged. "All I know is the score's locked up inside a hard target. Security's part physical, part occult, and he needs a pro with a foot in both worlds. Naturally, I thought of you."

"Naturally. And what do you get out of the deal?"

"Matchmaker's fee, that's all. Three percent of your cut."

I could live with three percent, but I wasn't sure I could live with doing business with Nicky again. We'd burned too many bridges between us.

"I'll think about it," I said.

"C'mon, just meet with the guy. Hear him out, see what he's offering. The job's not in Vegas, I know that much, which means you'll be out from under the feds for a little while."

I didn't let my temptation show. Instead I tossed back the rest of my drink and slapped the empty glass down on his desk.

"Said I'd think about it," I pushed my chair back.

"Yeah, well don't think too long. You're not a unique and beautiful snowflake, Faust. There *are* other guys who can do this kinda work."

"I'll call you," I said and saw myself out.

Nicky was up to something. His "liquor distributor" guest looked like a storm cloud of trouble just waiting to rain, and there were only two reasons for the twins to be more than ten feet away from Nicky: somebody was about to get hurt, or somebody was about to get dead. I tried to tell myself none of this had anything to do with me or mine, but those were long odds.

Agent Black's little war on the underworld hadn't made a lot of arrests yet, but everybody saw the writing on the wall. Nicky was cleaning house. He'd already made an object lesson out of a disloyal lieutenant, bringing me out to an abandoned house in the sticks and making me watch while the twins tortured him to death. Nicky wanted the underworld to know he was still the King of Vegas, ready and willing to fight for the throne.

We know each other's secrets, he'd said. *I need you quiet, just like you need me quiet.*

The idea of leaving town for a few days looked more and more attractive.

* * *

Sheets of gray satin swirled around me, and the weight of the comforter pressed me against the supple mattress. Warmth and pleasure beckoned me down into sleep, weighing my eyelids despite the spreading glow of sunrise behind the venetian blinds.

The pale woman in my arms wriggled back against my chest. The faint scent of musk perfume clung to her scarlet hair. I held her close, our naked bodies breathing in unison.

"This is nice," Caitlin whispered.

I held on to her for a while. Lying together like this, I could forget that anything existed outside her bedroom walls, forget the problems waiting for me right outside the door.

Most people wouldn't take solace in the arms of a demon, but I wasn't most people.

"How did it go last night?" she asked. The question I was dreading.

"Didn't," I said. "Harmony Black broke up the party. Don't worry, she didn't get anything she could use."

"She didn't *this* time, you mean. The woman has it in for you, Daniel. I think you should take a break. Go into hiding for a few weeks until things run their course."

"Can't do that. Winslow's already fixing to break my kneecaps over the cash I owe him. He's not going to wait much longer."

Caitlin rolled over, turning so we were nose-to-nose, sharing a feather pillow. She poked me in the chest with a sharp fingernail.

"I *have* money, you know," she said.

"I can't take your money. Not to pay a debt."

Four more fingers joined the first, nails pressing lightly over my heart.

"And why not?"

I tried to answer without seeing my father's face in my mind's eye. The old man sleeping in front of a television tuned to static, empty beer cans littering the stained carpet. Another six-pack in the fridge but not a damn thing to eat.

The first time I stole anything, I was eight years old, snatching food for me and my little brother.

"Because I need to know," I said, pushing away the memory. "I need to know that I can provide for myself."

Caitlin arched an eyebrow. "That's not all of it. What?"

"You know what I did when I worked for Nicky Agnelli. Helping his crews out, pulling down scores."

"Mm-hmm," she murmured, her nails digging into my chest a little harder.

"I was good. I was really good. Then, one night..." My voice trailed off.

It's strange, the things you remember. The ear-splitting klaxon of an alarm. The rotten smell of the blood from a buddy's gut wound, the way it made my hands slick and hot. The sound as he shrieked, biting down on a ballpoint pen, as I tried to shove his intestines back inside him.

"The intel was bad," I said, "and the whole thing went sideways in the blink of an eye. I brought a four-man crew on that job, two of 'em friends of mine, and I was the only one who got out alive. That was the end of working for Nicky Agnelli."

"Was it his fault?"

I looked up at the ceiling. I'd asked myself that question a thousand times. Usually around two in the morning, when the memories were the loudest.

"Doesn't matter whose fault it was," I said. "Point is it knocked me off my game. I floated around after that, pulling a few small grifts and selling vengeance for hire."

"Which is how you met me," Caitlin said, swinging up and straddling my waist. Her curls draped down, framing her face as she leaned in close. "So I'd best not hear any complaints."

I craned my neck to kiss her. Her lips tasted faintly of cherries.

"None. But then Lauren Carmichael and her cult came along. It feels like we spent so much time and energy fighting them—"

"Horseback riding," Caitlin said.

"Huh?"

"You were an accomplished horseman. Then you were knocked from the saddle, and you didn't get right back on again. Any teacher will tell you that's when the fear sets in. Making you wonder...can you still ride at all?"

I clasped my hands around her hips and looked up at her.

"You get it," I should have known she would.

She ran her fingers through my hair, grazing my scalp with her nails.

"Then ride, horseman." She brushed her lips against mine. "Find the reassurance you seek. But be swift. I'm going on a business trip in a few days, and I want to see you before I leave."

"Business trip? Where?"

"Home. My prince is having a celebration, and I've been asked to make a personal appearance. I won't be gone for long, just have to make a few courtesy calls, stand at his side and look imposing, that sort of thing. I'd invite you along, but...well, for *you*, that would be a one-way trip."

"Give my regards to your family," I said, half joking.

"Oh, I will. My sisters keep asking when they get to meet you."

I forced myself to chuckle, ignoring the chill in my spine. "What do you tell 'em?"

Caitlin flashed a toothy smile. "That depends entirely on you, pet. Do be careful out there."

* * *

I crashed in Caitlin's bed until noon and then myself up with a groan, staggering off to get cleaned up. She'd already headed out, leaving me a note on the bathroom sink written on a sheet of primly lined violet paper: "Hound business to attend to, call me later. Food in fridge. Don't eat out of the red Tupperware.—Cait."

While the twin heads in her shower pounded the soreness out

of my chest and back, clouds of steam clearing my head, I weighed my options. No matter how attractive the offer was, I didn't want to do business with Nicky. I'd find another way.

I wasn't lacking for choices either. All professional heisters carry a list in the back of their minds: places they've always wanted to hit, weak targets that look like a quick and easy payday, that sort of thing. Call it a thief's rainy-day stash, just waiting for the day we might need them.

Now felt like a good time.

An hour later I was cruising the streets of Vegas in my black Barracuda, fingers strumming the steering wheel in time with a Muddy Waters song. The sun rode high and kissed the dusty roads with a dry autumn heat. I followed the map of my memory, scouting my way across town, figuring out which of my old rainy-day scores were still good and which ones were busts.

Around three I found myself sitting in an outdoor cafe, nursing a paper cup of black coffee and pretending to read the *Vegas Sun*. The currency exchange across the street had my real attention, that and the two chuckleheads in tan uniforms who were taking their sweet time loading the armored car out front.

With that fence it's a total blind approach to the back door, I thought. *Anyone could be hiding around that corner. Guards don't care. They've run this route a thousand times for a thousand days; they can't manage to stay alert. Company should mix up their shifts better—*

"It's embarrassing, isn't it?" Harmony Black dropped into the chair beside me. She set down a cup of coffee and ruffled her own copy of the newspaper. "No operational discipline, not looking out for each other, it's almost like they *want* to get hijacked."

"Agent." My throat went tight.

"Don't mind me," she said. "I'm just getting some fresh air. Please, keep planning your armed robbery. Pretend I'm not even here."

She set down her paper and picked up her cup. Then she looked me in the eye and slowly, loudly, slurped her coffee.

I folded my newspaper and pushed back my chair. "It's fine. I was just leaving."

"Oh? Where to? The Athens Credit Union? That laundromat off Bonanza Road? The Ford dealership on Fairfax? Can I come with? No, never mind, just go ahead and I'll meet you there."

I gritted my teeth and walked away.

Harmony slurped her coffee again and gave me a finger wave. "See you soon!" she called out behind me.

I drove two blocks, pulled off to the side of the road, and took out my cell phone. Every instinct screamed that I was making a bad move, but that didn't stop me from punching in the numbers and making the call.

"Nicky," I said, "that job still available?"

5.

Nicky gave me a phone number. It rang through to voicemail. There was no message on the other end, just a few seconds of silence and a beep.

"This is Daniel Faust," I said. "Nicky Agnelli referred me, said you might have some work you need done. Call me."

My phone rang less than a minute later. A woman with a crisp British accent rattled off instructions before I could get a word out.

"Proceed to Henderson Executive Airport. It's just off St. Rose Parkway. Hangar four. Your flight leaves in thirty-two minutes. Be prompt."

"But what is—" The line went dead. I shrugged and threw the Barracuda into drive. I didn't have long, not with afternoon traffic clogging up the highway, and something told me this was a one-time offer.

Most of the tourist traffic came in and out of Vegas through McCarran International. Henderson Executive was for a better heeled crowd, mostly high-rolling whales and corporate bigwigs winging into town on their company jets for a weekend of expense-account-approved wining and dining. I had four minutes to spare when I jogged into the cavernous white confines of hangar four, and I whistled long and low when I saw what was waiting for me.

A Gulfstream G550 filled the hangar from wall to wall, painted golden tan. A small crew in white jumpsuits was working feverishly to get it air-ready, uncoupling fat yellow fuel hoses and going over the jet's underbody with penlights and clipboards.

"Mr. Faust," called out a voice from the far end of the hangar, the same woman from the phone call. She had dark brown skin and sharp eyes, and she strode toward me like she was on a mission. "I'm Ms. Fleiss," she said, "Mr. Drake's personal assistant. Come with me, please."

Fleiss wore her curly black hair pinned in a tight bun, and her tailored suit had shoulders sharp enough to cut glass. I followed her up a wheeled staircase and into the Gulfstream, suddenly feeling like a bum who had wandered into a taping of *Lifestyles of the Rich and Famous*. Drake's ride was an expanse of white leather and cream, with wall-mounted HDTVs and plush swivel chairs.

It looked like they were doing some remodeling. Toward the back of the jet, a heavy sheet of white plastic dangled from painter's-tape anchors, and another sheet draped the floor. I was distracted by a new arrival, a tanned wall of meat with chiseled muscles and razor-cut blond hair. He wore a shoulder holster over his tight white T-shirt, showing off a fat chromed .45.

"Mr. Pachenko," Fleiss explained with a nod. "Mr. Drake's head of security. Hold your arms out to your sides, please."

I knew the drill. I stood there while Pachenko's meat hooks slapped my hips, chest, and back, working their way down to my ankles. Most people don't know how to do a proper frisk, or they half-ass it, but not this guy. If I'd been carrying anything bigger than a deck of cards, Pachenko would have found it.

"Please, sit down and buckle up," Fleiss said, walking me over to a chair right in front of the dangling tarp. The plastic crinkled under my shoes. She sat down in the swivel chair opposite mine. A small lacquered table inlaid with a swirling gold leaf design stood between us.

"You haven't told me where we're going," I said.

"Austin. Provided you pass the job interview, you'll be well compensated for your time."

"And if I don't?" I said.

She didn't answer. The jet's engines throbbed as it taxied out of the hangar, taking a sharp right turn and pointing its nose toward the runway. I didn't like this, didn't like a thing about it, but at least Agent Black wouldn't be waiting for me at the airport on the other end.

And if she is, I thought as the jet rolled forward, picking up speed and pushing me back in my chair, *I quit*.

The jet lifted off, took a shuddering turn over Vegas as we hit a pocket of turbulence, then rose over the clouds and into a pale sky. It wasn't long before we leveled out and a gentle chime sounded over the cabin speakers.

"Good," Fleiss said, glancing at her wrist. Her watch was a slender gold Cartier, the oblong face encircled with a dusting of diamonds. "Mr. Pachenko? We're ready to begin the test."

I didn't like the sound of that, either.

The slab of beef came back with a wooden box in his hands, about a foot across and half as deep. He held the thing like it was a sleeping rattlesnake, and I didn't blame him. It radiated power, a purple vortex of seething malice that felt like it might lash out at any moment.

He set it down on the table between Fleiss and me.

The wood was pitted, old and gray, like it had been carved from some dead and lightning-seared log. Engraved symbols covered the face and circled the sides, prickling my memory. Glyphs from old European witchcraft, mostly, but a handful were out of place or misinscribed. While I studied the box, Pachenko unrolled a cloth napkin next to it, revealing a handful of tools. A pair of steel lockpicks. A Phillips-head screwdriver. A tiny mallet, like doctors use for testing reflexes, and a coiled steel spring.

"As I'm sure you can imagine, Mr. Drake deals with a great number of opportunists," Fleiss explained. "Impostors, pretenders, poseurs. As such, before he takes you into his confidence, he would like to verify that you live up to Mr. Agnelli's claims. A test of skill."

"I'm listening," I said.

Fleiss shot another glance at her watch. "We will land in two hours and fourteen minutes. You have until that time to open the box before you. You may use any of the tools in front of you to accomplish this task."

Pachenko moved to stand at Fleiss's shoulder. Then he pulled his .45. I thought his gun was big before. It looked a lot bigger pointed at my face.

"If the box is not open at the moment our wheels touch the runway," Fleiss added, "Mr. Pachenko will execute you."

Now I knew what the plastic sheeting was for.

"I suggest you move with haste," she said.

I took a few deep breaths and weighed my choices. I figured I could spare enough time for that, at least.

The hard way wasn't an option. If I gave Pachenko the bum-rush, he'd gun me down before I unbuckled my seat belt. I was going to have to play it their way.

The box then. Nicky had told me Drake wanted someone who knew his way around physical and occult security. I'd take this test one piece at a time. I let my eyes slip out of focus and narrowed my concentration, studying the box with my second sight. Violet lines of power wrapped around the wood like a spiderweb or a cargo net, sealing it tight and thrumming with malice. Some kind of potent curse, set to lay a whammy on anyone who opened the box without defusing it first. Simple enough.

Taking it apart wasn't so simple. The longer I studied the web, the more daunting it became. Every intersection of lines was a trigger, every bend and knot a hammer waiting to fall. If I snipped a single line, the others would trigger and blast their deadly payload right in my face.

Fleiss, emotionless and still, watched me as the minutes slipped away.

I needed to find the trailhead. The place where the curse weaver had started his work. If I could isolate that one single strand of magic, I could cut off the spell at its knees and render it harmless. I stared at the lid and the sides of the box, following this line and that, running into dead end after dead end. The lines seemed to emerge from a wellspring in the middle of the lid, but that wasn't the trailhead. So how...

I half smiled. Then I turned the box over. There it was. One little clot of concentrated magic, tied off and drilling up through the heart of the box from the bottom to the top. Plain as day and unconcealed, for anyone who could think beyond the pointless maze on the other side. I called a spark of power to my left hand, hovering over the knot, and exhaled sharply as I snipped my index and middle fingers together like a pair of shears. The air tingled as the curse strands whipped away and dissolved, burning to nothing in the space of a few quick heartbeats.

"Occult competence and three-dimensional thinking," Fleiss murmured, as if taking notes under her breath.

I turned the box back over. The ornamental lock on the lid was kid's stuff, nothing compared to a serious padlock.

That was what worried me.

It was too easy. Anyone with a delinquent teenager's grasp of lock picking could get through that thing in two minutes flat. After they'd gone to so much trouble with the curse on the box, I couldn't believe this part would be that simple. They'd even given me lockpicks.

My gaze flicked to the white cloth napkin and the spread of tools Pachenko had so generously laid out for me. Something was off about them. A faint chemical smell hung in the dry cabin air, and the metal was a little too shiny.

I picked up the edge of the napkin and gingerly lifted it up, peeking underneath. Pinpricks of moisture dotted the underside, soaking through from above.

Not long ago I'd gone up against a sorcerer who had a thing for brainwashing his victims with contact poison. He'd spread his happy juice over business cards, doorknobs and pens, anything he could get his victims to touch. Once they did, and the custom toxins seeped into their skin, it was all over.

The lock was as simple as it looked. The picks—and all the

other useless tools they'd offered me to overcomplicate the puzzle—*those* were the trap.

Still, I needed something to get through that lock. Fleiss stared at me, unblinking, almost reptilian, as I worked it through. *You may use any of the tools in front of you*, she'd said.

I unbuckled my seat belt.

Pachenko took a step back and raised his gun as I got up from my chair. I kept my hands easy and open, right where he could see them.

"Stay cool, big guy," I said. "I'm following the rules."

Fleiss didn't move a muscle as I reached for her hair, plucking out the bobby pin that held her bun in place.

"This was in front of me," I told her, sitting back down.

She shook her hair out. "So it was."

I snapped the bobby pin in two, carefully bending one half to give it an L-hook, and got to work. This was the easy part. Thirty seconds' work and the tumblers clicked. I reached for the hasp, then froze.

I was missing something. The test should have been over and done, but Fleiss was still watching me like a mouse in a maze. Like there was something left beyond pulling that hasp and opening the lid. I couldn't hear a thing but the pounding of my pulse and my instincts screaming in my ear, telling me danger was close enough to kiss.

I lightly touched the sides of the box, keeping it closed, and rotated it to face Fleiss.

She flinched.

She had a hell of a poker face, but she couldn't hide that. I said, "Thank you," and turned the box ninety degrees so the lid would open away from the table, toward the far side of the cabin.

I pulled the hasp and opened the lid. The box jumped as two darts launched out, whining through the air and digging into the baggage compartment. One dripped a few beadlets of slime-green venom down the ivory plastic.

A pristine envelope of bone-colored paper sat nestled in the box between the empty launching mechanisms. I scooped it out and offered it to Fleiss.

"I believe this is yours," I said.

"Yours, actually. Congratulations, Mr. Faust. Out of four candidates for this position, you are the first to successfully complete the interview assignment."

Pachenko holstered his gun.

I thumbed open the envelope, peeking in on a stack of crisp green bills.

"Two thousand dollars," Fleiss said, "simply for meeting with Mr. Drake. Whether you accept his proposition or not, the money is yours to keep."

With the box in front of me like a bomb on a timer, I'd been too focused to feel the strain. Now, with the lid open and the danger gone, I had to squeeze the envelope tight to keep my hands from shaking. Misspent adrenaline flooded into my veins, looked for a fight, couldn't find one, and started a riot instead. The stress turned to anger, and I wanted to start throwing punches. Instead, I swallowed it all down and focused on my breathing.

I came this far, I told myself. *I can go a little farther and hear the guy out.*

The wheels thumped down on the runway, and I sank back in my chair as the wing flaps rose and the turbines screamed. I hadn't even noticed we were going down.

6.

Another private airport, another rolling staircase to see us off the jet. The Texas air wasn't like the desert back home. It was hot but wet, a clammy dampness that clung to my lungs. Prickling beads of sweat stained the back of my shirt. A sticky heat. Sparse, cotton-ball clouds hung in a pale blue sky, with a storm broiling in the distance.

A sleek gray limousine waited on the tarmac. Privately owned, no livery plates. I got in back, and Pachenko filled out the bench seat beside me. Fleiss sat facing us, absorbed by her phone, fingers dancing across the touch screen as she rattled off a text message.

I thought we were going to Austin, but the limo turned away from the city limits and headed south. The rolling hills swallowed us up, sprouting clumps of cedar scrub and rugged Texas oaks. I was a long way from anything that looked like home.

I took out my phone, wanting to hear a friendly voice. I figured I should let Bentley and Corman know where I was, at least. Fleiss shook her head, not looking up from her own screen.

"No calls, please."

I glanced to my right. Pachenko loomed with a frown permanently chiseled on his face, like he was a wall of stone ready to crash down on top of me. I put the phone away.

"We're almost there," Fleiss added.

"Almost there" turned into another twenty minutes of hills, but eventually the land leveled out and the road turned from asphalt to dirt, leading us to the hickory-wood gates of a ranch in the heart of nowhere. With bunkhouses and what looked like a turn-of-the-century plantation estate rising up ahead of us, it could have been a relic of the Old West. But there weren't many boxy gray security cameras in those days, bristling from every rough-hewn post and rooftop, and the eagle-eyed men who patrolled the grounds in teams of two weren't exactly carrying antique six-shooters. From their headsets and pressed uniforms to the assault rifles slung over their shoulders, everything about Cameron Drake's security was state of the art.

As the limo rolled through the gate and onto the ranch grounds, I started angling for a way out. My alarm bells were ringing louder by the second, and if Fleiss could be believed, they'd already murdered three other people who hadn't gotten as far on the "job interview" as I had. Until circumstances proved otherwise, I stood on hostile ground.

We rumbled around a circular drive lined with gravel and pulled up in front of the plantation house. The chauffeur hopped out to open the door for us. While I got out, stretching my legs and squinting against the sinking sun, a middle-aged man in denim and rolled-up sleeves jogged down the mansion steps to greet us.

"Mr. Faust!" he called, flashing movie-star teeth and giving a wave. "Cameron Drake. Welcome to Eastern Pines. So glad you could join us."

His handshake was dry and firm. He had a strong Texas twang in his voice and a confident swagger. Maybe there was still a little adrenaline in my system from the flight, or maybe it was his too-friendly grin, but I struggled with the sudden urge to punch him out.

"I didn't have much of a choice," I told him. My eyes eased out of focus as psychic tendrils uncoiled from my spine, brushing over his hand, licking the sky and taking their measure of the place. Cameron was magically inert. So was his slab of beef, Pachenko. Fleiss, though, she had some tricks up her sleeve and an iron wall around her soul. My senses slid right off her, like she was made of glass.

Cameron's house was what really caught my eye, glowing black and throbbing in my second sight. Something was in there—no, *under* there—something that felt hungry and cruel and stank like sulfur.

Cameron furrowed his brow at me, like he didn't know what I was talking about.

"We put Mr. Faust through the usual test," Fleiss said pointedly, as if she was feeding a bad actor his lines.

"Oh, the *test*." Cameron's gaze darted between us. "Of course, right. Well, I...I take it he passed with flying colors?"

If I hadn't, I wouldn't be breathing. Apparently Cameron didn't know what his own people were up to.

"You have a conference call in thirty-eight minutes," Fleiss told him.

"Right. Thank you, Ms. Fleiss, we'll take it from here." He gave me a nervous schoolboy smile. "Lose my own head, if she wasn't watching it for me. C'mon, lemme give you the grand tour."

Pachenko followed us, a lumbering shadow, as we mounted the porch steps and crossed a foyer lined with flowery Spanish ceramic tiles.

"Grew up watching reruns of *Dallas*," Cameron said. "Always wanted my very own ranch."

I stayed close to his shoulder, only half listening, sending out feelers for trouble. The house felt cold. Unloved. Like a museum pretending to be a home. The malevolent thrum underneath worried me most, leaking up through the tile and itching at the soles of my feet.

"Heard you came into some money," I said. "Lucky play."

"Lucky me, yeah. Everybody tells me I'm a lucky guy. Born lucky."

Cameron grabbed a pair of wooden door handles and shoved them wide. The office on the other side was bigger than my old apartment. An oval cherry-wood desk sat angled toward a bank of wall-mounted televisions, each muted screen showing a feed from a different channel. Money-green carpet draped the floor, and vintage movie posters—mostly '80s action flicks, a few signed by the stars—lined the walls.

Cameron turned, looking like he had something to say, then froze in Pachenko's shadow. "Drink?"

"No thanks."

"Mind if I do?"

I gave a noncommittal shrug, and he led me over to a minibar by the desk. From the looks of his collection, the local liquor store must have been running a sale on near-empty bottles. He took down a cut-crystal glass and rummaged until he found half a fifth of Southern Comfort. He filled his glass almost to the brim. No mixer, no soda, just five fingers of high-proof liquor. He tossed back a mouthful like it was tap water.

"It's five o'clock somewhere." He looked just embarrassed enough that I knew he had a problem. Not embarrassed enough to stop himself from topping off his glass, though.

I felt my impatience trying to get the better of me. I decided to let it. "So what's the job?"

He blinked. "Oh. The job. Right. Nicky says you're good—I mean, really good. He says you're his best man."

His best man? Wow, I was going to have words with Nicky when I got back to Vegas. For now I kept my irritation to myself.

"Depends on what you're in the market for," I said.

"What do you know about...stealing art?"

"That it's strictly amateur hour, for the most part. Punks hear that a Picasso is worth twenty million, so they pull a smash and grab. Never occurs to them that a one-of-a-kind artwork might be *worth* twenty mil, but that doesn't mean anyone's going to *pay* 'em a dime for it. There's exceptions. Ransoming it back to the insurance company—that can be done, but it's risky as hell. It's safer to cross the feds than it is to cross an insurance company."

"But you can do it?"

"A score is a score," I told him. "It's not what you're stealing, it's who you're stealing it from and how far they'll go to protect what's theirs. What are you after, anyway?"

A manila folder lay on his desk blotter. Cameron flipped it open and rested his fingers on the photograph inside, twisting it around to face me. The glossy picture made my skin crawl. Worse, I couldn't figure out why.

It was just a knife, propped up in a wooden cabinet, with a gleam suggesting the photographer had shot it through a pane of glass. The knife had a flared, black blade like a diseased leaf. Pits and craters marred the blade's rough face, making me think of a cold and distant moon. The handle was carved from some yellow-green stone, with the pommel forming the roaring mouth of a lion and the grip wavy like a serpent's coils. A strip of black punch tape stuck to the bottom corner of the photo read, "Museum File 3397-8C."

"It's a sacrificial dagger from the Aztec empire. Carved from obsidian." Cameron's voice dropped, like he was whispering in a library. "Dates back to the fifteenth century."

I tapped my fingertip against the punch tape. "Museum?"

"Not anymore. Private collector. He won't sell."

"You contacted him about a buy and got shot down?" I said, glancing up from the photo. "Recently? You do realize that once it goes missing, you'll be the number one suspect."

"Yes, I mean, no. No. I just know he won't sell it."

He was talking to me, but he only had eyes for Pachenko, glancing over at the slab of muscle like a schoolkid hoping for a gold star from the teacher. There was one question I'd normally never ask a client—it was bad etiquette—but I needed a better read on this guy.

"Why do you want it?"

Cameron swallowed hard. "I'm a collector, too. Mesoamerican antiquities are a...a passion of mine."

Which was why he had an office full of movie memorabilia, where the closet thing to going south of the border was a framed poster for *The Good, The Bad, and The Ugly*. In my experience, people kept their passions close and loved to put them on display. Cameron? Not even a turquoise paperweight on his desk.

I wished I'd studied up on the Aztecs; I had a hunch I could stump him cold with an easy trivia question or two. One thing I knew for sure: Cameron had the cash, but his "personal assistant" and his muscle were calling all the shots around here. I just couldn't figure out *why*.

"Who's the mark?"

"Mark?" Cameron said.

"This private collector. Who is he, and where's he keeping the knife?"

Cameron turned over the photograph. Another one waited underneath, a wide-angle shot from a telescopic lens. One man walking down a crowded sidewalk, nice suit, dark skin, and big, expressive eyes, circled in red Sharpie.

"Damien Ecko," Cameron said. "Chicago. He owns a boutique on Jewelers Row, D. Ecko and Company. He sells custom rings, pendants, he's big in the diamond trade."

"How about the antiquities business?"

"Just his personal collection. He's a buyer, not a seller. He keeps the dagger in his loft on the second floor, above the shop."

I gave him a hard look. "You think this? Or you know this?"

"I'm certain."

"How?"

He bit his bottom lip.

"I've got people," he said. "Close to him."

"Just not close enough to touch."

"That's right."

Nothing about his story played straight. Just because my client was bogus, though, didn't mean the job was—and neither were Cameron Drake's lottery winnings. My better judgment told me to walk away, but Cameron had my curiosity firing on all cylinders and the smell of his money kept my feet rooted to the cash-green carpet.

I should have walked away.

7.

"Chicago's not my usual stomping grounds," I told Cameron, "and knocking over a jewelry store isn't exactly low risk."

"Twenty thousand dollars," he said. "Paid in full when you bring me the knife."

I ran the numbers in my head. I'd need a box man—and this would be a good chance to make things up to Coop, for Harmony Black stepping on our score the other night. I'd also want a local for a wheelman, somebody who knew the streets of the Windy City forward and back. Twenty grand on a three-way split.

"Make it thirty," I said.

"Deal."

I blinked. Apparently winning Powerball meant forgetting the meaning of the word *haggle*. Fine by me. If I didn't take his money, somebody else would. My cut still wouldn't be nearly enough to pay my debt to Winslow, but it'd keep him happy—and my kneecaps intact—while I lined up another job.

"One last question," I said. "You wanted an occult-security specialist. Why? What's he got up there?"

Cameron looked at Pachenko. No help there.

"Well," he stammered, "it's, um, complicated—"

"Damien Ecko is a necromancer," Fleiss said, appearing in the doorway. She stood on the threshold with her arms crossed, shooting a dour look at Cameron. The actor must have forgotten his lines.

"You don't say."

"We don't know how he's defending his business, beyond mundane locks and alarms, but you can safely assume his...area of study will factor into it. Is that a problem?"

"I'll need a few things," I told her. "Specialty items. You'll pay for my expenses, on top of the thirty G."

"Keep good receipts." She turned to Cameron. "Mr. Drake, it's time for your conference call."

Suddenly Cameron's mask was back in place, that confident Texan swagger, and he shook my hand like he wanted to crush it. *Saved by the bell*, I thought. *He's fine, as long as nobody's asking him any questions. Poking holes in the illusion.*

Fleiss hustled me back to the limo as fast as she could manage it. She wasn't stupid. She had to know I'd figured out something wasn't right down on Eastern Pines Ranch, but I took her poker face and shot it right back at her. We rode in silence all the way back to the plane.

* * *

When the sun went down over Vegas and the neon ignited, Fremont Street turned into a drunken carnival. The air smelled like cheap beer and stale sweat as I blended in with the milling crowds, just another anonymous face under the cherry glow of the canopy light show. Streamers of color swirled and exploded overhead, timed to the rhythm of a Beatles medley pumping out over bass-heavy speakers. My mind went slack and I let my feet carry me along, leading me to—

—sudden silence broken by the jingling of a tiny brass bell as the door to the Tiger's Garden swung shut behind me. Every big city had its own haven for the occult underground, a place where the clued-in could talk shop without worrying about the wrong word landing in the wrong ear. The Garden had an extra layer of protective camouflage: the only way to get there was *not* to look for it.

The odors of the street gave way to the rich aroma of fresh-baked naan and curry wafting through the tiny restaurant. The decor was 1970s chintz, from the cigarette-burned orange carpet to the ratty paper lanterns dangling over the tiny tiki bar in the back, and heavy wooden shutters shrouded the windows. There was an unspoken agreement among the regulars that nobody should peek behind those shutters. Given that the Garden was only vaguely connected to the real world, I think we were happier not knowing what was out there.

Jennifer had already commandeered our usual table in the corner, her tattooed arm lazily draped over the back of a chair while she bit into a scarlet slice of tandoori chicken. Mama Margaux, draped in a white frock and nursing a tall glass of rum punch, sat beside her. I walked into the room and killed the conversation.

"Something I said?" I asked, wandering over.

Margaux and Jennifer shared a look.

"Just talking some business," Jennifer said.

"Since when do you two do business?"

Margaux crossed her arms. "*Some* people respect what I'm capable of."

Amar, the Garden's sole employee—that we knew of—stepped up alongside me with a brass-rimmed tray. One Crown and Coke, mixed to perfection. I took the glass, nodded my thanks, and he disappeared into the kitchen again. You never had to order at the Garden; Amar already knew what you wanted, usually a few minutes before you arrived.

"You're still mad at me about the Enclave thing." I sagged into a chair on the far side of the table.

"You benched me, Danny."

"I needed to make sure Bentley and Corman were safe—"

"They could have gotten here themselves," Margaux said. "Their legs weren't broken. You *benched* me. I could have helped in that fight."

"The stakes were too high, Mama. Hell, I didn't even want to bring Jennifer. I didn't want to risk your life, any of your lives, going up against that...*thing*. Given what Lauren was capable of, I couldn't take that chance."

Margaux's brows knitted as she took a long sip from her drink.

"Ain't your decision to make," she muttered. "We're either family or we're not."

Jennifer stretched languidly and shook her head. "Nothin' wrong with feeling protective, sugar, but it's a matter of trust."

I slid my fingertip around the rim of my glass.

"I'm sorry." I looked up at Margaux. "I fucked up, okay? You're right. It wasn't my decision to make, and if you wanted to be on the front lines, I should have let you. It's not...it's not that I think you're not capable, okay? There just aren't a whole lot of people in my life who matter to me. When it comes to the ones who do, hanging on to that is more important to me than anything."

Margaux studied her fingernails. "Hmph. Apology accepted."

"I suppose Bentley and Corman are pissed at me, too?"

Jennifer flashed a smile. "Hell, they're just glad we put Meadow Brand down like Old Yeller. That was pretty much a community service kinda killin', any way you slice it."

"I wish Agent Black felt that way." I paused, something occurring to me. "Hey, Mama, let me make it up to you. I've got a job. One night, in-and-out kinda deal, and the mark's a necromancer. Just your kind of problem. You want in? I'll split my take with you."

"Means a lot that you'd offer, but no. Jenny's keeping me busy this week. Besides," Margaux said, glancing up at the ceiling, "she pays better."

"Doing what?"

"Just a little fail-safe," Jennifer said, "in case a certain somebody gets too big for their britches."

"And speaking of Nicky," I said.

"More useless than nipples on a bull."

"You've gotta stop baiting him, Jen. You're pushing too hard—"

One eyebrow shot up. "More like I spent years *gettin'* pushed when I never shoulda let him get away with it in the first place. You've got an ear to the ground. You know well as I do that

Nicky's on his way out one way or another. Either he's gonna cut his losses and run to Rio with a suitcase full of cash, or one of his own guys is gonna take him for a ride before Nicky can talk to the feds."

"Then let it play," I told her. "If you're so sure, then cool your jets and *let it play*. You know what Nicky's like. When he gets nervous, bodies drop. And he's plenty nervous right now. You need to pull over into the slow lane, keep your head down, and see what—"

The door jingled. I turned, expecting to see Bentley and Corman rounding the corner.

"Well, look who we have here," Harmony Black said with a smile.

Margaux pursed her lips and rested her hands in her lap, under the table. Jennifer narrowed her eyes to razor slits.

"What are *you* doing here?" I asked. Harmony walked over, dropping into an open chair at our table. Amar swooped in, his tray bearing a can of Diet Coke, a glass filled halfway with ice, and a paper-wrapped straw.

"Having a drink, obviously." Harmony took the can and glass and tossed a couple of singles onto Amar's serving tray. He bowed deeply and faded into the kitchen.

"This is a private club," Jennifer said.

"Right. A private club for magicians only. I'm a magician." Harmony cracked the can open and poured her soda over the ice. The silver bangle on her wrist glittered. "So. Jennifer Juniper. Haven't seen you since, oh, your last arrest. How's the narcotics business?"

"Who, me? I'm a florist."

Harmony's gaze swung my way. "Have fun in Texas today, Faust?"

"I wouldn't know."

"Sure you would. You flew in and out of Henderson Executive on Cameron Drake's private jet. You are so predictable, you know that? Drake's some rube who wins the lottery, and not even a year later, he's spending money like it's his full-time job. Perfect target for a grifter like you. What kind of scam are you running on the poor schlub? Worthless real estate? Bogus stock investments? Or maybe you're playing up the magic-man angle. Let me guess: his money is cursed, and only you can cleanse it."

I almost protested my innocence. Then I got a better idea. I shrugged. "You're just not gonna cut me a break, are you?"

"Not until you're behind bars where you belong." She looked over at Margaux. "And you are?"

"Leaving," Margaux said, pushing her chair back. "Danny, call me. I'll send you off with a goody bag. For that thing we talked about."

Jennifer followed her out, glaring daggers at Harmony the whole way. The door jingled behind them. I sipped my drink.

"I like this place," Harmony said, taking a long look around the empty restaurant. "Nice ambiance. I think I'll start coming here *every* night."

I fished in my wallet, pulled out a five-dollar bill, and tossed it on the table between us.

"What's this?" she asked, eyeing the bill.

"A bet. You think you've got it all figured out, huh? Put your money where your mouth is." I leaned in toward her and lowered my voice. "Five bucks says I get my hands on Cameron Drake's money, and you can't stop me."

She mirrored me, getting nice and close.

"Just try it. You won't even make it on the flight to Austin."

"Five bucks."

She hesitated for a moment, then smiled.

"I don't gamble when I'm on duty, Faust. And I'm always on duty. Keep your money. You'll need it for buying cigarettes in the prison commissary."

I left the cash on the table and walked out, letting the world fade as I neared the door, whisking myself out in a blur of mental static. Suddenly I was on Fremont again, keeping pace with the tourist traffic under the whirling lights, as if I'd never left.

As usual, Harmony knew too much for her own good. This time, though, she'd taken a handful of puzzle pieces and put together the wrong picture. It wouldn't take long for her to figure out where she'd gone wrong, but in the meantime, her mistake—thinking Drake was my target instead of my client—was the only edge I had.

I could work with that.

8.

I found Coop at his usual watering hole, an eastside pool hall called Della's. A pack of bikers played eight ball through a haze of stale cigar smoke, and the backs of their leather vests displayed a skeletal eagle swooping in for the kill. Winslow's crew. I kept to the edge of the room, keeping it casual, making sure their boss man wasn't with them before I made my way over to the bar. That was one conversation I didn't want to have tonight.

Coop sucked on a longneck bottle of Bud, staring listlessly at sports replays on the TV behind the bar. I swung up onto the stool next to him, and he gave me a bleary-eyed nod.

"Watch yourself," he said. "Those boys from the Blood Eagles are feeling feisty tonight. They already stomped some tourist into a mudhole after he tried hustling 'em at pool. You know Winslow's been asking about you, wanting to know where you're at."

"I'll take it under advisement. You looking for work?"

"With you? Oh, no. Not as long as that lady fed's got a hard-on for ya. You're too hot, Dan. You need to go underground for a while. Maybe a long while. You're radioactive until this blows over."

"The score's not here. It's in Chicago."

Coop took a pull on his bottle. "I'm listening."

"Jewelry store. Snatching a particular item for a particular client. In-and-out job, no muss, no fuss. Maybe a little weird stuff. I'll handle that, though."

"I don't like the weird stuff, Dan."

"And I said I'll handle it. The payoff's thirty grand on a three-way split. We'll need a local for a wheelman. Three percent, off the top, goes to Nicky Agnelli. He's playing matchmaker on this one."

"And five percent for Augie," Coop said. He tilted his head and looked at me, bottle lightly touching his lips, like he was daring me to say no.

"And five percent," I said, resigned, "for Augie."

"When's it going down?"

"As soon as possible."

Coop squinted, doing the math in his head. "Two days. I can't exactly fly with my gear as carry-on luggage. I'll load up a van and drive to Chicago. Me and Augie'll take shifts, get us there faster. You find your wheelman yet?"

"Haven't started looking. Why? You know one?"

"Might," he said. "Guy named Stanwyck. I've worked with him a couple of times. He's reliable. Originally from Chicago, but he relocated to Vegas about two years ago."

"Can't imagine the streets have changed that much in two years. Okay, if you vouch for him, he's in. Do the honors?"

Coop finished his beer. He set the empty bottle down on the edge of the bar.

"I'll have him get in touch. See ya in Chi-Town, Dan."

* * *

The next morning, I made a little detour on my way to the airport. The doors of St. Jude's opened with the sun, inviting Las Vegas's down-and-out to start their day with a hot meal. I crossed the scuffed parquet floor of the dance-hall-turned-soup-kitchen, edging around the serving line, and waved at one of the servers.

Pixie and I had gone through some rocky times lately, but she still called over another volunteer to take her spot so she could come around the tables and talk to me. Streaks of icy white adorned her dyed scarlet hair, and she wore a camisole top that showed off the fairy wings tattooed along her slender shoulder blades.

"I'm here to make a donation," I told her, peeling off a couple of hundreds from the wad of cash Fleiss had given me.

"In exchange for?"

"There's this guy, Cameron Drake. He won the lottery in Texas about a year ago, withdrew all the money in a lump sum, and bought a ranch outside Austin. I took a job from the guy, but something's hinky about the whole situation. I want anything you can dig up on him: what he knows and who he owes."

"Yeah, all right." She flashed an X drawn in black Sharpie on the back of her hand as she curled her fingers around the bills and tugged them away. "I'll be your Google."

"Keep an eye out for the names Fleiss and Pachenko. Supposedly they work for him."

"Supposedly?"

"Like I said, something's hinky."

"St. Jude's," she said, turning back towards the serving line, "appreciates your generous donation."

Out on the street, keys in hand, an idea hit me. Harmony Black was good. Really good. Obviously she was using magic to track me, but I didn't realize how thick a net she'd woven until I started looking. A chalked sigil on the sidewalk outside Bentley and Corman's bookstore, another etched in blue dust on a wall halfway down Fremont Street. Everywhere I went, all my usual haunts, I'd started catching the signs. That wasn't enough, though. To know about my trip to Henderson Executive Airport yesterday, she had to be tracking one of two things: me, or my ride.

I went over the Barracuda inch by inch, holding my open palms over the sleek black steel and concentrating like an occult auto mechanic, until I finally found her handiwork. She'd placed it under my back bumper, an enchantment veiled under layer after layer of gossamer illusion. I never would have found it if I hadn't been looking, and looking hard.

The witch-eye would have been invisible to most people. In

my second sight, it looked like its name: a disembodied, veiny eyeball stuck to the inside bumper with a lump of watery tissue and clotted blood. The eye lolled left and right, its blood-red iris taking in everything around it. As long as the eye was in place, Harmony could find my car anywhere just by concentrating on it.

Good. I was counting on that.

I drove over to McCarran International, parked the Barracuda in long-term, and pocketed my parking ticket. I kept an urgent stride on my way to terminal one, a canvas messenger bag slung over one shoulder, moving with purpose but not so fast I'd stand out in a crowd. I'd flipped over an hourglass by coming here, and I could feel the sand draining away with every passing second.

People like me don't get along with banks too well, but they have their uses, especially when it comes to building a cover as a solid citizen. On paper, Daniel Faust was a self-employed "street entertainer" who operated right below the poverty line. He had a bank account with a tiny balance, a debit card, and he filed his papers with the IRS every April like a good taxpayer should.

I had a pretty good hunch that Harmony was watching that bank account like a hawk, which was why I made a beeline for the Southwest Airlines desk and bought a 2:15 ticket for Austin with my debit card.

Peter Greyson was another good citizen, though he'd been unemployed for a while since his software company out in Los Angeles went belly-up. He had a bank account of his own and bulletproof papers, courtesy of my buddy Paolo. Peter Greyson and Daniel Faust had never met. Peter bought himself a ticket to Chicago on American Airlines, due to leave in an hour, and dumped the Austin ticket in the nearest trash can.

I shuffled through security as Peter, flashing my bogus driver's license and a harmless smile, taking off my belt and shoes to trudge forward with the rest of the crowd. Solid fake IDs were a lot harder to come by post-9/11, but there were still plenty of loopholes the feds hadn't gotten around to closing. My messenger bag slid through the scanner like silk. There wasn't much in it but a change of clothes, toiletries, and a few pieces of gear for the job. Nothing too eyebrow-raising, much less illegal.

The Austin flight was leaving from gate A8. My Chicago flight was D10, on the far side of a tram ride. I stood at the glass tram doors in a milling, listless pack of tourists, waiting for the next car to arrive.

The back of my neck prickled. I tensed, sending out psychic tendrils—then immediately yanked them back like I'd brushed my fingertips against a hot stove. Fifty feet away, Harmony Black cut through the crowds at full steam, trailed by three junior G-men in off-the-rack suits.

If she so much as glanced to her left, I was finished. I could see her own senses reaching out, touching the faces around her like a thousand wavering violet sea anemones, hunting for my scent. I locked down. Pulled my magic in hard, threw up walls of iron around my mind, and shuffled deeper into the waiting crowd, trying to cut the line of sight.

I could see the tram coming through the tunnel of glass, puttering toward the station. Twenty seconds. I just needed to hold out for twenty seconds—

Harmony froze in her tracks. Her pals almost tripped over each other, stumbling to a halt. One asked something and she waved him away. She tilted her nose up in the air. *Sniffing.*

I felt her senses touch mine, drifting over me like a lace veil. I crouched down inside my own mind, throwing up a confusion of symbols and images, a burst of random mental static to throw her off.

The veil paused, resting over me for a heartbeat. Then it moved on.

The tram doors slid open. I hustled on board and grabbed a standing pole, clenching every muscle in my body until the doors rattled shut again and the tram pulled away from the concourse. I watched the concourse slide away, leaving Harmony Black behind. Even so, I didn't feel safe until I was on the plane, nestled in a window seat near the wing and feeling the engines rumble as we taxied up the runway.

* * *

We hit turbulence somewhere over the Rockies, and then the silver clouds turned black like mottled iron. The "fasten seat belt" light chimed on and never turned off again. While the jet rattled and shook and lightning flashed off in the distance like the cannons of a pirate galleon, I tried to focus my attention on the in-flight movie. It was a romance flick where the hero got cancer and died in the end. I was not comforted.

Three hours later we broke through the clouds. Chicago sprawled below us, a bristling parasite of steel and stone clinging to the curve of Lake Michigan. Skyscrapers rose up from the urban expanse like the pistons of a mighty engine, standing tall and sharp in the rainy gloom.

Home was sin and sleaze and glitz in the desert sun. Vegas would steal every penny in your pocket, but it'd make sure you had a great time on your way to the gutter. Chicago didn't have time to play games. It was a machine for printing money, moving at the speed of industry, and it only offered two choices: keep up or be left behind.

Las Vegas was born from a gangster's dream of fleecing tourists in paradise. Chicago was born from a trading post, built on the bones of an Indian massacre. Neither city has ever forgotten this.

We touched down on the runway at O'Hare, the jet screaming as it put on the brakes, and I let out a breath I hadn't realized I'd been holding. I was a stranger in a strange land, but at least now I had both feet on the ground.

There was a message from Stanwyck on my phone. He kept it short and sweet. "This is Coop's friend. He gave me your number. I'm interested in that project you talked to him about. Give me a call."

Good, one less problem to deal with, now that I had a full crew for the job. Overfull, if you counted Augie. My stomach grumbled as I joined the conga line to shuffle off the plane, inch by inch and toe to heel. *Food first*, I thought. *Then call him back. Then figure out where I'm sleeping tonight.*

O'Hare felt like a relic of the 1970s. Plenty of white paneling, white floors, the kind of white that gets grimy ten minutes after it's been mopped clean. It felt like an overcrowded office building buried under a thin layer of grit. I found a small food court and grabbed a cheeseburger and an order of fries at a McDonald's kiosk. I'm all for sampling the local cuisine when I travel someplace new, but at the moment I just needed something solid in my stomach.

I sat at a round plastic table on the edge of the food court, idly people-watching while I dug in. I was down to the last couple of stubby fries when I took out my phone and called Stanwyck back. He picked up on the first ring.

"Yes."

"Faust here," I said. "You in town?"

"Not yet. Flight leaves in two hours. Green light?"

"All systems are go. I just got off the plane. Any suggestions for a safe house?"

"Motel in the south 'burbs," he said, "about twenty minutes from downtown. I've used it before. The management has selective amnesia: slip him an extra twenty and he'll forget you were ever there."

"Sounds good. Let me get something to write down the address—"

My voice trailed off as I looked across the concourse and saw who was heading my way.

"Have to call you back," I said and hung up the phone.

9.

The last time I'd seen Mack and Zeke, I was stealing their keys at gunpoint behind a family diner in Richfield, Utah. Mack had a weightlifter's build, but with a little bit of pudge around the belly. He was dumb but reasonable. Zeke was a scrawny guy with cropped ginger hair and a fascination with knives. He was dumb but bloodthirsty.

They had sold their souls for rock and roll. I mean that figuratively: souls were a buyer's market. Nonetheless, they were the welcome wagon for Prince Malphas and his Court of Night-Blooming Flowers, and they looked about as happy to see me as I was to see them.

At least they'd stopped dressing like Mormons, but I wasn't sure the death metal concert T-shirts were an improvement.

"You're a long way from Utah," I said as they walked up on my table.

"And you're a short way from the *grave*, asshole," Zeke hissed.

"You," I said, "have been working on your quips. I'm impressed."

"We lost our old jobs after we ran into you," Mack said. "That car we were driving? Wasn't ours, man. It belonged to our manager. When he got the bill for the locksmith, he was *pissed*. I mean, dude's from the Choir of Wrath, so he's basically pissed all the time, but still."

Zeke loomed over me. "We got transferred and busted down to airport duty. Know what that means? We patrol the airport. All day, every day, looking for enemies of the court trying to sneak into Flowers territory. Know how many we've found?"

"A dozen?" I shrugged.

"One. *You.* You're the first one we've caught, and now you're gonna help us get our old jobs back. It's a sign. A sign from our infernal master below."

"We gotta get out of here," Mack said, shaking his head. "I've put on six pounds since we started this gig. It's those Auntie Anne's pretzels. You get one of those big, soft, salty pretzels with the dipping cup of cheese sauce...I just can't say no."

"Every time we pass by, he's gotta buy a pretzel. That's *your* fault, Faust."

"Could be worse," I said. "Could be Cinnabon."

Mack and Zeke shared a sidelong glance.

"We don't talk," Zeke said, "about the Cinnabon."

I held up my open hands. "I'm not looking for trouble, guys. Here on personal business, nothing to do with you or yours."

"That's what a spy would say," Zeke muttered.

"You know my face, and you know my name. That'd make me a pretty lousy spy, wouldn't it?"

"That," Mack said, "is *definitely* what a spy would say."

I sighed and slumped in my chair. "Okay, fine, you caught me. What now?"

They shared another glance.

"We could—" Mack started to say, then fell silent.

"You know," Zeke said.

"No, I—I mean, you were the one taking notes at the briefing—"

"I'm calling it in." Zeke looked at me and puffed out his chest. "I'm *calling it in.*"

He stomped off to find a quiet corner of the food court, and I weighed my options. Obviously I wasn't letting them take me anywhere. As far as I understood it, I occupied a strange and unfortunate niche in the infernal courts. It was no secret that Caitlin and I were an item, and that made me an obvious target for anyone wanting to put a hurt on her. At the same time, since I didn't actually work for her prince, I couldn't claim diplomatic rights or any of the good stuff that came with being one of hell's made men.

All the danger, none of the reward. Or as I like to call it, Tuesday.

A fight, then? Two against one was a sucker bet. Mack had a good six inches of height and fifty pounds of muscle over me, at least, and Zeke was quick with a knife. I didn't have anything in my pocket but a deck of cards, and I wasn't about to show off my special tricks in front of all these civilians.

For that matter, I had to think about collateral damage. I knew Mack and Zeke were crazy. Crazy enough to pull a piece and start blasting away in the middle of a crowded airport? Zeke might have been, and I wasn't going to risk innocent lives to find out. No, fighting my way clear was a bad play. I needed something smarter. Evasive action.

I pushed back my chair and stood up. Mack's eyes went wide.

"Hey, where do you think you're going?"

"To get a cup of coffee. It was a long flight."

He jogged around the table to catch up as I walked away. "You can't leave!"

I nodded toward the Starbucks kiosk, twenty feet away. "I'm not leaving. I'm getting a cup of coffee. You want one? Maybe a blueberry scone or something?"

He squinted at me.

"Yeah...maybe a scone."

I ordered a double shot of espresso macchiato and told Mack to pick out anything he wanted. I wasn't paying attention as I handed a twenty to the cashier and took my cup, the cardboard hot against my palm. I was already working on my spell.

Magic was strong in places of purpose. The longer people gathered someplace for a common goal, the more the essence of their work seeped into the foundations. It was what gave a place its "soul," like the way you could walk through a stock exchange long after closing and still hear the ringing of the bells and feel the money sliding through your fingertips. It was why old libraries felt like temples.

O'Hare International was one of the biggest and busiest airports in the world. The essence of travel and all that came with it—speed, flight, freedom—saturated its steel pores. Lying dormant, waiting to be tapped.

I called on that power now, with one hand on my cup and the other in my pocket, fingertips resting on the glossy face of my boarding pass. An unused ticket would have made the bond stronger, but it was good enough to open the tap and let the energy flow. I reached out and gathered up the surface hopes and tensions of the minds around us. *Going on vacation getting away from it all getting away...*

Zeke came back, holding up his phone.

"We're supposed to take him straight to the hound."

Mack nudged my shoulder. "You heard him. Get moving."

Now I was a plane on the tarmac, a 747 loaded with high-octane jet fuel. I walked between Mack and Zeke, turning down the concourse like it was a runway. The flow of energy coursed through my body like gasoline through a hose, running from the boarding pass up my arm, pumping through my heart, across and down my other arm, and pouring full-strength into the cardboard cup. I felt slow, so painfully slow, held to the ground. I ached for flight.

Zeke frowned at me. "You look weird."

A people mover lay just ahead, a hundred-foot-long treadmill track that quietly hummed along between a pair of glass railings, inviting tired commuters to put their bags down and ride for a minute or two.

"What are you doing?" Zeke looked at Mack. "Is he doing something?"

I tossed back the espresso in one long chug. The caramel-tinged coffee burned down my throat, carrying a caffeine payload spiked with raw magic. Nitrous for my brain.

"Three words," I said.

They looked at me. My foot came down on the people mover track.

"Cleared for takeoff."

The spell ignited.

I walked, that's all I did. To the tired tourists and road warriors lugging their suitcases, I was just another face in the crowd, walking briskly along the people mover. There was no magic speed-blur, no gust of wind, nothing out of the ordinary.

And yet, in the space of two steps, I was somehow fifty feet ahead of Mack and Zeke. Two more, and I crossed the far end of the track.

I heard Zeke shout. I didn't look back. I strode, fast and free, toward the next people mover. Before I finished drawing my next breath, I stepped off the other side. A sign up ahead pointed toward an escalator down, leading the way to the baggage claim and the taxi line.

Have to slow down, I thought. My heart pounded against my ribs, pulse racing. Then I was suddenly at the bottom of the escalator, and I could hear blood roaring in my ears. I'd stolen too much of O'Hare's magic, pushed the spell too far, and now my body was straining to keep up like an old junker racing on the redline.

A cluster of hard plastic seats stood near a rent-a-car booth, about fifty feet away. I looked at them. Then I took a step and was standing next to them. Then I fell to the cold linoleum floor.

I pushed myself up into the seat, put my hands on my knees, and squeezed my eyes shut. I visualized my heart as it pounded faster and faster, veins pulsing on the verge of eruption. Seizing on the memory of an old breathing exercise, a meditation on a Tibetan sorcerer's mandala, I fell back into my training. As symbols and colors spun in my mind's eye, I regulated my breathing with a careful rhythm. Four seconds to inhale. Four seconds to hold the breath in my trembling lungs. Four seconds to release. And again. And again.

My heartbeat slowed.

My mouth was dry and my hands trembled, but I'd surfed the spell's wave until it broke against the shore. I pushed myself up on wobbly legs and walked, this time at a speed that didn't violate space and time. No sign of Mack and Zeke. I'd lost them in the crowd and put some distance between us, but that didn't mean they'd stopped hunting.

A chill wind ruffled my hair as I stepped through a sliding glass door and onto the grimy pavement. A long line of cabs, most of them painted canary yellow, waited in a receiving line. High above our heads, a concrete shelf rumbled and the air whined with the sound of another plane taking off into the stormy sky.

My watch said it was a little after three in the afternoon. Plenty of time to get some work done. I waited in line, jumped into the first cab that'd have me, and told the driver to take me downtown.

10.

By the time the cab dropped me off on the edge of Millennium Park, the rain had turned to a slow drizzle drifting down from gray velvet clouds. The mist felt good against my cheeks, cool and clean, and the air smelled like fresh-cut grass. The *Cloud Gate* was the first thing that caught my eye: a giant curving sculpture of mirrored metal, like a kidney bean made of liquid mercury, reflecting the city back at itself.

I walked the other way. Too much self-reflection can be bad for you.

I waited for the crossing light, jogged across six lanes of traffic, then followed East Madison for a block. Chicago was cavernous, skyscrapers looming around me like art deco mountains, and the crowds on the sidewalks could give the Vegas Strip a run for its money.

Money, again. The smell of it hung in the air, stronger than the rain. Back home, I was used to being the fastest thing on the street, moving like a shark through the packs of tourists in cheap sunglasses and flip-flops. Here, everybody had a little hustle in their step. Phones to faces, charging straight ahead, chasing that money down.

I turned south onto Wabash Avenue. Here it was: Jewelers Row, two solid blocks filled with the stuff that dreams are made of, cast in the shade of the elevated train tracks. I drifted past diamond wholesalers and custom wedding-ring designers, trying to figure how much cash flowed along this street on any given day.

An "L" train rolled by overhead, rattling the iron rails and sending a shower of sparks down onto the street below.

Ecko's shop looked like it catered to a discreet crowd. No big marquee out front, just a marble plaque reading "D. Ecko and Company" over a thick glass door. I pretended to window-shop, eyeing the necklaces on display while looking past them to the showroom. Security was no joke, not that I'd expect it to be. Even from outside I could see a wide-angle camera and a motion-detector box high up in the back, and the corner of the window glass was rigged to a tiny plastic disc and a cord that snaked out of sight. Seismic alarm.

The keypad inside the door bore a stylized lapis lazuli *P*. Polymath Security. I gritted my teeth. Polymath was the best in the business: multiple backups, rock-solid security systems, and a reaction time measured in seconds. I knew a few heisters who would just walk away and look for an easier score the instant they saw that logo. I didn't have that luxury.

I hooked a right down an alley barely wide enough to fit a car through, looking for another angle. Much as I liked the idea of robbing Ecko's *entire* castle, the only thing I needed was supposedly up in his second-floor loft. If I could find another way in, and bypass the shop altogether, it'd make my life that much easier.

No such luck. What I found around back was a small parking nook and a couple of overstuffed Dumpsters. The windows of Ecko's loft looked down from a flat brick wall devoid of a fire escape. I could even see the empty bolt holes where an emergency stairway used to be.

I called Stanwyck back, got the address for his favorite motel, and went looking for another cab. I'd done all I could as a solo act.

* * *

The motel manager had deep jowls, a potbelly, and more hair on his cheeks than on his head. I waited on the other side of the check-in desk as he hunt-and-pecked his way around his computer, one glacial tap at a time.

"Two nights," he said, like he was thinking hard. "That's $59.98, plus tax."

"I'll be paying in cash."

He squinted at me. "I need to get a credit card. Even if you pay cash. In case of damages."

I counted out six crisp twenties from my envelope and laid them out side by side on the counter between us. Making the math easy.

"So how about I put down a nonrefundable security deposit, and we skip that step?"

Three twenties went into the register, and three went into his back pocket. He handed me a key clipped to a heavy plastic tag.

"Room four," he said. "Enjoy your stay, Mr. Smith."

I walked along the edge of the lot, trying to ignore the drug deal going down in plain sight between a couple of parked sedans. Between that and the empty beer cans scattered around the dirty asphalt, I obviously wasn't in the best part of town. The first thing I did in the room, after throwing the deadbolt, was check for bedbugs. The mattress was clean, but I couldn't say the same for the musty sheets or the mildew spots clinging to the shower stall in the bathroom.

I unpacked my messenger bag. Inside were toiletries, a change of clothes, my laptop, a camera I'd borrowed from Bentley, and a set of batteries. I thumbed open the camera's battery compartment and tugged out a small plastic baggie filled with glittering red dust. Mama Margaux couldn't come along on this job, but she still made sure I had a little something special to work with. Her spirit powder had saved my life back when I ran into Stacy Pankow's wraith in the storm tunnels under Las Vegas. I figured it was the perfect thing to have in my hip pocket if Damien Ecko really was a necromancer.

After that there wasn't much left to do but sit on the edge of the bed and watch local television on a grainy, twenty-inch screen while I waited for a knock at the door. When the knock finally came, I jumped up and took a look through the peephole. The man outside was stocky, clean-cut, and standing at parade rest.

"Faust?" he said as I cracked the door.

I nodded. "Stanwyck?"

"May I?"

I let him in. He moved like ex-military, someone who hadn't been out of the service long enough to forget old habits. I gestured to the round table by the window and he pulled back a chair, but he didn't sit down until I did.

"Coop says you're dependable," I told him.

"And he says you've got a pedigree. Nicky Agnelli?"

"Not anymore. This job is for a private client. I need a wheelman who knows the streets here."

"That's me," he said.

"Done anything I might know about?"

"Palmidero Street Currency Exchange in '09, First Boston Federal in winter of 2012. You should have seen that one. Blizzard rolling through and the streets were carved from sheets of black ice. Silent alarm blew, Boston PD rolled in, and I still got the whole team out clean. Not even a scratch on the fenders."

"Palmidero." I frowned, trying to remember why that name was nagging at me. "That went sideways, didn't it? I remember there were a couple of hostages."

"Wasn't my fault."

"Those hostages wound up dead."

"They shouldn't have played hero." Stanwyck shrugged one shoulder. "It happens."

"Not on my crew. No civilian casualties, no cowboy bullshit. I do it clean or I don't do it."

"Whatever you say. I'm just the driver." He gave me a lopsided smile. "Clean, dirty, you call the shots. Long as I get my cut, I'm a good soldier."

"Fair enough. Got a car?"

"A rental under a fake name, but we won't be using that for the job. I'll boost something on the day of. We exfiltrate in the stolen car, drive it a few blocks, dump it, and switch to the rental once I know our trail's clean. What's the target?"

"A loft above a store on Jewelers Row," I said. "Coop told me you used to be a local here. Ever hear anything about a guy named Damien Ecko?"

His eyes narrowed, just a bit.

"Nothing good. Word is—and this is all secondhand, mind you—Ecko runs a backroom banking operation for half the drug dealers in the city. See, you give him something for collateral, usually something high-value but hard to fence, like a piece of stolen art. He fronts you a stack of cash. You go buy a brick of coke or whatever your poison is, sell it on the street, and buy back your collateral—plus twenty percent interest—with part of the profits. Everybody wins."

And now I knew why an ancient Aztec knife, once kept in a museum, was sitting in a jewelry merchant's safe. *Private collector, my ass*, I thought. It looked like Nicky Agnelli wasn't Drake's only contact in the underworld. This job had been sketchy from the start, and it just kept getting sketchier.

"Is he connected?" I asked.

"What, to the Outfit? On the outside edge, maybe. Gotta assume he pays out for the right to do business in Chicago. Lots of people do, though. Doesn't mean he's a made man."

Those familiar old alarm bells in the back of my mind, ringing strong and loud.

"You still have any local contacts? Somebody you might ask?"

Stanwyck nodded. "Sure, a couple."

"I just want to be certain, if we do this thing, that nobody *but* Ecko is gonna come looking for us."

And if it turns out Cameron Drake tried to con me into stealing from the Chicago mob, I thought, *I'm flying straight back to Austin to kick his head in.*

"Knowing's half the battle," Stanwyck said. "I can make some calls tomorrow, before Coop and Augie get here."

"Good. Can you help me with something else tomorrow morning? I need to do a little more recon, and it's a two-man job."

Stanwyck pushed his chair back. "Just say when. I'm in room seven. Got any objections to drinking the night before a score?"

"Long as you aren't hung over tomorrow, it's no business of mine."

"Good," he said. "Then I've got a date with a six-pack. Come on by if you're feeling thirsty. Otherwise, I'll see you in the morning."

I let him out, slid the deadbolt, and sat back down. I had some thinking to do.

The client was weird. Now the score was weird, too. Didn't make the job any less real, though, and it didn't change what I'd come here to do. I decided it would all come down to Stanwyck's contacts. If they said Damien Ecko was protected from on high by the Outfit, I'd pull the plug and send everybody home. I needed cash, but I didn't need it badly enough to go toe-to-toe with the mob. On the other hand, if the local wise guys wouldn't shed any tears over Ecko getting ripped off, we'd give it our best shot.

A family diner stood across the street from the motel. I walked over and ordered the pot roast dinner, with mashed potatoes and macaroni and cheese on the side. It was midwestern food, basic stick-to-your-ribs fare, and the meal left me feeling stuffed and vaguely drowsy.

I headed back to my room and went to bed early, keeping my clothes on and lying on top of the musty blankets. I had a lot of work to do, and tomorrow was going to be a very, very long night.

11.

"We're golden," Stanwyck told me, turning the key in the ignition. His rental was a plain blue Camry, the kind of car that blends into traffic. I sat on the passenger side, still waking up, feeling the morning sun on my face. Yesterday's storms had given way to clear blue sky, but it was still about twenty degrees cooler than back home. Bentley's camera rested on my lap, fitted with a zoom lens.

"You asked around?"

"Yep. Ecko doesn't have a whole lot of friends in the Outfit. They wet their beak in his wallet, but that's about as far as that relationship goes. I wouldn't say it's open season on the guy, but they're not gonna put too much effort into avenging him unless he raises a major squawk."

"And we'll be in the wind long before that happens. Good. Game on, then."

Stanwyck drummed his fingers on the steering wheel. "Glad I didn't come all the way out here for nothing. Where to, boss?"

"Downtown. I want a closer look at that loft."

Our stop was almost directly across the street from Ecko's store. The words chiseled into the pink granite mantle above twin revolving glass doors read The Cantor Building in block capitals. The Cantor looked like a jewel of the 1800s, all rough-cut stone and vintage architecture, but the old girl had fallen on hard times. Half the window displays were curtained off and gathering dust.

Inside the front door, a marquee with slots for fifty names displayed a paltry twelve, the last few gem merchants and jewelers able to keep their doors open. The rest were blank slates, locked doors and dark, empty shops. I gave the antique elevator cage a dubious look. We took the stairs instead.

I'd called ahead. The Cantor's rental agent, a skinny bundle of nerves named Elaine, was already waiting for us on the second floor with a clipboard in her hands and an anxious bounce in her step.

"Elaine," I said. "Peter Greyson. We spoke about the rental. This is my finance manager—"

"Joe," Stanwyck offered.

She had a fluttery handshake. "It's so good to meet you both, and you've picked *such* a great time to expand your business. The Cantor is one of the most competitive addresses on Wabash. I expect we'll be filled to capacity by the end of the year."

Stanwyck snorted into his hand, disguising it as a cough. I just smiled and gestured down the silent hallway.

"Well, if it's still available, we'd love to see that street-facing unit."

"Of course," she said, leading the way. A key ring jingled against her clipboard. "That would be...loft 2-C. An excellent choice. One of our pricier units, but—"

"We're good for it," Stanwyck said.

She unlocked a frosted glass door, still streaked with the scraped-off remnants of the last tenant's name, and let us in. Sunlight cascaded through tall windows spaced out along the long, narrow loft, laying warm fingers upon the dusty hardwood floors. Outside the window, another "L" train rumbled past.

I held up my camera. "Is it all right if I take some pictures? The investors are going to want to see everything before they commit."

"Of course!" Elaine's head bobbed like a metronome. "Please, feel free."

I gave Stanwyck a nod. His turn.

"While he's doing that," Stanwyck said, "I need to go over some particulars with you. First, let's talk about the utilities..."

Stanwyck took Elaine aside, turning so she had to face the door to talk to him. I'd prepped him with about ten minutes' worth of legitimate-sounding questions to ask her, and he was a quick study. I snapped a couple of shots, just to look professional, and stepped through an open partition into the next room.

Ecko's loft sat directly across the street, with only the elevated train tracks between us. I stepped close to a window, out of Elaine's sight line, and took aim. One twist of the telephoto lens and I found myself staring right into Ecko's living room.

It looked like a five-room loft, maybe six. I could only peer into the street-facing rooms, and bamboo shades shrouded two windows, but I could see plenty. The place wasn't cheap. Ecko went in for dark wood, high ceilings, and leather furniture, and his decorating style screamed, "Look at my vacation photos." From the African tribal drums by the couch and the wall-mounted wooden masks to what looked like an actual elephant tusk over his plasma TV, he apparently wasn't shy about visiting far-off destinations and coming home with trophies.

I panned slowly from right to left, snapping pictures, hunting for a safe. The lens zoomed in on an open doorway as I tried to get a good look at the room beyond it.

The air in the doorway blurred.

I glimpsed a curlicue of white light, like a frosty breath in the winter air. Then it was gone. For a second I wasn't sure if I'd seen anything at all. I slowed my breathing, focused, and stared intently into the camera's viewfinder. I moved the lens again, slowly sweeping across the loft.

Another blur. My index finger hammered the button like I was a paparazzo stalking an A-list celebrity. I caught a third blur, on the far side of the room, and snapped off another flurry of pictures.

I couldn't get a magical read on the blur—I'd need to get closer for that—but whatever it was, it was fast. Fast, nearly invisible, and guarding a necromancer's home turf. Great.

I scanned the rest of the loft. Over on the far left side I found

Ecko's home office. He'd gone all-in with mahogany fixtures, a plush high-backed leather chair...and a wall-to-wall bookshelf behind his desk, where I could barely make out the edge of a black steel safe.

While I tried to get a good angle on the safe, moving down to another window, something else caught my eye. Four clay jars, about a foot and a half tall and almost as wide, sat upon a glass credenza in his office. They lined up neatly side by side, each lid topped with what looked like a sculpted animal head.

Even from across the street, they radiated power. Their energy tasted like razor blades and misery, and just looking at them through the camera's lens set my teeth on edge. At maximum zoom, I could see the faded Egyptian hieroglyphs, inscribed in red pigment that spiraled around each jar.

The jars were bad news, I knew that much, but past that I was at a loss. Some kind of cursed artifact? A ward to keep people like me out of Ecko's office? Between the jars and the blur, I needed more than a handful of Mama's special powder before I walked up those stairs. I needed information.

I snapped a few final shots, slung the camera strap over my shoulder, and walked back out to join Stanwyck and Elaine.

"Think I've got everything we need," I said. We said our good-byes, promised to be in touch, and gave her a bogus address and a number for a burner phone about to be tossed into the nearest trash can.

Stanwyck didn't say a word until we were back in the car. As he cruised down Wabash, taking advantage of the sluggish traffic to take it nice and slow, I leaned low in the seat and got another few shots of Ecko's storefront from ground level.

"How's it look?"

"Dodgy," I said. "Once we get back to the motel, I'll dump these pictures to my laptop. That'll let me check for extra cameras, disguised motion detectors, all that fun stuff."

Specifically, I thought, *the "fun stuff" that only I can deal with.*

* * *

Stanwyck dropped me off. He wanted to prowl the neighborhood a little and work out our escape route. I sat at the table in my motel room, curtains drawn, with a takeout carton of General Tso's chicken and a lukewarm can of Pepsi at my side as I flipped through the photos on my laptop.

One picture, shot through an open door and giving me a clear view of the opposite side of the loft, exposed a rugged plastic box bolted under one of the back windows. That explained the missing fire escape. The box was for a rolled-up chain ladder, something Ecko could unfurl and climb down in case of an emergency. I knew it on sight because Bentley and Corman had one in their apartment too. All the benefits of a back exit and none of the risks.

We'd have to go in the hard way: through the shop downstairs. I pondered our options while I clicked through the pictures, frame by frame. No such thing as an impregnable security system. There was always a weak link, a crack in the armor. Finding it, that was the trick.

I clicked to the next photo, and a face stared back at me.

It emerged from the blur in the doorway, translucent and silver like a reflection on glass. A lunatic's face, mad-eyed and shrieking with what could have been horror, pain, or bloodlust.

In the next picture, taken a second later, it was gone.

I advanced slowly now, my finger hovering over the arrow key. The next few shots were empty. Just Ecko's apartment and his art.

I tapped the keyboard and called up the next picture. Two arms, fused at the shoulder and bent into impossible, bone-breaking angles, hovered in midair at the edge of a streak of light. A human head—not the first one, this one had long tangled hair and milky eyes—lay on Ecko's carpet. A bloated tongue protruded from its open mouth.

The next picture just showed the streak of light, fading to half its size. In the one after that, it was gone.

I retraced my steps. I remembered trying to catch the doorway blur, then the one in the middle of the living room...there'd been one last ripple in the air, the big one right near the door to Ecko's office. I rushed through the pictures, clicking through the photos racing headlong toward that final moment to see what I'd captured.

I hit the arrow key one last time and froze.

I'd captured it, all right.

It nearly filled the frame, so big it would have to squeeze through the loft's doors to move around. Or squirm through. I couldn't take it all in at first. My eyes darted around, trying to make sense of what I was seeing. There were broken arms and opposite-facing legs, a bloated torso lined with sewn-on hands that grasped and pinched. And there were heads. I counted five, sprouting like tumors from the creature's body, including the head on the floor being dragged along by a tentacle of meat.

A man's head and torso rose up from the back of the creature, spine curved like a scorpion's tail. His one arm aimed directly at the camera lens, pointing an accusing finger. That was when I realized all of the heads were staring right at me.

And screaming.

They had seen me photographing them from across the street. While I was watching the loft, they were watching *me*.

I shut the laptop's lid and sat very still, alone in my motel room. A moment later, I got up and turned on the television set, tuning it to some inane sitcom. The silence wasn't my friend.

12.

Hearing Bentley's reedy voice on the phone was a touch of home. I was a stranger in a hostile land, but I still had a compass to get me through.

"Dr. Halima Khoury," he said. "If anyone can advise you, it's her. Back in the...well, more years ago than I'd like to say, she helped Cormie and me with a sticky bit of trouble out in California. She moved east about a decade ago and took a position as a conservator with the Field Museum. We still correspond with her occasionally."

I hadn't given him all the gory details, just that I was going up against a necromancer with a passion for antiquities. Between Ecko's creature and the jars with the Egyptian hieroglyphs in his office, I needed some local expertise.

"And she's clued-in?"

"She's an accomplished sorceress, yes. You can be frank with her. In fact, I recommend it. She has precious little patience for dissemblers."

"Thanks, Bentley. Can you give her a call and vouch for me?"

"I'm thumbing through my Rolodex as we speak. Daniel...are you going to be gone long?"

"No, the job's going down tonight. Why? What's wrong?"

"Nothing, nothing," he said quickly. I heard the *but* coming before he said it. "But we saw Jennifer last night. One of her...close business associates, one of Nicky's men, has gone missing. Allegedly, he'd been seen meeting with Agent Black."

Nicky. The memories of my own visit to his kill-house in the suburbs, and the torture session he'd forced me to watch, were still fresh. I tasted bile in the back of my throat.

"She should stop looking for him," I said. "He's dead."

"She knows."

"Nicky's cleaning house. Black's stepping up the tempo, trying to scare him. Sounds like it's working. He'll go after anyone he remotely thinks might do him wrong."

Like Jennifer, I thought. The best thing Bentley and Corman could do was stay as far away from her as possible. I knew this, just like I knew they wouldn't do it. We protected each other. That's what families were supposed to do.

"You know Jennifer," Bentley said. "When she gets her dander up, there's no talking her down."

"Just sit tight. I'll get the job done, take a red-eye to Austin and drop off the package, and then I'll be on the next flight home. Then I'm going to do what I *should* have done weeks ago: sit the two of them down in a room together, and nobody leaves until they come to terms. Jen and Nicky don't have any reason to fight, especially not with the feds in town. If they'd just *talk* to each other, they'd figure that out."

"Shall I sweep up the back room at the shop?" Bentley asked, his tone dry. "Perhaps *two* chairs with handcuffs this time?"

"You know, it's not a bad idea. Don't worry, Bentley, I'll fix this. See you tomorrow."

* * *

The Field Museum reminded me of a Greco-Roman temple, with its sweeping flight of stone steps and towering Ionic columns. Fifty-foot banners draped down from the eaves, advertising a traveling exhibit in bright gold lettering with a picture of a roaring jaguar in midpounce.

The inside wasn't any less impressive. I pushed through the glass doors and felt cool air-conditioning wash over me as I stood at the edge of a lobby bigger than Grand Central Station. The reconstructed skeleton of a Tyrannosaurus rex loomed over the ticket counters, large as life, head turned as if sniffing out fresh prey.

"Her name is Sue," said the woman at my side. She looked to be in her forties, with almond skin and a long, narrow face framed by a pale blue headscarf that matched her eyes. She wore an employee badge clipped to the waist of her ankle-length dress. "One of the most complete Tyrannosaurus rex skeletons ever discovered. Our pride and joy."

I wondered, for a brief instant, what a necromancer like Damien Ecko could do with the skeleton of a T. rex. I shrugged the idea off. Nobody's *that* good.

"Dr. Khoury," I said, turning to face her. "I assume Bentley told you I was coming."

Psychic tendrils snaked through the air, violet and glistening, meeting between us. As they brushed, I tasted what little of her leaked out from the edges of her mental shields. Ink-stained hands and long hours in dark libraries. Sandalwood and ritual.

She read me the same way. I wasn't sure what she sensed—you never know how you look in someone else's eyes, much less their second sight—but she gave a faint nod as we reeled back our senses. A magician's handshake.

"It was good to hear from him," she said. Now she offered me her physical hand. Her grip was firm and dry. Almost oddly dry—her skin had the texture of wax cloth.

"I need to know about Egypt. Well, I think so, anyway."

"You came to the right place." She smiled and gestured for me to follow her across the vast lobby floor. "The ancient Near East is my specialty. Come, let's walk the exhibit. Maybe you'll see what you're looking for."

We walked through a recreation of an Egyptian tomb, where ancient walls—carved out of the original stone and flown across the ocean—stood on display behind sheets of Plexiglas. Faint traces of pigment still stained the rows of hieroglyphs, worn away by time, and I could only imagine how colorful they must have once been.

"I'm embarrassed to admit this is a blank spot in my education," I told her. "Everything I know about ancient Egypt comes from old Universal monster movies."

"The real history is infinitely more interesting. But less Boris Karloff. An unfortunate trade."

I decided that I liked Halima.

We descended a winding staircase to the exhibit hall below. As we strolled through the dimly lit cases, looking for a spot to talk away from tourists' ears, one display stopped me in my tracks. It was a sarcophagus, its top carved to resemble a young woman's face. Her sculpted hair flowed down over the coffin's husk, which was painted from end to end in ornate imagery. Animal-headed gods stood in procession under unfurled wings, while the young woman's wide, open eyes looked up at the heavens.

"Beautiful, isn't she?" Halima stared into the display case enraptured. "Her name is Chenet-a-a. She lived in the third intermediate period—about three thousand years ago—when elaborate mummifications were more popular than ever before. A good time to die."

"Why is her coffin so bright, while the tomb walls upstairs barely have any paint on them? Is it a reconstruction?"

"All original. This was an *inner* coffin. It was kept securely inside a larger, plainer wooden sarcophagus. This material is called *cartonnage*. Barely stronger than an eggshell. If we tried to open it, it would crumble to pieces at a touch." She looked over at me and smiled. "So we let her sleep."

I saw a couple of pots and jars on the ground around the coffin, but nothing like what I'd glimpsed in Ecko's office.

"What about sealed jars? Four of them, a little under two feet tall, with animal-head lids. That mean anything to you?"

Halima led me around the corner, past a massive stone sarcophagus, and pointed into another case. They weren't an exact match, but the jars in the case and the ones I'd seen at Ecko's were birds of a feather.

"Canopic jars," she explained. "Used during mummification

to store and protect the vital organs of the deceased. Those heads aren't animals. They represent the four sons of the god Heru, or Horus in the Greek idiom."

"So they'd put...brains in those things?"

She laughed. "No, the brain was discarded entirely. You ought to know, Mr. Faust: the *heart* is the seat of your power. As for the jars, they stored the liver, intestines, stomach, and lungs. They'd be interred along with a mummy's sarcophagus, keeping their body pristine and safe for their voyage into the West."

"So that's the historic use." I glanced over my shoulder, making sure nobody was close enough to overhear. "Next question: what could a necromancer do with canopic jars?"

Her smile vanished.

As she spoke, I could feel her probing me again, intently, like a finger poking at my chest. "Before I answer that, you must tell me something. And speak truly."

"Ask."

"Chicago, like your own city, I must imagine, has a very insular occult community. All of the influential powers know one another, or at least know *of* one another. And you are here to steal something. I can always smell a thief. Tell me: who is your intended prey?"

I thought of ten different denials and snuffed each one out before they could reach my lips. I remembered what Bentley had told me about her patience. Either I could take a chance and lay my cards on the table or walk. No middle option.

"Damien Ecko," I said. "That a problem?"

"I have known Damien Ecko for a very long time." The way she said it, I wasn't sure if that was a good thing or a bad thing. "Are you in the habit of making powerful enemies, Mr. Faust?"

"I wish I could say I wasn't."

"I'd be surprised if you've met one more powerful than Damien. He has his fingers in many different shadows."

"You should have met a lady named Lauren Carmichael," I said. "Trust me, I've been in some tight spots before. Besides, if things go right, he'll never know it was me. That is...assuming you aren't going to tell him."

The faintest ghost of her smile returned. "No. In truth, each of us would be pleased to see the other one gone forever. I am not a violent person by nature, though, and...well, he made an attempt on my life once, many years ago, and he learned a valuable lesson from it: peaceful does not mean weak. Since then, we've agreed to keep to our personal corners of the city and stay out of each other's business."

"Sounds like me and an old business associate of mine," I said. "Doesn't always work, though. So Ecko has jars like these in his office. He's also got this...thing."

"The abomination, yes." Her lips pursed tightly. "I've seen it. And your observations are not unrelated. There are paths of ancient Egyptian sorcery—*heka*—intended to pervert the rites of holy internment. With such knowledge, a magician could use the trappings of a sacred burial to *prevent* a soul from moving on. To keep it here, binding it in shackles of misery and pain, a slave to the sorcerer's will."

"Lovely. So if these jars are keeping that thing on a leash..."

"Breaking them will free its tortured soul. That's assuming you can even get close enough to try. I assure you, the creature has been ordered to defend those jars, and it will fight like a demon to keep itself in chains. And don't forget: one isn't enough. Until *all four* jars are sundered, it will still be under Damien's control."

"Fortunately," I said, "I'm really good at breaking things."

Halima gave me a small smile, but she looked anything but amused. "I would wish you fortune, but if fortune favored you, you wouldn't be here. I'll be praying for your soul tonight."

I cracked a smile. "You'd be the first."

"Then guard it well. For it would be better for your soul to fall into the depths of perdition than for it to fall into the hands of Damien Ecko."

13.

I got back to the motel right around sunset. Stanwyck was out in the parking lot with Coop and Augie, helping to unload canvas sacks from the back of a battered panel van. An animated and smiling cartoon faucet posed on the side of the van next to the words "Drip Bros. Plumbing, Las Vegas, NV, Est. 1978. We Do It All!"

I pitched in, grabbing a sack that weighed at least fifty pounds and clanked when I hauled it over my shoulder, and we all ended up in my motel room with the door dead-bolted and the curtains drawn tight. I turned on my laptop and pulled up the photos I'd taken at the loft—a selectively pruned collection, leaving out the shots of Ecko's pet monster.

"We're good on wheels," Stanwyck said. "I've got a place to stash the car, for the switch, and I found a perfect boost just a few blocks from here. A Lincoln with local plates, and the mail piling up says the owners haven't been around in days. Nobody will report it stolen until we're long gone."

"Catch us up," Coop said. "What are we up against?"

I brought up the shots of the storefront, taken as we cruised past in Stanwyck's car. "Seismic alarms on the windows, motion detector on the ground floor, and he's got a contract with Polymath Security. We can't *get* to the second floor without beating the security in his shop. Second-floor windows are alarmed too, probably on the same circuit."

Coop whistled. "Well, that's a pickle. We know anything about his safe?"

I showed him the picture of the upstairs office and the black steel door poking out behind Ecko's desk. He got closer, leaning in and squinting at the screen.

"Can't tell the make and model with that. We'll just have to load for bear and expect the worst. Ain't met a safe I couldn't crack, but that assumes we get in and have plenty of time to work uninterrupted. Don't suppose you got any friends at Polymath?"

"*Nobody* has friends at Polymath," I said. "They vet their employees harder than the Secret Service. No, our only option is to get in without triggering the alarm at all."

Augie sat on the edge of the bed, brow furrowed and lips slightly parted, like he was trying to do long division in his head.

"If the alarm box is at the bottom of the window display," he said slowly, "why not just cut the *top* of the glass away and not touch that part?"

I shook my head. "Like I said, *seismic* alarm. It monitors the tension of the entire sheet of glass. Break it or cut it—anything that gets the glass vibrating too hard—and the alarm goes off."

I tabbed back to a photo of the storefront. Something was bugging me, something I should have caught. And a slow smile spread across my face as I realized what it was.

"Good job, Augie. Didn't think to look until you brought it up. See, the windows have seismic alarms," I said, tapping the screen. "The glass on the door *doesn't*. The alarm will catch anyone trying to jimmy the lock...so how about we break through the glass and leave the lock untouched?"

"Looks like tempered double-pane." Coop stroked his goatee while he thought out loud. "Smash-resistant. Not smash-*proof*, though, and I can get us in nice and quiet."

"How long?"

"Five minutes buys us a hole we can wriggle through. What about that motion detector?"

"Hold up," Stanwyck said. "You want to bust through a

jewelry-shop door in full view on a busy street? Totally exposed for at least five minutes? First cop to cruise by is gonna make us, and that's assuming some helpful citizen doesn't call it in first."

The first rule of camouflage is to conform to local expectations. What looks natural in the wilderness sticks out like a sore thumb in a city, and vice versa. I thought back to when I first arrived in Chicago, walking the streets, taking in the local color.

"Construction." I snapped my fingers. "Lot of street construction going on, right?"

Stanwyck snorted. "Always. Always too much and always too slow. They stretch the jobs out until winter comes, then start all over again in the spring. I spent most of the day driving different routes, marking all the construction spots so they don't trip us up on the way out."

"Any of that work get done at night? Third shift?"

"Sure. Some."

"And if a local sees a couple of guys in reflector-tape vests hanging around a work site and taking a coffee break, do they think, 'Looks like a burglary in progress'?"

"Nope," Stanwyck said. He shook his head and smiled, catching my angle. "They don't even think twice."

I rifled the drawers until I found a flimsy notepad branded with the motel logo and a ballpoint pen. I sketched it out as I talked, working the problem.

"We get a city truck and park it right here, directly opposite the door. Construction sawhorses here and here, cutting off the sidewalk. Best if we can get the kind with the blinking amber lights. They're disorienting in the dark, and anyone who looks our way will focus on the lights instead of what's happening behind them. Coop and I slice the glass. Stanwyck, you and Augie stand guard, and if anyone comes close, warn 'em off."

"That could work," Stanwyck said, "but where do we get the gear?"

"You already found it. Like you said, you drove around all day noting where the construction sites were. We hit the closest spots, find the ones that don't have an overnight crew, and grab what we need. They won't even notice anything's missing until tomorrow morning, and we'll be back in Nevada by then."

"What about the second floor?" Coop said. "Any other security up there?"

My gaze flicked to the screen. I kept seeing the other photos, the ones I couldn't show them, fresh in my mind's eye.

"Yeah. But that's my job. Weird stuff."

"Weird stuff?" Augie asked.

"Kid," Coop told him, "something you gotta learn about livin' the life. Every once in a while, on certain special jobs, a guy like Dan here will say the words 'weird stuff.' It's...sort of a secret code. You know what you do when you hear those words?"

Augie tilted his head. "What?"

"You stand aside, you let him go in first and do what he's gotta do, and you don't ask questions. Trust me, your life will be a lot happier that way."

* * *

Pulling a heist is like going on vacation: you're never ready when you think you are, there's always one last thing to pack, and there's always something you forgot. If you're lucky, you remember it at the last minute. If not...well, you're either in for a bad vacation, or you're going to jail.

We used more of my cash envelope for a quick shopping run, buying bits and pieces from stores all over the suburbs. Thin leather driving gloves for me and Coop and sturdier workman's gloves for Stanwyck and Augie since they didn't have to do any delicate work. Next, masks. Ski masks might be traditional attire for a burglary, but buying four of them when there was no snow on the ground was a great way to stand out like a sore thumb. Believe it or not, cops follow up on that kind of thing, and cashiers remember it.

Fortunately, we were cruising into autumn and Halloween wasn't too far away. Seasonal party suppliers had already sprouted up like weeds in vacant strip malls, renting out empty stores for a few months before they would vanish again. We split our purchase between three different shops, picking up a few latex monster masks. Coop and Augie were zombies, and Stanwyck wanted to be a werewolf.

I considered my mask carefully, knowing Ecko would eventually see it on the playback from his security cameras. I ended up going with the Mummy.

We picked up prepaid phones for everybody. We used my burner as the master phone, punching its number into the other three. If we got separated for any reason during the getaway, it'd be my job to change the plan up and set a new rendezvous point on the fly. Of course, that meant something had gone horribly wrong, so hopefully it wouldn't come to that.

Our shopping spree ended at a Home Depot, where I picked up the last tools we'd need: some construction vests lined with reflective tape, orange hard hats, and duct tape. A *lot* of duct tape.

There was only one thing left to do. We needed an empty building, which meant we needed Ecko gone.

I called his shop. He picked up on the third ring.

"Ecko and Company," said a sonorous, cultured voice. I couldn't place the accent. South African? "How may I help you today?"

"Damien Ecko, please."

"Speaking."

"Mr. Ecko, call me Greyson. I'm new in the city, and some friends told me you're the man to see about certain short-term financial services."

"I'm not certain I know what you mean." He kept his tone polite and even, carefully enunciating every word. "I'm a jeweler. Who are these...friends of yours, please?"

"I'm hesitant to speak their names over the phone, but I can say they recently left a piece of collateral with you. An obsidian Aztec knife."

He didn't answer right away. I could hear the wheels in his head turning as he tried to decide if I was a cop.

"We can meet," he said. "But not at my shop. There's an all-night diner on LaSalle Street. Be there tonight, at ten sharp."

"I'll be—" I started to say, but he'd already hung up.

The store closed at seven. I figured he wanted the extra time to call his current clients and ask if they'd sent any new business his way. That could go one of two ways: either they had and he'd assume that was who he was going to meet, or they hadn't and he'd assume I was an undercover cop trying to set him up—in which case he'd want to make this look like a big misunderstanding and plead his ignorance. Either way he'd show for the meet, and while he was waiting at the diner we'd be cracking his castle walls. I had one more call to make before we left.

"Hey, Cait."

"Daniel." She sounded tired but pleased. "Are you back already?"

"Tonight. We're about to head out and get things done."

"Have everything you need?"

"It's a good crew," I said. "They know their jobs."

"And yet."

She always could read me like a book.

"The occult security," I admitted, "is a little tougher than I'd bargained for."

"You can still back out."

"No, I can't. You take a job, you do the job."

"I'm making preparations for my trip," she said. "Leaving Emma in charge while I'm gone. She should be able to keep the wolves at bay for a few days."

"Can't you stay home and send Emma instead?"

"I am my prince's hound. As you so aptly noted, you take a job, you do the job. Even when the job is to stand beside his throne at a gala and look vaguely menacing."

"You're good at that," I said.

"Yes, but the specific and targeted sort of menacing is much more fun."

"On that note," I said, "I ran into my old buddies Mack and

Zeke at the airport. Gave 'em the slip, but they know I'm in town. Do I need to be worried? Not about those two, I mean, but Chicago is Night-Blooming Flowers territory."

"Probably not. A move against you is tantamount to a move against *me*, and after their failure with Pinfeather and the Redemption Choir, they're not eager to earn another spanking so quickly. Don't be surprised if they watch you from a safe distance, but as soon as they understand you're not in town on hell's business, I expect they'll lose interest. Just to be safe, I'll give Naavarasi a call and ask her to keep an ear out. She's eager to be helpful."

Never for free, I thought.

"All right," I said, "time to gear up and get this over with. I'll call you as soon as I touch down in Vegas."

A familiar feeling sank its claws into me, like a vulture perched on my shoulder. A current of tension ran down my spine and brought back old memories. The last time I'd felt like this was a couple of nights ago, on the edge of the Laramie Brothers parking lot. Just before the feds swooped in.

The time before that had been the night of the last job I ever pulled for Nicky Agnelli.

False positive, I told myself. *You're rebounding from a bad break, you're rusty, and you're working in a strange city. Of course you're nervous. You'd be stupid not to be.*

There were nerves, and there were *nerves*. This felt like my sixth sense twitching its nose, catching the scent of a thunderstorm in the air, but all I could see was a cloudless blue sky. I knew I should walk away, right then and there, before things had a chance to go bad.

And then what? I thought. *Then you get a little uneasy and walk away from the next job, and the one after that? If you don't get back on that horse tonight, you might as well turn in your riding boots.*

There are three key ingredients to any crime: means, motive, and opportunity.

I had all three.

I bundled up my gear and headed out to the parking lot. Time to go to work.

14.

We loaded up the trunk of Stanwyck's rental car with all of Coop's gear and rode downtown. The first handover spot was over in Lincoln Park, where his stolen ride—a Lincoln Town Car with mud-smeared license plates—waited for us on a strip of metered parking outside a row of brownstone apartment buildings. We pumped as many quarters into the meter as it'd swallow and quickly swapped the sacks of gear, leaving the rental behind. We drove over to a parking garage one block away from Jewelers Row.

"Coop and I will head over and check out the storefront," I told Stanwyck. "Get the utility truck and meet us there. Take Augie with you."

Stanwyck gave Augie a dubious glance and shrugged. He didn't argue, though. Puppy-dog eyes run in Coop's family.

Ten after seven and the downtown traffic slowly eased up. The daily commuters were back home already, snug behind their suburban picket fences, and the party crowds didn't come out on Wednesday nights. Coop and I did a casual walk-by, checking out the darkened storefront and the tone of the street.

"I like it," he told me. "Damn shame we can only hit the loft, though. Hate the idea of breaking into a jewelry store and not coming home with something shiny for the missus."

I shrugged. "I don't like leaving money on the table, but unless you can figure out a way to crack those glass cases without setting off the alarm in the next ten minutes, we don't have much of a choice."

"More like five," he said, nodding up the street. "I think our cover's here."

Stanwyck came tooling up behind the wheel of a big blue utility truck, the back loaded with orange construction cones and sawhorses and the City of Chicago seal stamped on its door. Augie hopped out when he pulled up to the curb, already wearing his hard hat and safety vest.

"Somebody call for a little urban camouflage?" Stanwyck asked as he got out. He tugged his own vest on over his gray flannel sweatshirt, and I walked around back to help unload the truck. In three minutes, we had the sidewalk cordoned off and amber lights strobing against the darkness.

Time wasn't on our side. We'd rehearsed as best we could, making sure everyone knew their jobs and when to do them, but I felt the pressure building. My watch read 7:27 when we hauled Coop's sacks off the truck. Ecko's "meeting" at the diner was at ten, and it wouldn't take him too long to figure out he'd been stood up. I figured we had three hours, three and a half at most, to get the job done and get out of town. When you're facing the threat of prison time or worse, two and a half hours flies by faster than you'd think.

Coop took two rolls of duct tape from a sack and handed me one. We pulled on our masks. Then we crouched down on the sidewalk side by side, layering the bottom half of the shop door with strips of tape until it was one solid silver blob. Then we cross-layered it, building a fluffy tape blanket. Stanwyck and Augie kept a lookout, loitering around the truck and acting like a couple of bored Teamsters on a never-ending coffee break.

Coop brandished a rubber-headed mallet and squinted at the taped-over glass like he was Michaelangelo with a fresh block of marble. I gave him some room. He tapped, softly but quickly, following an invisible path across the glass with the hammer. When an "L" train rumbled by overhead, steel wheels screeching against the tracks, the staccato thumps became sharp, full-swinging *thuds* swallowed up by the noise of the train.

He swapped his hammer for a short chisel and forced it in at the upper corner of the pane, wriggling it firmly from side to side. I heard a soft crackling sound as he pulled the sheet of duct tape backward—and with it the two dozen broken chunks of glass on the other side. A few pieces had fallen loose, tumbling to the cornflower-blue carpet inside the door, but most of the glass peeled away clean. A few taps of the hammer to clear the odd jagged edge, and now the bottom half of the front door was nothing but an empty hole surrounded by a brushed metal frame.

"My turn," I said.

The stairs up to Ecko's loft were on the far side of the store. The only thing standing between us and the prize was the white plastic face of a motion detector. The box sat high in the back corner of the shop, tilted downward to keep a watchful eye over the glass cases.

Most modern high-end security systems run on passive infrared. They pick up temperature fluctuations, and they're a hell of a lot harder to beat than the old ultrasonic or microwave systems. You can't hide your body heat behind a wall or a counter. Ecko apparently wasn't big on modern science: his detector was an old Sakamoto model. Seventies-era tech, big and boxy, bouncing microwaves across the room like a traffic cop's radar gun.

He's got a monster upstairs, I thought, shooting an anxious glance up toward the second-floor windows. *Means he can cut costs a little.*

No matter the method, motion detectors are aimed to leave a little wiggle room near a store's front door. If they didn't, they'd go off the second a legitimate employee walked in and tried to shut off the alarm in the morning. I adjusted my mask, got down on all fours, and crawled through the broken door, then stood straight and pressed my back to the wall on the other side.

Maybe twenty feet of open space stood between me and the motion detector. With my palms pressed flush to the wall and my head turned to one side, making myself as flat as I could, I edged my way in. Microwave detectors only trigger at a certain threshold of movement. My job was to stay under that threshold.

"Slow" didn't begin to define it. I moved like an ice statue, melting droplet by droplet on a mild afternoon. Minutes rolled by as I crept along the wall, eyes fixed on the unblinking LED under the detector's face. One misstep, the tiniest involuntary flinch, and I'd set it off.

Ten minutes later I was almost halfway across the room, and my nose started to itch. The heavy latex mask heated my face up, coaxing beads of sweat on my brow that trickled their way down my cheeks, like tiny tickling feathers teasing the curve of my chin.

Trying to ignore it made it worse. As the minutes dragged on, it went from itching to burning. Then another itch in the small of my back flared up. I imagined thousands of tiny red ants crawling across my skin, but all I could do was keep my hands perfectly still. I focused on my breathing. Inhale for four seconds. Hold for four seconds. Release for four seconds. My breathing, and that LED light up ahead, became my entire world.

After an eternity I finally slipped in under the plastic box, just under its blind spot, and scratched like I'd been doused in itching powder. I slipped my gloved hand under my mask, not wiping away my sweat so much as smearing it, then tore off a strip of duct tape.

I stood on my toes, reaching to slide the tape up and over the motion detector's lens. If I'd moved like melting ice before, now I was chiseled from stone. My feet ached and my calves and arms burned, but as the minutes ticked by, the tape slowly passed over more and more of the lens without setting it off.

The eclipse was complete. I pressed the tape into place. I took an experimental step backward, giving the motion detector a wave. With its cyclops eye blinded, the green LED didn't even flicker. The alarm sat quiet. As far as the system was concerned, everything was working as intended and the building was secure.

As long as we didn't mess with any of the jewelry cases, it would stay that way.

I gave Coop a thumbs-up. He crawled through the broken door next, masked and gloved, and Augie passed the first burlap sack of gear through to him. It clanked against the carpet.

My watch said 8:13. We'd burned almost an hour just securing the room, and we hadn't even gotten to the safe yet.

"Going up," I whispered to Coop. "Don't follow me until I call for you."

"Whatever you gotta do, make it fast."

I crept up the stairs at the back of the shop. The lock on the second-floor door was child's play. After the molasses-slow slog downstairs, I felt like a bolt of lightning with a pair of lockpicks on the tip. The tumblers rattled and fell into place, and the door swung wide.

I traded my picks for the baggie of Margaux's spirit dust.

The living room stood empty. Nothing glimmered, not before my physical eyes and not in my second sight. On the far side of a tiger-skin rug, an open archway looked in on a darkened bedroom. Another wider arch led to the dining room.

I felt like the explorer in an old adventure movie moments after the natives' drums went silent. Waiting for the attack.

I crept through the living room, my shoes sinking into the plush, tawny rug, and let my eyes slip out of focus as I gazed from arch to arch. Ecko's creature had to be here. It had to know I was here, too. So where *was* it?

I heard something. Something like the droning of flies' wings, almost too soft to hear but growing steadily louder, more forceful, angrier. I realized what the sound was. *Growling.*

I looked around, my heart pounding faster, trying to spot it before it could get the jump on me. The creature was near, but the noise sounded like it was coming from everywhere at once.

No, I realized, *not everywhere. It's just very, very close.*

I looked up.

Nine arms clung to the ceiling above my head by their twisted, blackened fingernails. Five heads looked down at me and screamed as one.

15.

I felt the creature's scream more than I heard it, a rippling shockwave that scorched through the air and hit my heart like a fist. The shock sent me reeling, jumping backward as the arms let go and the creature fell, slamming onto the living room floor where I'd been standing a heartbeat before.

It was there and it wasn't, a vision in shimmering silver that swam in and out of reality. I saw a tangle of sewed-together body parts, ragged stumps, and bones twisted at impossible angles. It felt like my eyes were forcing themselves to slip out of focus, sparing me from seeing too much of the misshapen thing at once.

Abomination, Halima had called it. The name fit.

I scooped up a handful of Margaux's powder and dashed it across the floor, just as the creature launched itself at me like a starving panther. It slammed into an invisible wall, fell back, rolled and thrashed, then wheeled around and charged into Ecko's bedroom.

I shot a glance toward the dining room and its three connecting doorways Every room in the loft had at least two ways out.

It was circling around to cut me off.

I ran across the dining room, skirting the edge of a polished mahogany table as the creature lunged through a connecting doorway. Arms snapped at me and spectral teeth gnashed the air, missing me by a foot. I hurled the rest of the enchanted powder at the thing's faces like I was throwing a fastball. It squealed and fell back, tipping over and righting itself on centipede arms, and ran for the kitchen to intercept me.

Now we were in a race to reach Ecko's office. The prize: first one there got to live. As I charged for the open doorway, the canopic jars in plain sight, my deck of cards riffled into my outstretched hand. Adrenaline turned into raw magic, launching a quartet of cards across the room like a swarm of killer hornets. My four aces.

They hit the closest two jars, shattering clay and sending a clutter of painted shards and black, withered lumps of flesh cascading to the carpet. The creature screamed behind me, hands and feet pounding the floorboards in rage.

Then it caught me.

A clawed hand closed on my ankle and yanked me off my feet. I hit the floor hard, cards jolting from my grip and scattering everywhere. Before I could call them to my grasp, the creature flipped me onto my back and hauled me away, dragging me through the dining room. Three heads loomed over me on broken necks, shrieking their outrage.

My right hand flailed out, caught the leg of a chair and held on for dear life, pulling it toward me. I grabbed onto it with both hands and broke it over the closest head, smashing the ornate wood into kindling. The head reared back, stunned, and two more took its place. Heads with more teeth than any mouth should have.

I clutched the broken chair leg with both hands. It had snapped away from the seat at a rough angle, ending in a jagged spike of splintered wood. One of the heads lunged at me, mouth wide and drooling, and I thrust upward as hard as I could and rammed six inches of wood straight into its eye socket.

The hand on my ankle let go as the creature reared back, roaring in agony and struggling to pull the chair leg loose. I rolled onto my stomach, jumped up in a sprinter's launch, and ran for the office. Behind me, the creature got its footing back and charged.

I could hear it thundering after me like a wooly mammoth from hell, mad with pain and starving for my blood.

I threw myself through the narrow office doorway. The creature slammed against it a moment later with a brutal *thud*, hard enough to make the doorframe shake. Hands groped for me, clawing the air. I grabbed the third jar, held it high above my head, and hurled it to the carpet. It shattered on impact, scattering desiccated blue-black livers across the office floor like a sick piñata.

The creature just tried harder, squeezing through the doorframe, inch by agonizing inch. I heard bones cracking and saw wet, gluey blobs of ectoplasm spatter the floor.

"Sorry." My muscles burned as I hoisted up the last jar, holding it high. "Not your lucky day."

The jar burst at my feet and spilled its grisly payload over my shoes. The creature vanished in a pulse of silver light, unwoven in a heartbeat. Where it had stood, only a cloud of thick dust hung in the air. The loft stank of mildew, ancient linens, and rot.

"Then again," I said to the empty room, "maybe it was."

My lungs and arms were fighting to see who could ache more, but I didn't have time to catch my breath. I gathered up my cards, hustled to the door, and gave Coop a tired wave. I helped him carry his sacks up, dragging the heavy equipment one thumping step at a time. He froze at the door to Ecko's office and stared down at the wreckage.

"So, uh, do I even wanna—"

"No."

He shrugged and stepped around the mess, crouching behind Ecko's desk. The safe was on the small side, about two feet wide, set into the bookshelf and sporting a shiny chrome spin handle and a traditional combination lock.

"Okay," Coop said, "Whistler Model Seven. It's not bad. Not the top of the line, but it's not bad."

"Can you get through it?"

He put his hands on his hips. Behind his zombie mask, his eyes narrowed to slits.

"Forget I asked," I said.

He tugged a little spiral-bound notebook out of his pocket, flipping through page after page of numbers scribbled in faded blue ink.

"I will. Now let's try this the easy way first."

I watched while he twirled the dials this way and that, glancing from the notebook to the lock.

"Try-out combos," he explained, catching the way my head tilted at him. "Standard combinations that come straight from the manufacturer on a brand-new safe. Any locksmith can get ahold of these, because only an idiot buys a safe and doesn't change the defaults. Still...sometimes, you catch a break."

He ran through the last number and shook his head. "Nope, not an idiot. Okay, we do this the hard way. Drag that sack over here and help me set up the Pornstar."

I wasn't sure I'd heard him right. "The...what?" I said, lugging the heavy sack. He grinned and tugged the burlap aside, revealing its contents: a power drill on a stout, telescoping tripod. The drill's body was as long as my arm and twice as thick, with a diamond-tipped bit nine inches long and an oversized battery pack.

"He *always* gets the job done," Coop deadpanned, setting up the tripod. The drill kicked to life with a shrill whine, chewing into the safe's black steel face as Coop held the rig steady and watched it like a surgeon evaluating a heart transplant.

"Model Seven's got cobalt plates inside," he called over the drill's hungry chewing. "Turn most drill bits into scrap metal. We don't gotta go that far, though."

More time slipped away while the drill did its work. I looked at my watch and wished I hadn't. 10:08. By now, Ecko had been at the diner for at least eight minutes, and he had to suspect his new "client" wasn't going to show up.

"How are we doing on time, Coop?"

The drill shut off with a grating clang. He tugged the bit free and blew on the slender hole it left behind, puffing out a cloud of black steel dust.

"Don't rush me," he said. "You got your magic, I got mine."

His next tool was a tiny display screen, about the size of a phone, connected to a long flexible tube. He waved me over, and I crouched next to him as he pressed the screen into my hands.

"Here," he said, feeding the tube into the hole. "Keep the screen facing me, so I can see what I'm aiming for. Ah, there you are. That's the sweet spot."

To me, the blurry image on the screen was a mishmash of ghostly gears and rods like a robot's x-ray, but to Coop it was the key to the kingdom. While I held the screen, he went to work on the combination dial, slowly turning it and watching the safe's inner mechanism move. One by one, tumblers fell into place.

He gave the chromed handle a spin. The safe door made a *chunk* noise and swung open.

The knife looked just like its picture, from the flared black obsidian blade to the wavy and serpentine hilt to the roaring yellow-green stone lion on the pommel. The safe's only occupant, it rested on a pillow of black velvet.

"That what we came for?" Coop asked.

"That's it. Let's pack up and get the hell out of here."

We had started bagging up the drill when my burner rang, buzzing against my hip. Augie was calling.

"What?" I said.

"You gotta come downstairs. You and Uncle Coop need to come downstairs, right now."

There was a tremble in his voice.

"What's going on, Augie? Where's Stanwyck?"

"*Please*. Come downstairs."

He hung up. I looked over at Coop and grabbed the knife.

"Something's wrong," I said. He was already up and on his feet, heading for the door, leaving his gear behind.

We jogged down the steps and into the showroom below. Augie stood there, halfway into the shop, unmasked and exposed to the security camera. Stanwyck stood behind him, wearing his gloves and his werewolf mask.

"Damn it, Augie," Coop said. "You're on camera! Where's your damn—"

Stanwyck took one step to the right. Showing us the revolver in his hand, pointed at Augie's back.

16.

"Stanwyck," I breathed. "What the *fuck*."

"Sorry, guys," he said. "See, I asked around like you wanted me to, seeing if anybody would come after us for ripping off Ecko. And while I did, I ran into somebody who wanted that cute little knife. They made me a better offer."

"Let him go," Coop growled. He took a step closer, skirting the edge of a display case. Stanwyck pressed the barrel of his gun to Augie's temple.

"Uh-uh. You stay right there, unless you want to pick bits of your nephew's skull off the carpet. Same goes for you, Faust. I've heard you're tricky. Think you can outsmart a bullet? Best be sure, for little Augie's sake."

I kept my hands where he could see them, nice and easy, the knife in full view.

"Stanwyck," I said, "I'm gonna tell you this once, and once only. Nobody stabs me in the back and gets away with it. Nobody. I'm feeling generous, so I'll give you one chance: put the gun down and *leave*. You forfeit your cut. That's your punishment for being a greedy asshole. Walk away, and I won't go after you."

"I might," Coop said through gritted teeth.

"Shut it," I told him, then looked back at Stanwyck. "*We* won't go after you. My word on it. Just let the kid go and walk away."

"I've got a better idea," Stanwyck said. "You slide that knife over here, I trade it for Augie, and we *all* walk away. This doesn't have to get bloody, Faust. I'm not looking to kill anybody. I'm just looking to get paid."

"Then you should have stuck to the plan."

I could feel time slipping away. How long before Ecko came home? How long before a patrol car prowled by on the street outside? Every wasted second made it less and less likely that any of us would get out alive.

Stanwyck laughed. "Can you do math? I can. Tell me, what's bigger: all the money, or one share of a three-way split? Seems like a no-brainer to me. Now slide that knife over here."

"Take that gun off my goddamn nephew *right now*, you son of a bitch," Coop snarled. He took another step closer, his hands balled up in leathery fists. Everything was sliding out of control, and all I could hear were the psychic klaxons in my head. The ones taking me back to another job gone bad. Another job I should have walked away from.

"Stay cool, Coop," I said. "Look, Stanwyck, we don't have a lot of time—"

Stanwyck nodded. "You're right. I don't think everybody appreciates the pressure we're working under. Let me help with that."

He smashed the lid of a jewelry case with the butt of his revolver, then pressed the barrel back against Augie's head before the kid could squirm away. As the glass shattered, my psychic alarms were muffled by a very real one, squalling out as the store security system blazed to life.

"Five seconds. The Chicago PD is getting an emergency call from Polymath Security," Stanwyck said. "Seven seconds, another operator is calling Damien Ecko and telling him his store's just been broken into. Are you *getting* this now, Faust? *Give me the damn knife!*"

"Let him go!" Coop shouted, moving up on Stanwyck now, a grizzly bear protecting his sister's cub. Augie's eyes bulged with panic, flashing left and right. I laid the knife on the closest counter.

"Fine. You want it? Take the damn thing."

I slid it over. It spun in razor-edged circles, gliding along the polished glass to rest near Stanwyck's hand. Stanwyck flicked his gaze away, just for a second. I saw the disaster coming before it happened. Time lurched into a slow molasses drip as Coop saw his chance and lunged at him.

Stanwyck pulled the trigger and shot Augie in the head.

Augie's body tumbled to the carpet. Specks of gray and scarlet glistened on the jewelry-shop wall. Stanwyck swung the gun around, fired again, and blasted Coop square in the heart from three feet away.

I ducked low as he took two shots at me, blowing out chunks of drywall just over my head. My cards fluttered into my hand, but I didn't have time to return the favor. Stanwyck snatched up the knife and ducked through the broken doorway, fleeing into the night.

Coop was still breathing, if you could call it that. More of a wet, ragged rattle as he stared up at the ceiling with a confused look in his eyes. I ran over, keeping low, and pulled up his shirt to survey the damage.

Coop tugged off his mask. His face was fishbelly-white and drenched in sweat. I tried to shield him from the security camera, stubbornly pretending it mattered, but he knew better.

"Forget it," he croaked. "Ain't exactly a flesh wound. I'm done."

I bundled up his shirt and pressed it against the guttering hole in his chest with both hands, trying to slow the bleeding. "Hold on, just hold on. All you need to do is last until the cops get here. They can call an ambulance—"

"And then I do a twenty-year stretch. I ain't got twenty years left in me. Don't wanna die behind bars. Don't want that, Dan. I don't *want* it."

He tried to push my hands away. He was weak as a kitten. In my mind I was back on my last job for Nicky. Back with my friend

Max, alarms screaming and cops on the way, and trying to push his guts back into his stomach.

It was happening all over again, like a nightmare on permanent repeat.

"You gotta live, Coop. You gotta—"

"Not behind bars," he said. "Dan, hey, you gotta run. You gotta do two things for me. Promise me. You gotta get my share to my old lady. She's gonna need the cash, with me gone. *Please*. You gotta promise me."

Coop was good as dead. He knew it. I knew it. Only difference was he accepted it. I couldn't let him go out like that.

And I couldn't get the cash to his wife if I was hauled out of here in handcuffs. I had to choose, and choose fast. I could keep him alive, so he could spend the rest of his life in prison—with me sharing a cell right next to him—or I could let him rest easy, knowing his family would be okay.

"Yeah, Coop," I told him. "I'll do it. I promise."

I pulled my hands away and let him bleed.

"The other thing." He let out a racking, high-pitched cough, wincing. "You find that son of a bitch, Dan. You find him and you send him straight to hell."

The swell of police sirens rose in the distance. I looked down at Coop.

"He's already dead," I said. "He just doesn't know it yet."

Coop nodded weakly and twitched his fingers at me. "Go on, then. *Get*."

I wanted to stay until the end—it seemed like the thing to do—but I couldn't argue with him. Couldn't argue with the sirens either, and they sounded like they were less than a block away. I gave Coop's hand one last, long squeeze.

Then I ran.

Out the door, into the night, and around the corner, ducking into the back alley. I ripped off my mask and my gloves as I ran, holding them close to my chest in a wadded-up ball. The alley kinked on a diagonal, curving behind the building and opening one street up. I froze in the shadows with my back pressed to a cold brick wall as three squad cars roared past, lights blazing against the dark. As soon as they rounded the corner I made my move, breaking from cover and running across the street, diving into another alleyway.

Distance. The more distance I could put between me and the crime scene, the safer I was. A stairway up to the elevated train tracks looked inviting, but I knew better. There were security cameras on the platforms, and the cops would be pulling all of tonight's footage to look for suspects. I had to figure they'd canvass the local cabbies too, so that meant hailing a ride was a no-go. I kept moving, alley to alley, backstreet to backstreet, with no direction in mind but "away."

About three blocks out, I found an open Dumpster piled high with last week's trash. I held my breath and shoved the mask and gloves as far under the mounds of moldering plastic bags as I could reach. Unless some eagle-eyed cop got incredibly lucky, they were good as gone.

Another couple of twists and turns, and I wound up on Michigan Avenue. Even this late at night there was plenty of traffic on the street. I could pass myself off as some faceless middle manager, stuck working late and on his way home.

Home. I wanted my desert, my neon, my tourist crowds, not this desolate, cold canyon of stone and glass. I wanted to catch the next flight west and leave this horrible night behind me. Couldn't do that, though. Not now.

I'm a professional liar, but some promises you just don't break. I promised Coop his wife would get his share of the score, and I'd be damned if I went back on that. Then there was Stanwyck. Between killing Augie and Coop, and thinking he could bushwhack me and get away with it, I had three good reasons to put a bullet between Stanwyck's eyes. Getting the knife back made four.

And he'll be lucky if I let him die that fast, I thought. He said he found another buyer. It'd have to be someone local and somebody who knew Damien Ecko's business. That couldn't be a huge pool of suspects. I gave Halima Khoury a call, got her voicemail, and left a message asking her to call me back right away.

The sky rumbled. More rain on the way. I took shelter in a tavern called Keefe's, where St. Patrick's Day was a year-round sort of celebration. The brick-walled pub felt like a cellar, cool and dark, and the air smelled like beer and fresh-roasted peanuts. There were worse places to wait out a storm. I found an empty table in the back where I could rest my feet for a while. Most of the crowd was up toward the bar, and I didn't feel too sociable.

A tired-looking waitress in a short plaid skirt came around, and I ordered a club soda with lime. I wanted hard liquor like a man in the desert wants ice water, but I had a feeling my work tonight was just getting started.

Sitting still gave me time to think. That was the last thing I needed. I played the night back in my mind, over and over again. If I'd been a little faster, a little sharper, if I'd done this thing or that thing differently, would Coop and Augie still be alive? I ran it down a hundred different ways, and it all ended in a hundred different pulls of the trigger.

A shot of the storefront came up on the TV behind the bar. My stomach clenched, waiting for a police-artist's suspect sketch, but none came. All I could make out over the chatter of the crowd was something about "mysterious circumstances" and a dead body found at the scene of the break-in.

My burner phone buzzed twice against my hip. I should have thrown the damn thing away with my mask and gloves, but in the heat of the moment I'd forgotten I had it.

It was a text message. Sent from Coop's phone.

17.

For just a second, my heart soared. He'd gotten out somehow. Crawled away from the store before the cops got there, or maybe bribed somebody into taking him to the hospital instead of a prison infirmary. Coop was okay.

Then I read the message.

You have something that belongs to me.

Ecko. He'd gotten there before the cops, most likely. Plucked the burner from Coop's pocket. I didn't answer him. Ecko didn't know me from John Doe; all he had was a number for a throwaway phone, one that was heading for the bottom of a trash can the second I walked out of here. Out of all my problems right now, he was at the rock bottom of the list.

The waitress brought over my club soda, and I pretended to enjoy it. A few minutes later, another message came in.

I have something that belongs to you, too.

And underneath, in a blue bubble of text: *File Attachment: friend.avi. Would you like to open it?*

One body, I thought. *The news said the cops only found ONE body.* My stomach clenched like a fist.

I cupped my hand over the phone, holding it close, and pressed play.

The video was taken from Coop's own phone, grainy and shaky, as the person holding it strolled down a dim corridor walled with cinder blocks. An overhead light hung dead, its bulb burned out, and the person taking the video clicked on a flashlight as he rounded a corner. As the camera slowly swept from left to right, I realized what the openings lining the hallway were: steel cell doors with tiny barred windows.

The director stopped at a door at the end of the hallway. He held up the camera and the flashlight together, sending a thin, pale beam of light into the cell. Letting me see what waited inside.

Coop's eyes were like a pair of white marbles, the pupils gone pale and dead. Mortician's thread stitched his lips shut, but they could only muffle the mewling animal noises he made as he flinched at the sudden light, throwing up his hands to hide his face. He was naked and sitting cross-legged on the dirty stone floor, one ankle shackled to a ring set into the floor. I could see the black clotting on his chest, blood congealed over the wound that killed him.

Coop wasn't dead.

He wasn't alive either.

Call me, the next message read.

I got up and walked into the men's room.

A naked fluorescent light bar crackled softly above the sinks. I stood under the harsh light, took a long look at myself in the grimy mirror, and waited for a drunk washing his hands to finish up and leave. I needed some privacy for this. Ecko picked up on the second ring.

"Mr. Greyson, I believe. Unless that was the gentleman with the bullet in his head, staining my carpet."

"This is Greyson," I said. No point denying the alias. He'd recognize my voice from the last time I called him. "I want my man back."

"And I want my property returned to me. It was a fortuitous thing, you know. Your friend had just breathed his last when I returned to my shop, but his soul hadn't quite left the body. I made sure he'd stay that way. And let me answer your unspoken question: he *is* suffering. He's suffering the torments of the damned, shackled inside his own dead meat. You should move with haste. Before he starts to rot in earnest."

Damn you, Stanwyck. Hell with the money, I'd give the knife back in a heartbeat if it meant setting Coop free.

"I don't have it," I said, "but...I'm working on that. Fine, you want it? It's yours. Just let him go."

Ecko chuckled.

"Oh, it's not that simple. There are damages. The violation of my shop, the destruction of my front door, not to mention the mess you made in my home." He paused. "You know, it's funny. There was a time when I'd pursue a thief to the ends of the earth to enact my vengeance, but I've been in this game for a long, long time. Perhaps I've mellowed with age, but I'm honestly more amused than angry. Perhaps I'll just keep your friend as an *ushabti* and we can call it even."

"Get to the damn point," I told him. "You've got a price in mind for letting him go, so let's hear it. What do I have to do?"

He giggled before he answered, a capricious little laugh, and that was when I knew I was in trouble.

"I want the Judas Coin."

"I don't know what that is."

"No," he said, "I imagine you don't. That's what happens when you go to a city where you don't belong and rob a stranger. Nonetheless, that's my price. Bring me the dagger and the coin, and you can have your friend back."

"If you'll just tell me—"

"We don't have anything else to talk about." He hung up.

I stared at the useless lump of plastic in my hands. I wanted to throw it against the wall. I wanted to break something. Instead I shoved it in my pocket, trudged back out into the bar, and drank my damn club soda.

Halima called me back. "I saw the news," were the first words out of her mouth.

"Things didn't go according to plan."

"I warned you," she said.

"Ecko wasn't the problem at the time. *Now* he's the problem."

I filled her in. She didn't answer right away, lost in a pensive silence.

"*Ushabti*." She said the word as if she'd swallowed a mouthful of sour milk. "In ancient Egypt, they were figurines. Little statuettes, imbued with funerary magic. The idea being that they would serve you for eternity in the afterlife."

"So when he called Coop one..."

"He's making it very clear he has your friend's soul in his power, and he means to keep him."

"But if I bring him this coin thing—"

Halima sighed. "He's playing with you. The coin isn't something you can...you know, it'd be easier to show you. Where are you? I'll come pick you up."

I waited outside under the glare of a streetlamp. A cold mist rode on the night wind, prickly and wet. It kept my senses sharp. Halima rattled up in an old brown Datsun with an NPR bumper sticker.

"I'm not doing this for you," she said as I got in on the passenger side. "That is to say I am, but...this isn't the sort of thing I get involved in, you understand? I'm doing this for your friend's sake."

"I'm grateful," I told her. "Stanwyck—the guy who bushwhacked us—said he got a better offer while he was asking around about Ecko. So it had to be someone local, somebody who deals in hot antiquities. Know anyone like that?"

"Possibly. What were you sent to steal?"

"An Aztec dagger. Obsidian blade, and the hilt's some kind of yellow-green stone with scallops and a lion head on the pommel."

"Sacrificial knife? Not good. Does it have magical properties?"

"For what I'm getting paid, I can't imagine it doesn't. My buyer is in Texas, so word about this thing is spreading fast."

"Stolen magical antiquities." She wrinkled her nose. "As it happens, I know a likely suspect, but getting the truth out of him won't be easy. It never is. Hold on, we'll be there in a few minutes."

"There" was at the end of a twisty drive through the backstreets, down empty roads lined with construction cones and along narrow alleys littered with chunks of asphalt. A murder of crows watched us from telephone lines and rusty fences, their eyes glittering in the dark.

"I understand there's a private club for the occult underground in Las Vegas. Is that right?" She gave the birds a narrow-eyed stare as we rolled past.

"The Tiger's Garden," I said. "It's picky about who it lets in. Magicians only."

"I've heard a rumor that there's a nightclub not far from the Vegas Strip, too. Allegedly operated by one of the courts of hell and exclusively catering to *their* particular...needs."

"I've heard that rumor, too."

The Datsun turned into a parking lot, pulling into a vacant space between a battered old pickup and what was, unless my eyes deceived me, the sleek fire-orange wedge of a four-hundred-thousand-dollar Lamborghini.

"It's important to understand, first and foremost," Halima explained as she killed the engine, "that in Chicago, the occult community is rather...desegregated."

A three-story brownstone, all of its windows boarded over, turned its back to the parking lot. My shoes crunched on loose gravel as I followed Halima over to a battered metal door.

"There are rules," she said and ticked them off on her fingers. "Take nothing that does not belong to you. Lay no hand on another, except by their invitation. Speak no true names and tell no secrets, save those which are yours to tell."

"Halima, where *are* we?"

She rapped four times on the metal door. I glanced up, spotting the eye of a closed-circuit camera set high on the wall. A moment later, the door buzzed and she pulled it open. A gust of warm air washed out over us, carrying the distant, muffled strains of violin music. Halima looked at me, grave.

"A place I do not care to visit very often," she said. "Welcome to the Bast Club."

18.

"Stay close to me," Halima warned as we walked down a short hallway lined in burgundy wallpaper. The floor was an elaborate mosaic expertly carved into solid oak, a sea of interlocking puzzle pieces. Sconces under globes of green glass cast pale light, but something about the hall set my nerves on edge.

Too many shadows, I realized, glancing from the lights to the walls. *Shadows without anything casting them.*

The vestibule opened onto a lounge done up in grand Victorian style, baroque wood and brass, with red velvet divans gathered in discreet sitting nooks. Another pair of green glass sconces dangled over antique billiard tables in one corner of the lounge, and a lacquered bar with brass runners curved in an L-shape stood on the opposite side. Lush velvet curtains and lace chintz shrouded the boarded-over windows.

Raw sensation hit my psychic senses so fast I couldn't keep up with it. The room was a vortex of strange magic and confused signals. A couple of cambion wearing bikers' leathers played pool, openly displaying their runny-egg eyes and purple-veined faces. A petite Chinese woman in a tailored black suit held court in one of the conversation nooks, a briefcase at her side. Sitting opposite her, a pair of young women in matching blue hoodies watched intently while she demonstrated items from her case—a tiny brass spinning top, a bell, a pair of bone dice. Sandalwood incense and something musty, like the smell of a library filled with old and rare books, hung in the air.

If I let my eyes slip out of focus, I could see tangled serpentine snake-trails of glowing fractal runes flitting around us. They whirled and danced and mated, giving birth to impossible mathematics.

"It's a bit much at first," Halima said, unimpressed.

I nodded toward the bikers at the pool table. "I thought the Flowers had an open-season policy on cambion these days?"

"Did. From what I understand, a rebel faction called the Redemption Choir stirred up a hornet's nest. Then their leader disappeared, and things calmed down again. Cambion still aren't exactly welcome in Chicago, but violence is forbidden within these walls."

Halima confirmed what I'd suspected all along, that the "pogrom" was a feint to force the Redemption Choir west into Prince Sitri's territory. Didn't matter now. Their leader didn't disappear. I knew exactly where he was: buried twenty feet under a parking lot.

A squeal of delight broke my concentration. The woman steaming toward us had a lopsided mop of curly hair dyed fire-engine red. She wore a gray raw silk halter dress that could have come from Caitlin's closet, belted with a twist of gunmetal black chain. An envelope-sized purse dangled from the crook of her arm, her hand currently occupied with an oversized martini glass.

"Lady H, you came out of hibernation!" She stopped, turned, and gave me a curious head-to-toe look. "Hey, who's your date? Not bad."

A faint blush colored Halima's cheeks. "Not my date, Dances. Just a friend of an old friend. This is Daniel. Daniel, this is Freddie."

"Fredrika Vinter." She offered me her free hand. Her skin was morbidly cold to the touch, like she'd just pulled it from an ice bucket. "My good friends call me Dances. Wanna be good friends?"

"Daniel's from Las Vegas," Halima said. "He's in town on business, and I thought I'd show him the sights."

"I've got *my* sights set on that couch," she said, eyeing one of the empty conversation nooks, "and another appletini. Come, come, drinks are on me."

Halima's fingernails gently touched my back as we followed her across the lounge. "Dances is a good friend of mine," she whispered. "You can trust her. Nobody else here, though. And I mean *nobody*."

Freddie draped herself across a red velvet divan, a fresh drink in hand. I ordered a whiskey sour from the bar—at this point in the night, I needed to limber up a little—and Halima asked for a club soda. We sat in high-backed wooden chairs set at an angle to the divan, all clustered around a little round table and a handful of felt-lined coasters.

Freddie gave Halima a look over the rim of her glass. "Swear to God, when are you going to let me dress you properly? You're too pretty to have a wardrobe that frumpy. You should look like a model. You should be one of *my* models."

Instead of answering her directly, Halima rolled her eyes and looked my way. "Fashion designer," she said, as if that explained everything.

She was more than that. I couldn't miss the shiver that rippled down my spine as I sat close to her—not from nerves, from cold. The air around Freddie was cooler than the rest of the room by at least ten degrees. It felt like I was standing next to an open freezer.

"House of Vinter, *dahling*," she told me, punctuating it with a diva-esque twirl of her hand so over-the-top it had to be deliberate. "And what do you do, Mr. Las Vegas?"

I looked over at Halima. She shrugged.

"I'm a thief," I said.

Freddie blinked. "Ooh, and I thought tonight was going to be *boring*."

A couple strolled by behind my chair. For a moment, they got between us and the closest light, casting Freddie in a patch of shadow. As the light peeled away, so did the facade. A desiccated corpse reclined on the divan, with skin turned blue and chapped by arctic windburn. The corpse grinned at me from a lipless mouth, showing sharp yellowed teeth. Her nose and most of one cheek had rotted away, the ragged wounds black with frostbite, and iron talons three inches long curled around the stem of her martini glass.

Then the light flooded back and the moment was gone. Freddie must have caught the look on my face. She smiled and gave me a wink.

"So is this a post-robbery celebration?" she asked. "Because if so, I'm getting us a bottle of something expensive."

"Not a celebration," Halima said. She would have said more, but she glanced to one side and hushed up. I recognized the man strolling our way from his photograph, dressed in a tailored tweed suit and bow tie. Even with bags under his eyes and wrinkles on his dusky skin, there was something regal about Damien Ecko. He wasn't old so much as *antique*, a refined style from another time.

"I thought I heard a voice I recognized," he said, looking my way. "You must be the illustrious Mr. Greyson. And I cannot express how *shocked* I am to find you in the company of my dear friend Halima."

Halima glared at him. "Before you say one more word, I had nothing to do with this man's crime. I'm merely trying to keep this situation from getting any worse."

"Yes, you're helpful that way. So good-intentioned." His gaze slid from her headscarf to her glass of club soda. "Still pretending to be a Muslim?"

"Hey, Damien," Freddie said, "still pretending to be a man?"

"Dances-with-Knives, a pleasure as always." He lowered his voice. "I could ask you a similar question, *wendigo*."

"I was commenting on your lack of genitals." Freddie leaned closer to me, cupped one hand to the side of her mouth and stage-whispered, "*Nothing down there. Smooth like a Ken doll.*"

Ecko swung his attention back my way.

"I just had the most illuminating discussion with your friend," he said. "Of course, it was mostly one-sided, but he contributed his share of agonized whimpers. The rigor mortis should be setting in soon. I have to imagine it would be like...intense cramps in every muscle in your body, all at the same time. Unendurable. Most people would choose death over pain like that. Pity he doesn't have that option."

I was on my feet before I thought about it. My hand balled into a fist, but Halima grabbed my wrist and clamped down hard.

"Not in here," Halima said, her voice low and urgent. "No fighting in here. I told you, it's forbidden."

Ecko grinned. All around us, the shadows seemed to weave. Tighten. Grow thicker and darker as they crawled across the Victorian wallpaper.

"Go ahead," he said. "Take a swing. Test your luck."

"*Daniel*," Halima said, squeezing my wrist harder. "*No fighting*. Management doesn't give second chances."

"God," Freddie groaned, rolling her eyes at Ecko. "You are *so fucking boring*. And you are dismissed. Go. Leave. Away from my table."

Ecko narrowed his eyes at her. "I may go wherever I—"

"This is the Cool Kids' Table. I am the Queen of the Cool Kids, and I hereby use my magic chalice of office to banish you into the hinterlands of boredom." Freddie waved her martini glass at him. "Go suck somewhere else."

"Insufferable woman." He wrinkled his nose at her. I couldn't help but crack a smile. Halima eased up on my wrist as my hand unclenched. Ecko turned and started to walk away.

"Just one thing," I said.

He stopped and looked back at me, lifting a curious eyebrow.

"The name's not Greyson. It's Faust. Daniel Faust."

"And," Ecko said, "should that mean anything to me?"

"It will, real soon. You just guaranteed that."

He shook his head. "You are a very small fish in a brand-new pond. I suggest you swim with more caution. And in better company."

Halima and I waited until Ecko was long gone before we sank back into our chairs. Freddie let out an excited little squeak and drummed her high heels against the divan.

"Oooh, you pissed off Old Dusty. Points for style, points for brashness, now give me all the scandalous details."

I walked her through it. When I was done, Freddie sighed and looked over at Halima.

"He's trying to get him killed."

"That was my thought," Halima said.

"The Judas Coin thing?" I asked. "What is it, anyway, and why is it so dangerous?"

"Because you can't steal it," Halima told me. "It's impossible. Come on. We'll *show* you."

Freddie led the way up a side hallway that ended in a pair of double doors. A discreet brass placard on one door read "Gaming Parlor."

The room beyond was almost the size of the main lounge and laid out better than some casinos back home. Empty, except for us and the shadows. Crescent-shaped tables with green felt tops circled the room, ready for action. The lights, simple squares set into the vaulted ceiling, were dimmed down to give the room a dusky ambiance.

As we walked farther into the parlor, our footsteps echoing in the silence, I looked to one wall and counted. There were three of us.

Six shadows stood on the wall.

As I watched, one of the shadows turned and elongated, its arms becoming spears. Two more appendages sprouted from where its stomach would be. It scurried up the wall and climbed onto the ceiling, disappearing into a patch of darkness.

"Management," Halima said softly, "is not to be trifled with."

I spotted the prize right away, once I could tear my eyes from the shadows. It stood at the heart of the room, a wooden pedestal topped with a box of polished glass. Inside the box, resting on a black silk pillow, sat a single silver coin.

I walked closer to take a better look. The coin was small, about the size of my thumbnail, and age and wear had stolen its gleam away. The face depicted some kind of vulture-headed creature, encircled by an inscription in ancient Greek.

"Tell me something," I said, "has anybody ever stolen anything from this place and lived to talk about it?"

Halima crossed her arms. "Allegedly, a bartender was once short on cab fare home. He borrowed five dollars from the till, intending to pay it back the next day. He was found in his apartment, torn into so many pieces the police had to scoop his remains up with a shovel."

"Zero-tolerance policy," Freddie added.

19.

The three of us stood around the glass case, eyeing the tiny treasure within.

"So what's the deal with the coin?" I asked. "They just keep it on display here?"

"It's this year's grand prize," Halima said. "Daniel, what do you know about the courts of hell?"

"More than the average joe."

"Management rents the place out for special occasions," Freddie said. "Weddings, parties, black masses, all that jazz. Once a year, Royce throws a big tournament. The buy-in is steep, but the winner walks away with a nice chunk of change, plus whatever that year's grand prize is. It's always something weird and rare, no idea where he gets the stuff."

I had a feeling I wasn't going to like the answer, given Halima's lead-in, but I had to ask. "And this Royce is...?"

"He works for Prince Malphas," Halima said. "His hound, if you're familiar with the term."

Yeah. I was familiar with it. The princes of hell were too old, too powerful to operate on Earth. They couldn't even set foot here without kicking off the apocalypse ahead of schedule. So every prince had a hound: the one demon in their court who was smart enough, tough enough, and mean enough to take care of their court's business and scare all the other hellspawn into submission.

Caitlin was Prince Sitri's hound, and on a good day, she could give the Terminator a run for his money. Now Damien Ecko wanted me to rip off her less-friendly counterpart.

No way, I thought. *Even if I could pull it off, even if I could get out of Flowers territory and back to Vegas in one piece, I'd bring a political shitstorm down on Caitlin's head. It's impossible.*

Then I thought about Coop, locked in a cell in the darkness, trapped inside his own rotting corpse.

There's no such thing as impossible if you've got the right motivation. And I had it in spades.

Freddie rested her fingernails on the display case, lightly stroking the glass. "Supposedly it's legit. The Judas Coin. A Tyrian shekel, formerly owned by a Mr. J. Iscariot, one of thirty, gotta collect 'em all. Creepy, huh?"

"This tournament," I said. "Is it open to anybody?"

Freddie nodded. "Sure. There are thirty-six seats, first come, first served. Just pay the buy-in and you're on the list. Five thousand dollars, cash. You playing this year, Lady H?"

Halima cringed. "Dances, I'm a museum conservator. How much money do you think I make?"

"Indiana Jones never had cash problems. C'mon, couldn't the Field front you some money? It'd be worth it, just so you could say the line."

"What line?" Halima asked.

Freddie leaned against the case, sinking down until her big, bright eyes were level with the coin. "*It belongs in a museum*," she stage-whispered.

"So what's the game?" I asked.

"It changes every year," Freddie said. "This time around? Texas Hold'em. You any good at poker, Mr. Vegas?"

"I've been known to play, now and then."

"Better bring your A-game. Royce goes hunting for the best of the best to fill his tables. He wants to put on a good show for his boss. Me, I just play for fun and to provide color commentary."

"And you have to play *clean*," Halima added. "No magic, no

tricks, just pure cards. Royce personally provides security for the event, and if anyone's caught cheating...management steps in."

I glanced up, watching an eight-legged shadow the size of a car squirm across the ceiling.

It was a shot. A long shot, sure, but a shot. If I won the coin fair and square, I could hand it over to Ecko with no problems. I'd just have to take down the thirty-five other players in my way first. No pressure. Then there was the five-grand buy-in, which I didn't have.

"One problem at a time," I said. "I've got to track down that dagger while the trail's still hot. You said there might be a local here who deals in stolen antiquities?"

"Two that come to mind," Halima said. "Let's go back to the lounge. I'll point them out."

I didn't object. The longer we loitered in the gaming room, the bigger the shadows got. And the hungrier they felt.

* * *

Back in the conversation nook and armed with a fresh martini, Freddie surveyed the room.

"Okay, nine o'clock. Look but don't be obvious. See the one in the Dolce and Gabbana tunic dress and the Saint Laurent heels? About forty pounds soaking wet? That's Amy Xun."

I'd already noticed her when I came in, the Chinese woman with the briefcase full of oddities. Her customers in the hoodies were long gone, leaving her alone to sip a glass of red wine and tap at her phone with rapid-fire pecks.

"Amy's the local go-to for all things esoteric and creepy-crawly," Freddie said. "She's hooked up from here to Dubai, and if she can't get it, you don't need it. Not just occult gizmos either. When it comes to sourcing some primo party favors, she's my girl. She'll wring your wallet dry, though, and she'll expect you to haggle over *everything*."

Halima leaned closer to me, lowering her voice. "Amy has...a bit of a fetish, I suppose you might call it, when it comes to her work. She lives for the art of the deal. It truly is an art, in her reckoning, and she's relentless in her pursuit of perfection."

"Now over by the bar, check the weasel on the end." Freddie waved her glass in his general direction. "Your eyes do not deceive you: he is wearing a black sports coat and a black pair of slacks he bought separately. They're not even *close* to the same shade, and he thinks he looks good."

I squinted, but in the dim light I couldn't tell the difference. I deferred to her superior fashion sense.

"Also, that thing on his head is not a dead badger, as you might reasonably surmise, but a toupee, which I believe he purchased in a thrift store. This sad, sad example of manhood in decline is Trevor Manderley, owner of the Hermetic Inquiry. It's a niche store in Wicker Park that mostly caters to the new-age and neopagan crowds, but Trevor does a brisk backroom business in contraband with a harder edge."

"Even odds," I said. "Which one's more likely to give a straight answer?"

"Neither, but one won't go out of her way to screw you." Freddie stood up and waved, raising her voice. "Amy! Amy, Amy, Amy. Come *here*. Meet my new friend."

Amy made her way over to us, still absorbed by her phone. When she glanced up, I felt like she was weighing me on a butcher's scale. Her eyes flicked toward my shoes, my fingernails, my haircut, taking everything in and assigning a dollar value. She set her wine glass down and gave me a measured handshake, firm and dry.

"Amy Xun," she said, "acquisitions and sales."

"Daniel Faust," I replied, "mostly acquisitions."

"You're not a local. Here for the tournament? I'll tell you the same thing I told Ms. Vinter. If you win the grand prize, please come see me at once. I'll give you a better price for it than anyone in Chicago, guaranteed."

"Lot of people want that coin. Doesn't seem like such a great prize, though."

"I don't speculate as to the motives of others," Amy said, "but I want it sheerly for the symbolism. The Judas Coin is an icon to build a business around."

"What symbolism? Betrayal?" I asked.

She gave a polite little chuckle. "I'm a merchant, Mr. Faust. If you believe the story, Judas made the greatest sale in history."

"I'm looking for a Judas myself," I told her. "Man going by the name of Stanwyck. Didn't happen to visit you, did he?"

"All client relations are confidential," she said, pursing her lips.

"Let me rephrase. Maybe you just bought a knife from somebody, doesn't matter who. Aztec dagger, with an obsidian blade. If you happen to have that knife, I'll be happy to take it off your hands, no questions asked."

"A buy?" she blinked. "*This* week? Tournament week? Absolutely not. I need to be as liquid as possible if I'm going to get my hands on that coin. You should ask Mr. Manderley."

"Just count your fingers after you shake his hand," Freddie added.

No worries there. Trevor wasn't offering any handshakes, with his fingers glued to his whiskey glass. I slid onto the stool beside him and waved over the bartender.

"One of those," I said, gesturing to Trevor's glass, "for both of us."

"Unexpected generosity," Trevor grunted, barely looking my way. "But nothing's free."

"Not in this life. I'm new in town. I hear you're a man who can get things. Exotic things."

He glanced over his shoulder toward the conversation nook where Amy had taken my chair.

"Xun couldn't help you out, huh? Not surprised. This week she's only got eyes for that damn coin."

"Not you, though?"

He sipped his whiskey. "It's a piece of junk, doesn't even *do* anything. Besides, I don't play cards. I don't believe in gambling.

That's why, when people in this town need a sure thing, they come to *me*. Sure, ol' Trevor is everybody's last stop, but at the end of the day? Their cash, my pocket. Turning disbelievers into satisfied customers is what I do. What's your poison?"

"I'm looking for a knife," I said and watched the pads of his fingers turn white as they tightened around his glass.

He talked to the bottles behind the bar, not looking my way. "Yeah? What kind of knife?"

"Aztec. Sacrificial dagger. Obsidian blade. It belongs to me, and I'd like it back."

"Small world," Trevor said. He tossed back another mouthful of whiskey. Drinking faster, now. "Small world indeed. A man tried to sell me an item just like that. Didn't say who it belonged to, though."

"And you didn't ask. Which I understand. Business is business, and normally that's not your problem."

He slowly turned his head to look my way.

"Are you saying it's my problem now?"

"Maybe," I told him. "Fortunately for you, I'm one of those problems that goes away easy. This isn't a shakedown. I don't want to step on your toes, and if you've got the dagger I'll buy it at a fair price. I just want the blade and the man who sold it to you."

"I'm not in the habit of selling out the people I do business with. I'm sure you can understand. Get a reputation for telling tales about your customers, and soon you don't *have* any customers."

"Look," I said, "I'm trying to help you out here. Save you some needless pain and suffering. I hope you'll let me."

"Stow the tough-guy act." Trevor gestured around us with his glass. At the corner of my eye, a new shadow crawled along the edge of the bar. "You can't touch me in here. And as far as outside goes? Buddy, I know everybody in this town, and everybody knows me. I can make your visit a short one. *Real* short."

"You know Damien Ecko?"

"Course I do," he said. "Why?"

“Maybe you should keep up on current events. Somebody broke into Ecko’s store tonight and left two corpses on the carpet. They took that dagger from his personal safe.”

Trevor didn’t answer. He just stared at me while the color leeched from his face.

“Two ways this can go,” I said, “both of them bad. The cops can catch my ex-partner, and the dagger’s trail leads right to your doorstep. Or Ecko catches him, and the trail leads right to your doorstep. I don’t see either of those options building up to a happy ending for you.”

“Hey, I didn’t know. I talked to the guy yesterday. All he said was he needed a bundle of quick cash, and he was about to get his hands on something that might be up my alley. I had no idea who he was going to steal it from.”

“I believe you,” I said. “But Ecko? He’s gonna think you set this whole thing up. I can help you, all right? I can make this problem just—poof—go away. But you’ve gotta level with me.”

He squeezed his glass harder, to stop his hand from shaking. It didn’t work.

20.

"The meet is supposed to go down in about two hours," Trevor said, sounding defeated. "He's bringing the dagger, and if it checked out, I was going to give him fifteen large. I've got a contact in New Orleans who's big on Mesoamerican stuff, figured I could spin it and make a quick buck."

Fifteen large. If Stanwyck had stuck with me and stayed loyal, I would have paid him just shy of nine. Augie was dead with a bullet in his brain, and Coop was trapped in his own rotting corpse, all for the sake of six thousand dollars.

"He said he needed the money fast, huh?"

Maybe my tone had changed, or maybe it was the look on my face, but Trevor edged away from me on his barstool.

"I didn't...I didn't ask for details," he said. "None of my business. Look, you've got to keep my name out of this—"

"We never had this conversation. Just tell me where the meet's going down. I'll take care of everything. You'll never hear from this guy again, I promise you that."

Trevor drummed his fingers on the bar, thinking.

"I don't like doing business with new clients at my store," he said. "Too risky. Never know who you're really gonna meet. There's a place off West 79th, down on the south side. It's a shuttered-up convenience store owned by some friends of mine."

He rested his hand on the bar and slid it my way. When he pulled his fingers away, a tarnished set of keys sat next to my glass.

They dangled from a cheap tag with a street address scrawled under translucent plastic.

"He'll be expecting me there," Trevor said. "Waiting for him."

"Hope he likes surprises," I said and scooped up the keys.

Back in the conversation nook, Amy had already made herself scarce. Halima and Freddie gave me a curious look. I jingled the keys.

"I know where Stanwyck's going to be. With the dagger. If you ladies will excuse me, I need to go have a word with him."

"Call me when it's over, so I know you're all right," Halima said. She glanced at Freddie. "Want to get a late dinner?"

Freddie smiled, but there was something sad at the edges of her eyes.

"You know me," she said. "I'm always hungry."

* * *

The cabbie, an Armenian with bushy black caterpillar eyebrows, stared at me in the rearview mirror when I read him the address.

"That's in Auburn Gresham."

"Problem?"

His lips twisted in a patronizing smile.

"You're not from around here." It wasn't a question.

"Not a big tourist crowd there, I take it."

"I don't go to Auburn Gresham after dark." He shook his head. "No way. Closest I can get you...mmm, three blocks from that address."

"Then I guess I'm going to get some light exercise."

He muttered something under his breath. I assumed it was Armenian for "crazy asshole." Still, true to his word, he drove me down to the south side of the city and pulled over on the edge of a dark, lonely backstreet.

"Walk that way," he said, pointing straight ahead as I passed him a rumpled twenty. "Three blocks, on your left. Don't get shot."

"I'll make an effort."

He responded with a shake of his head and muttered under his breath again. I didn't need a translation. He pulled a U-turn and left me standing alone.

The dark smooths things out, hides the blemishes that show under a noonday sun. I walked along a row of brick bungalows that wouldn't have looked out of place in a Norman Rockwell painting. Neatly cut lawns, not a stray brick or a scrap of trash in sight. Cities talk, though, and you can get the lay of the land if you learn how to listen. The bars behind vintage windows, the alarm-company signs on reinforced front doors, those were the first hints that I was in troubled territory.

The gunshots were next. One dull, basso thump and then three quick reports, a staccato burst coming from a block or two away. Then silence. No lights went on. Nobody came running out of their houses. It was as if nothing had happened at all.

I hit a commercial corridor cutting down the middle of the neighborhood. Heavy iron grates sealed the front door of a jerk chicken joint. Across the street, sheets of plywood covered the broken front window of a camera shop, the wood freshly tagged with the letters *GD* in thick calligraphic script. The street felt like the diseased pulp at the heart of a rotten tooth.

Red and blue lights strobed along alley walls. Cops had a trio of shirtless, sullen teenagers in blue bandannas up against their car, the hood piled with confiscated steel. I walked faster. I wasn't afraid of the neighborhood, but I didn't have an excuse for being there. Not one a cop would want to hear, anyway.

The convenience store stood on a desolate corner, windows shuttered and lights dead. It butted up against an abandoned dry cleaner's on one side and an abandoned cell-phone store on the other, nothing left but corroded bars, broken glass, and dust. I shot a look over my shoulder, making sure I was alone, and let myself in. The front door—all the glass broken out and replaced by layers of thick plywood—swung shut at my back.

My eyes slowly adjusted to the gloom. Maybe the store had thrived once, but now nothing was left but aisles of empty shelves and some stray dented tin cans a few years past their sell-by date. A door hung open behind the checkout counter, leading farther into the building. I crept toward it, listening to the warped linoleum crackle under my shoes. I needed to make sure the place was empty. Didn't want anyone interrupting the fun once Stanwyck showed up.

Like I'd told Halima and Freddie, I needed to have a talk with the man. And I was going to take a good, long time doing it.

Beyond the door was a stub of a hallway ending in two opposite-facing openings. A stockroom and a washroom, I figured. The doors were long gone, nothing but bare hinges left on the dingy frames.

In the darkness, a child giggled.

I froze. A faint glow emanated from the left-hand doorway, like a lit match shrouded in a stranger's hand.

I eased my way toward the opening and peeked around the corner. In the middle of a filthy bathroom, the fixtures ripped out and nothing but exposed pipes left behind, light glowed from a crack in the world. It hung in the open air, a jagged cut in space.

Tiny hands reached out from inside the crack and forced it wide. Inch by inch, the creature on the other side wrenched itself halfway through. It looked like someone had taken a cherubic baby doll and tossed it in a furnace, charring its waxy skin. It looked up at me with wide red eyes and giggled again, falling through the crack and tumbling to the bathroom floor with a wet *plop*.

The imp stood up on wobbly, fat little legs and raised its mangled hand. A gush of heat washed over my face, carried on a wind that stank of excrement. Then came a billowing *crump* of superheated air as the floor around the baby's feet ignited.

Trevor. Instead of giving up Stanwyck, he'd lured me to the middle of nowhere and summoned up a demon to take me out. Assassination by proxy.

Fine, I thought with a snarl. *Everything Stanwyck's got coming, you get it too.*

One card leaped from my hip pocket. The ace of spades. I twirled my fingers and sent it lancing through the air, straight for the imp's throat. It never made it. A globe of air shimmered around the squat, misshapen body and the card ignited, leaving nothing but a pile of ash.

The baby raised its hand and wagged a tiny clawed finger at me as it giggled.

A half dozen banishing rituals flickered through my mind, like a chef contemplating a recipe book. I had plenty of ways to get rid of the thing—and every one of them required gear I hadn't brought with me. Time was my only advantage. Without a body to hijack, the imp wouldn't be able to stay for long before getting sucked back into hell.

Discretion was the better part of valor. I ran for the front door. I hauled it open, tasting fresh air, just long enough to see three things: the sedan parked at the curb, Stanwyck in the driver's seat, and the silenced pistol in his hand. I jumped back as his gun coughed and a bullet whined past my ear like an angry hornet. I slammed the door closed.

The imp had followed me into the store. It performed a clumsy cartwheel and a pirouette, pointing this way and that, and more *crumps* of air made my ears pop as the walls and ceiling burst into fast-growing blossoms of fire wherever it gestured.

Stanwyck had his gun on the door, and he wouldn't miss a second time. Those were my options: burning or a bullet.

I sprinted past the imp and down the back hallway, jumping a streak of flame as it erupted under my feet. The stockroom was as empty as I feared. A few broken metal shelves rusted in the gloom, and moonlight streamed through a couple of windows set high in the wall, each one about the size of a shoebox. No way out. I spun around.

The imp stood on the threshold. It gave me a playful grin, flashing flame-blackened teeth, and stretched out its claws.

21.

At the imp's unspoken command, tiny fires exploded from the walls and floor around me, filling the stockroom with lethal clouds of roiling black smoke. The building rumbled as something crashed out in the storefront, the fire loosening chunks of ceiling and lashing at the foundations.

I stumbled back against the sidewall, my shoulder hitting peeling white plaster. It bent.

I blinked, put my hand to the wall, and pushed. The rotten wood underneath flexed and a chunk of plaster fell free. As I grabbed one of the broken shelves and pulled it over, sending it crashing to the floor, I tried to picture the building's layout. If I guessed right, this room butted up against the back of the dry cleaner's next door.

Building's an antique, I thought feverishly as I grabbed the shelf with both hands and wrenched at the groaning metal. *Cheap materials. Nobody checking for fire-code violations. Walls weren't strong to begin with.*

The shelving support snapped free, leaving me with a stout metal pole about three feet long. I braced it like a spear and slammed it into the wall where it felt weakest. Then again and again, as the growing smoke flooded my stinging eyes with tears.

The imp chittered and cooed, dancing in the fire. It could have ignited the ground under my feet, but the creature was just smart enough to be sadistic. It was taking its time, enjoying the struggle.

On my third hit, the pole pierced through the wood and left

a fist-sized hole in its wake. Coughing, I pressed my mouth to the breach and sucked down a quick lungful of fresh air, then dug my hands in and grabbed the rough edges of the wood. I braced one foot against the wall, knee bent, and hauled back with every ounce of strength I had left.

The rotten plywood buckled, driving jagged splinters into my palms. I gritted my teeth against the pain and did it again. One more try and I'd torn open a gap wide enough to squirm through. The imp let out an enraged squeal when it figured out what I was doing, but not before I pulled myself through the opening with bloodied hands.

Smoke and firelight followed me into the abandoned dry cleaner's. Hulks of old laundry machines sat silent in the dark. I vaulted a rusted folding table and ran all-out, my sights on the back door. I threw my shoulder into it at full speed. It felt like I'd been kicked by a mule, but the door burst open, sending me stumbling over my own feet and tumbling onto the concrete in the back alley behind the store.

I pushed myself up on my knees, coughing until my throat felt like a piece of raw meat, and forced myself to keep moving. I clutched my sore shoulder as I stumbled up the alley, leaving the imp's furious squealing and the flames behind.

Sirens in the distance. I walked as fast as my body would let me, trying to get away from the oncoming lights. No sign of Stanwyck out front. He must have figured the imp killed me. He'd regret that. He'd regret a lot of things. I picked splinters from my hands in the dark and tossed them to the sidewalk, each jagged wooden needle leaving drops of cherry blood in my wake.

* * *

I made it to the Hermetic Inquiry, Trevor Manderley's shop in Wicker Park, about half an hour before sunrise. He was too cheap to spring for a decent alarm, but he'd wrapped the entire building in barbed-wire coils of warding hexes. He should have paid for the alarm. I sliced through his spells like a red-hot scalpel, fueling my power with adrenaline and anger, and let myself inside.

The place was pure dabbler kitsch, with shelves of lurid paperbacks promising to teach the mysteries of the universe, grant cosmic occult power, and make your acne disappear overnight. A wall held racks upon racks of herbs in big glass bell jars, and I could tell at a glance that half of them were mislabeled or cheap substitutes at best. "Genuine consecrated amulets" hung on a rack up front, fifty bucks each and about as magical as dry toast. Trevor made his money selling dreams that came pre-broken. At least when I robbed somebody, they knew they'd been taken.

I found what I was looking for in the back, in Trevor's office: a magic circle drawn on the concrete floor in bright orange chalk, with little piles of grainy yellow sulfur at the points of the star within. A bronze idol stood at the heart of the circle, about a foot tall and depicting a leering man with hair of flame. *Moloch*, read the chiseled inscription at the base.

I picked up the idol. It was heavy. Warm, too, like it had lava in its belly.

Out front, keys jiggled in the door's lock. I killed the light, stood to one side, and waited for him to come in the back room. Trevor was just sharp enough to realize something was wrong. I knew, because I saw the look on his face change and his eyes widen a split second before I swung for the fences and cracked the base of the idol against the back of his skull.

I was nice enough to bandage his head while he was unconscious. Didn't want him bleeding out. Then I dragged him into the storefront. When he finally came to, he was down on the floor with one wrist tied to a radiator by thick strips of knotted leather. I'd used a few of his "magical" amulets. Bound his ankles, too, to keep him from kicking too much.

"It's not what it looks like," were the first words out of his mouth. Maybe it was just the fear, but even he didn't sound like he believed it.

I leaned against the counter by the cash register and crossed my arms.

"Really? Is that how we're going to play this?"

"You—you backed me into a corner! I already have a buyer lined up for that dagger. I'd paid Stanwyck. I couldn't trust you wouldn't lead Ecko or the cops to my front door."

"Well," I said, "that's good. Because you definitely don't have to worry about Ecko or the cops anymore."

I stood aside, letting him see what I'd brought with me, sitting high on the counter.

A red plastic can of gasoline and a brand new lighter.

"Wait," he said. "Wait, wait—" And that was when I strode over, upended the can, and poured gas over his head. He sputtered and shook his soaked hair wildly, pulling against the radiator and kicking out with his bound feet. I gave him a few more dollops and walked away, setting the can down, picking up the lighter.

"What are you *doing*?" he cried.

I shrugged. "You were going to burn me, Trevor. Just returning the favor."

"You don't have to do this. I can *pay* you!"

"The dagger," I said. "Where is it?"

He squinted at me through teary eyes. "You don't understand. The guy I promised it to, my guy in New Orleans, he's not the kind of person who does take-backs. He's already wired the payment—"

I held up the lighter.

"Fun science fact," I told him. "In a gasoline fire, it's not actually fire *touching* the gas that ignites it. No. It's the gasoline vapors that ignite first, and the fire flows back to the liquid from there. You can ignite gasoline from a lot farther away than you'd think."

I flicked the lighter's wheel, showing him the tiny flame from ten feet away. Then I took a step toward him.

"Wait! We can make a deal. I can give you Stanwyck—"

"What do you think?" I said, taking another step toward him. "How close will I get before you go up like a Roman candle? Nine feet? No, not nine feet, so let's try eight—"

Trevor's free hand flailed, holding out his open palm like he could stop me by force of will. "*Stop!* Okay, okay, *damn* it. Under the cash register. There's a safe behind the wood."

I clicked the lighter off and crouched down behind the front counter. Sure enough, a black iron safe with a rotary dial hid behind a sliding panel.

"Combination?"

He curled up his knees, wet and miserable. "You're killing me here, you know that? You're literally killing me."

"That remains to be decided," I told him. "Combination."

"Thirty-five, twenty-two, thirty-five."

Marilyn Monroe's measurements. Nice. The wheel spun like silk under my fingertips, and the door swung wide. The Aztec dagger rested inside, along with a thumb-thick stack of bills bound with a rubber band. Tens and twenties mostly, but nothing to sneeze at. I helped myself.

"You said you could give me Stanwyck," I said as I stood back up. "Now would be a good time to do that."

"I can't—I can't *give* him to you—" I reached for the lighter and he squirmed. "I know where he'll be! I know exactly where he'll be!"

"You better be right."

"I am," he said. "Remember when I said he was hard up for cash? Stanwyck's got a gambling problem. He's in deep with this south-side bookie who he used to deal with, back when he lived here. Heavy action. This guy's all mobbed up, and he's getting ready to tap-dance on Stanwyck's kneecaps if he doesn't get paid soon."

"So you know where this bookie is?"

Trevor shook his head. "No. The fifteen I paid for the dagger won't make a dent in what he owes. So I told him—I told him about the poker tournament at the Bast Club. Convinced him he could sweep the tourney and quadruple his money in one night."

"Stanwyck's barely clued-in. He's not one of us."

"Don't have to be for this gig," Trevor said. "Just need a sponsor who is. So I said I'd sponsor him. He'd just have to put up the five-grand entry fee to play...and another five as a sponsorship fee."

I cracked a smile. "In other words, you end up with the dagger *and* a good chunk of the money you paid him for it."

"Hey, a guy's desperate enough, even a sucker bet looks like a life preserver. So yeah, he'll be there, but only if I can get him into the club. You kill me, he disappears. You *need* me."

I shook my head. "Nah, Trevor, I don't need you. But if you can play it cool and help me get what I want, I *might* manage to forget that you tried to kill me tonight."

I strolled over to a rack of "ritual knives" with dull blades and pentacle-inlaid hilts. I picked one out, set it on the floor, and slid it over to him.

"Cut yourself loose," I told him. "And in case you feel like taking another shot at me? Just remember: next time, you won't have anything *left* to trade for your life."

* * *

Dawn, and the streets filled up with bright yellow cabs ready for the tidal wave of commuters. I flagged one down, fell into the backseat, and struggled to stay awake. I'd been running too hard, too long, and the night was a blur of fear and fire.

I felt like treating myself with Trevor's money, so I had the cabbie take me to the Four Seasons on East Delaware Place. They gave me a room on the thirty-third floor, facing lakeside. I could look out the window and stare down at a white-sand beach and an endless expanse of crystal water, but I barely gave the view a second glance. Instead, I dead-bolted the door, stripping off my clothes as I walked and leaving them in a trail on the pristine slate-colored carpet. I staggered into the bathroom.

My hands were pulpy red, scabbed up from the scrapes and splinters I'd taken, and an ugly purple-black bruise blossomed across my left shoulder like a patch of mold. Everything hurt. I turned the shower on full blast, drinking in the white-hot steam, letting the water pound my skin like a masseuse.

I almost fell asleep standing up. I killed the shower, pulled the curtains tight across the windows, and set the alarm for a four-hour nap. I slid naked into the soft, warm, king-sized bed, and I was gone before my head hit the pillow.

I woke to the sound of a local radio station, some morning DJ talking about a traffic jam on Lake Shore Drive and a four-car pileup. I just lay there, drifting, letting my mind work the problem.

The dagger was mine. Halfway there, halfway to paying Damien Ecko's blood price for Coop's soul. I couldn't pat myself on the back. Getting the knife had been the *easy* part.

Now, somehow, I had to get my hands on the Judas Coin. A prize belonging to a demon prince's right-hand man and secured in a building nobody had ever been able to rob. A prize Ecko obviously expected I'd die trying to get my hands on.

I didn't want to drag any of my friends into the trouble I'd earned. Still, no matter how I sliced it, I came to one inescapable conclusion: I couldn't do this alone.

I forced myself out of bed, crouched beside my fallen slacks, and fished out my phone. There were a few calls to be made.

22.

Six hours later, I waited in the baggage claim at O'Hare in a stiff blue vinyl chair, idly watching a bank of monitors. Flights came and flights went, white block numbers flickering and shuffling by the minute. Every now and then, one of the conveyor belts in the vast room would kick to life, sending suitcase after battered suitcase to the clustered waiting crowds.

I was surprised when I saw Mack and Zeke steaming my way. Not that they found me, but that it had taken them so long. I didn't bother getting up. They loomed over me, triumphant.

"We've got you now," Zeke said with a sneer.

"Curses," I deadpanned, rolling my eyes. "Foiled again. I would have gotten away with it, too, if it wasn't for you kids and your meddling dog."

"Hound," said the man who casually strolled up behind them, speaking with a breezy English accent. "The proper title is hound."

Mack and Zeke parted to make room.

"We spotted you twenty minutes ago," Mack said. "We called the *big* boss."

The "big boss" glowed like a black diamond and felt like a barbed-wire whip on the edge of my psychic senses. He could have been a retired supermodel, with cheekbones carved from marble, an aquiline nose, and eyes the color of fresh-cut grass on a summer morning. A jet-black tattoo poked out from underneath his tight V-neck sweater, caressing his neck and left wrist with the curling tips of a thorny rose vine.

Him, I stood up for.

"Daniel Faust," he said, squinting just a bit. "You have a penchant for dangerous living."

"We haven't been properly introduced," I said.

"I won't tell you my full use-name, because you wouldn't be able to appreciate its history. Or pronounce it. You may, like most, call me Royce. A simple name for simple minds"—his gaze flicked left and right, toward Mack and Zeke—"but I'll admit to growing fond of it over the years. You're in the wrong place, sport."

"Still a free country, last I checked."

He chuckled and shook his head, giving me a condescending smile.

"Freedom. You humans do love to prattle on about freedom, and you barely understand the word. How much agency do you think you actually have? From the cradle to the grave, you're bombarded with media, advertising, cultural and social pressure to conform...it's amazing you can think at all."

"I'm sorry," I said, "what choir did you say you belong to?"

He inclined his head and held up an open hand. "Touché. Yes, like my prince, I am a child of Greed, and my bloodline has shaped me well. But I posit that I'm more aware of the outside influences in my life than you are. And I can prove it. Right here, right now."

"Go for it." I wished I felt as confident as he looked.

"I've been following your exploits," Royce said, "and there's a question I've been *dying* to ask you. One simple question."

He inched closer to me. His voice was a low, intimate purr.

"Wasn't it *easy*?"

I frowned. "What do you mean?"

"If I understand what happened—this is largely secondhand, so please correct me if I'm wrong—you rescued Caitlin, my counterpart in the Court of Jade Tears, from enslavement."

"That's right."

"Knowing she could, and likely would, reward your kindness with a horrible death."

I put my hands on my hips. "I didn't care who or what she was. I wasn't going to stand by and watch any woman be treated like that."

"And I believe you," he said. "But...she did kill two men in front of you. Slowly. Made you watch, right?"

"I was in a protective circle at the time. I didn't have a whole lot of travel options."

Royce shook his head. "No, that's not the interesting part. The interesting part is...how quickly you fell in love with her. You dreamed about her that very night, didn't you? Kept thinking about her scent, the fall of her hair?"

I didn't know how he knew any of this, but I didn't like where he was headed. "Get to the point."

"It's so convenient, love at first sight, isn't it? Especially when the Ring of Solomon was still in play, and Caitlin *needed* a willing human to do what she could not. She couldn't get near the ring without risking her freedom again. But *you* could. And then...ah, the *pièce de résistance*. There you were, with the ring in your hand. Power. Glory. You could have been the savior of Earth. Then Caitlin just batted those beautiful eyes of hers, and what did you do? *You threw it away*. You even thought it was your idea."

"It *was* my idea," I said. "That ring would have put a bull's-eye over everybody I care about. It wasn't a gift. It was a time bomb that would have started a war. Taking it off the table was the best choice I could have made."

"But you did it for her," Royce said. "You actually think you're in love."

"We *are* in love."

Royce kept smiling, but there was something wistful in his eyes.

"She got inside your head, sport. That's what she does. That's what she is. I've known Caitlin a long time, a *very* long time, and let me tell you, she's one of the best. You're nothing special to her.

You're just another useful human, in a very long line of useful humans, and they were all the apples of her eye...until she wrung them dry and tossed them aside."

"And *you*," I said, jabbing my finger into his chest, "are full of *shit*. I don't know what your deal is, Royce. I don't know if you're too broken to get the concept of love, or maybe you're just jealous. Maybe this is how you get your rocks off, trying to drive wedges between people. You're forgetting something. I've *seen* Caitlin use her powers on people. I saw what she did to Carl Holt. If she snared me like that, even if she hid it from me somehow, it'd be obvious to everyone *around* me, just like it was with him."

Holt had been a junkie with an insatiable craving for Caitlin's heroin kiss. The addiction had destroyed him from the inside out, turning him into Lauren Carmichael's pliable puppet. There wasn't any love there, not even kindness. Holt took what he needed from Caitlin's body and left her bleeding.

That wasn't me. That *wasn't* me.

"You're starting to see the light," Royce said, looking deep in my eyes, "but you're not a true believer, yet. I can fix that. I have a houseguest who I'd like you to meet. She'll open your eyes. I'd appreciate it if you'd come along peacefully, so I don't have to force you."

"*We'll* force him," Zeke said, eyes narrowed to slits. Mack gave him an uncertain nod.

Royce arched one thin eyebrow. "Zeke? If you touch this gentleman without my say-so, I'll tear your fingers off. We're trying to *help* him."

"You can understand," I said, "why I find that hard to believe."

Royce chuckled politely. "My motives are entirely self-serving. Which is why, though I mean you no harm, *making* you come with me is still an option. I'll hurt you only as much as I have to. So are you going to raise a fuss, or can we do this the easy way?"

"Don't let him have *any* coffee," Mack warned. Royce slowly turned his head and blinked at him.

My eyes flicked to the flight display. Then I glanced to my left, toward the nearest bank of escalators, and smiled.

"Sorry, Royce. Going to have to take a rain check. I've got five good reasons you aren't taking me anywhere."

Royce sighed, glancing down at my hands.

"Please," he said, "tell me you aren't about to punch me. I'm the hound of Prince Malphas, Daniel. I won't even feel it, and you'll probably break your fingers."

"Huh?" I looked at my hand. "Oh. No. Reasonable assumption, but no. I mean *them*."

Caitlin strode toward us, wrapped in her white leather trench coat and wearing high camel-tone boots. On her left, Bentley and Corman kept up the pace, pulling a pair of Burberry rolling suitcases. Corman wore his old Dodgers cap, slung low over his eyes. On Caitlin's right, Margaux lugged a bulky woven tote over one shoulder, head craned to look at something on Pixie's phone as the two women walked close together.

"My crew just got here," I told Royce. "So can we do this the easy way?"

Royce's smile vanished. "Mack, Zeke, disappear."

They didn't need any more prompting, rushing to fade into the crowd. As Caitlin approached, Royce extended his hand.

"Ah," he said, "*Caitlleanabruaudi*, my old lover."

She reached for my hand instead. Her skin was velvet soft and chased away the chill. Or maybe the warmth came from the faces of my family, the people who had dropped everything to fly into danger at my side.

I couldn't go home until the job was done, so home came to me instead.

Caitlin gave him a bitter laugh. "We were never lovers, Royce. We fucked. For recreational purposes. It was fun, but you ruined all that when you turned traitor."

He looked genuinely pained. "Me? It's not treason to want to better yourself. I needed upward mobility. I couldn't exactly become Sitri's hound without killing you first, now could I? So I went where I had better job prospects."

"You swore an oath to our prince."

"Malphas has a better benefit plan. What *are* you doing here, Caitlin? This is our territory. You weren't invited. A less generous man might see this as a hostile act."

"Of course I was invited," she said. "I heard about your little poker tournament. It's open to everyone."

"That doesn't mean you can just—"

Caitlin cut him off with a dismissive wave of her hand. "It does, in fact. Proviso four-four-point-three of the Terms of the Cold Peace, article seven. This qualifies as a 'tournament, revel or moot,' one which you have specifically designated as open to all comers. If *any* demon from a foreign court is allowed to attend, we *all* are. It's an anti-collusion measure."

"*Collusion*," Royce echoed. "Really?"

"It's my job to know the law. That's what a hound is *supposed* to do, anyway."

"Well." Royce wrinkled his nose. "Hell prevails."

"It certainly does."

"You don't even play cards."

Caitlin brandished a sealed envelope of glossy, brass-colored paper. She slapped it into Royce's hand.

"I'm not going to. Daniel is. I'm just putting up his entry fee. The Court of Jade Tears is officially sponsoring him as our champion."

Royce cast his gaze across the rest of my crew, assessing them as he weighed the envelope in his palm.

"And these people are...?"

"Cheering section," I said.

Royce looked like a man who knew something was deeply, terribly wrong, but he didn't have the first clue about how to identify the problem, let alone fix it. He stood there for a moment, eyeing the envelope in his hand, running his fingertips over the shiny paper.

"Fine," he finally said. "I'll even note who he's playing for, so we can all have a good laugh at your court's expense when we send you home penniless."

"I don't know about that," I told him. "I'm not bad at poker."

"Perhaps, but you can't bluff against me."

"Oh?" I tilted my head. "Why's that?"

Royce's smile was a malicious thing, almost a leer as he looked from me to Caitlin and back again.

"Because if I want to know what *you're* thinking," he said slowly, "all I have to do is look in *her* eyes."

I clenched my jaw and tried not to make a fist. Caitlin reached up, her fingertips caressing the back of my neck with long feathery strokes.

"See you at the tournament," she told him.

23.

"What did he say to you?" Caitlin wanted to know as soon as Royce was out of earshot.

I shrugged. "Just a bunch of bullshit."

"Hmm," she said. "He hasn't changed at all, then."

I tried to take the doubts Royce had planted in my head and shove them in a closet. I didn't have time for that now. Or ever. If the memories of Carl Holt weren't enough to prove Caitlin hadn't tampered with my mind—and they were—the way her hand felt in mine did the job just fine.

I looked to the others. "Thanks, everybody. I know this was short notice, and I'm asking a lot—"

"Kiddo," Corman said, "you apologize and I will smack you upside the head. Don't think I won't."

Bentley rubbed Corman's shoulder. "It was a turbulent flight, drink service was canceled, and *someone* didn't get his vodka and orange juice."

"Jenny sends her best," Margaux said. "With Nicky being Nicky and Agent Black being, well, *everywhere*, it's not safe for her to leave Vegas right now."

"Thanks, Mama. I'm not sure it's safe for her to be *in* Vegas either, but she's a little headstrong."

Margaux snorted. "Granite's easier to crack. Left some of my spirits watching over her. Anything goes wrong, I'll know before *she* does."

Pixie had been fidgeting this whole time. "What about Coop?" she blurted out.

Pixie had worked with Coop before, the night we hit Lauren Carmichael's mansion and made off with the Ring of Solomon. If it hadn't been for them, cracking Lauren's safe and planting a fake while I kept Lauren's dinner party distracted down in the dining room...well, I didn't like to contemplate what-ifs too much.

"Not a conversation for a crowded airport," I told her. "C'mon, let's all head back to my hotel room."

Corman grumbled. "Just glad to be back on terra firma. I hate flying. Your room got a minibar?"

* * *

Back in my room at the Four Seasons, I gave them the grisly details. Not *too* grisly. Pixie didn't need to hear that, and everyone else had a damn good idea of what Coop was going through.

"That kind of zombie," Margaux mused, "is easy to raise up, if you know what you're doing. Even easier to put down. Remember those soul traps Lauren passed out to her followers? The little leather pouches? Same thing, it's just that Coop's own *body* is the pouch. Force his mouth open, his soul flies free."

Pixie sat beside her at the end table by the window, powering up her laptop. She glanced at Margaux over the screen. "That kind? How many kinds of zombies *are* there?"

"There's the kind that eat people, the kind that don't eat people..." Margaux's voice trailed off as she thought it over. "Two. Two kinds. Plenty of variations, but when you're looking at a dead man walkin' your way, that's the one question you need answered fast."

"And don't shoot for the head, that just pisses 'em off," Corman said, nursing a whiskey and Coke he'd assembled from the minibar. He sat on the edge of the bed. Behind him, cross-legged, Bentley kneaded the tension from his shoulders.

Caitlin's hands mirrored Bentley's, though she was gentle with my bruises. We stood at the window, the sun slowly setting and coating Lake Michigan in sparkles of golden light, and she massaged the back of my neck while we talked. It felt like she'd had one hand on me at all times since she'd arrived. I wasn't sure if she was trying to smooth my ruffled feathers, or if she was feeling awkward after running into an old flame. Either way, the nearer we stood, the more relaxed I felt and the happier she looked.

"Damien Ecko is keeping Coop in some kind of industrial building," I said, thinking back to the video he'd sent. "Concrete floors, cinder-block walls, maybe a warehouse or an abandoned hospital. Looked pretty big. Pixie, he contacted me by phone and sent over a video file and some texts. Is there any way to locate him with that?"

"Might be, unless he covered his tracks. Is he tech-savvy?"

I rubbed my chin, dubious. "Don't think so. He's more into the twenty-first dynasty than the twenty-first century."

"Most modern cell phones have a built-in GPS chip, even if you don't have any kind of GPS software. Allegedly to make it easier for emergency services to find you when you dial 911."

"Allegedly?" Caitlin asked.

"It also makes it easier for our burgeoning police state to keep tabs on innocent citizens," Pixie said. "Have I told you what the NSA does with voicemail—"

I cleared my throat. "So we can track the chip in his phone?"

"He tracked himself *for* us. Everything you record on a smartphone—pictures, video, whatever—has geotags embedded in the metadata. You can't see it, unless you know how to look, but it's there. It's a little hidden chunk of text that says not only when the image was recorded but where, latitude and longitude. It's easy to scrub—even easier to fake if you want to make it look like you're someplace you aren't—but most people either don't know about the geotags or don't care."

I thought back to Ecko's jewelry store and his outdated motion sensor. Then I held up the burner phone and tossed it over to Pixie.

"I have a hunch he's a little behind the times," I told her. "See what you can get off that. And, uh...you don't need to watch the video, okay? Nothing you want to see. So, next problem. Getting that coin out of the Bast Club."

"We went there a couple of times in the nineties," Corman said. "Does it still look like Jules Verne built a brothel?"

I nodded. "I think they call that steampunk now, but yeah. It's also got free-roaming man-eating shadows for a security system. And does anyone know who owns the place? The locals just call it 'Management.'"

"It was the same, back in the day," Bentley said. "According to Halima, folks claim the club just *appeared* sometime in the 1950s. She's fairly certain the lot it sits on didn't exist before that either, like the streets moved overnight to accommodate it and all the maps changed to fit. Whoever Management is, he or she prefers to work from the shadows. And with the shadows."

I glanced out the window. The lake was turning to turquoise as dusk slithered over the city, and the streets blazed with a thousand pinpricks of electric light.

"Can't count on getting the coin the fair way," I said. "I'll play my best, but they call it gambling for a reason. Besides, I'm pretty sure Royce will do whatever he can to knock me out of the game, short of blatantly cheating. It's a cheap way to insult Caitlin's court."

"Don't rule out the cheating," Caitlin muttered. Her fingertips squeezed the back of my neck a little bit harder.

Margaux shrugged. "I don't see any other way to get at that coin, unless we pull an all-out siege like we did at the Silverlode Hotel. And then they'll know we took it. You can't cover tracks that big."

"How do you steal from a theft-proof building," I mused aloud, "especially when the guy who owns the prize already knows you're after it?"

I snapped my fingers and pointed at Bentley and Corman.

"We pull a Kansas City Shuffle."

Bentley's eyes lit up. "Kansas City Shuffle."

"Excuse me," Pixie said, holding up her hand and looking back and forth between us. "What's a Kansas City Shuffle?"

Corman grinned. "Bet you five bucks you can't tell me what state Kansas City is in."

Pixie frowned and furrowed her brow. "Well, it's obviously not Kansas. Let me think, maybe a neighboring state...God, I suck at geography. Kansas River, drains from...Missouri? Is that right? I'm guessing Missouri."

"Bzzt. Sorry, kiddo. There *is* a Kansas City in Kansas. But here's the important question: why was that the first answer you thought of, and the first one you threw away?"

"Because it was too easy. You were obviously trying to trick me into thinking the answer was Kansas," Pixie said. "Wait. It *was* Kansas."

Bentley chuckled. "Most confidence games depend on the mark not knowing they're being conned. The Kansas City Shuffle depends on the mark *knowing* it. Not only do they have to see you coming, they have to figure out your entire plan before it happens."

"Problem being," Corman said, "they're working to stop the *wrong con*. You get 'em looking left, while you rob 'em blind on the right."

"We can't take the coin out of the building," I said, "but Royce can. So let's give him a reason to do it."

* * *

My stomach growled, and I wasn't the only one running on empty. We moved the party downstairs to the seventh floor. Allium, the Four Seasons's in-house restaurant, invited us in with warm, dusky mahogany and candlelight. We didn't have to wait long for a table.

"Forty-two-dollar strip steak?" Pixie murmured, looking over the menu. "For real?"

"Don't worry about it," I told her. "Trevor Manderley, our kindly benefactor, is paying for everyone's dinner tonight. And for your rooms. Serves him right."

"And that's the next piece of business," Corman said. "So he's sponsoring this Stanwyck guy for the tourney. I got two questions, kiddo."

"Shoot."

"Number one, can you keep it together when Stanwyck sits down at your table to play cards?"

I had to think about that.

"Yeah," I said. "Payback will keep. That's for later."

Corman rapped his fingers on his closed menu. "Second question. What about later?"

"I promised Coop two things before he died," I said. "One, I'd get his cut of the score to his wife. Two, I'd send Stanwyck to hell where he belongs. I'm keeping those promises."

"The latter," Caitlin said dryly, running a sharp red fingernail down her menu as she read it over, "can be arranged, with pleasure."

"I'm in," Pixie said. "Let's kill him."

The table fell quiet.

"You're here to run intel," I told her. "Then you're going back to Vegas."

I'd seen Pixie angry, and I'd seen her determined, but until that night I'd never seen her eyes that hard and cold.

"I said, I'm *in*. For all of it."

I shook my head. "Pixie, you don't...that's not your kind of work."

"Once you cross that bridge, you don't walk back," Margaux told her. She reached out and put her hand over Pixie's. Pixie didn't pull her hand away, but the cold resolve in her eyes didn't soften.

"I worked with Coop," she said. "He was a good guy. I liked him. And this man, Stanwyck, he just...he shot two people for what, a lousy six thousand dollars? And now Coop's some kind of *zombie*? He needs to go. That's all. Stanwyck needs to *go*."

"Yeah, he does," I said, "but that's not your job to handle."

I gave Caitlin a look. She shrugged.

"Don't know what you want *me* to say," Caitlin said. "I don't understand why humans get so worked up over killing in the first place. This is pest control. You kill him, he goes to hell, he hopefully gets put to good use. Nuisance solved."

"Listen to Daniel and Margaux," Bentley said, his voice gentle. "Please, young lady. You're no killer. That's not a burden you should have to carry."

The waitress swung by our table with a tray of drinks, throwing a blanket over the conversation. Still, as I took my Crown and Coke and waited for her to leave, I realized this was one more wrinkle I'd have to iron out. No way in hell was I letting Pixie anywhere near the Stanwyck takedown.

In the circles I ran in, innocence was a rare and precious commodity. Pixie was a criminal, sure, but her crimes were bloodless and her heart was usually in the right place. More often than mine was, anyway.

Damned if I'd drag her down to my level.

24.

When the waitress returned to take our orders, Caitlin's smile lit up the room.

"I'll go clockwise," Caitlin said, nodding my way. "*He* will start with the buffalo rock shrimp. For the entree, the Wagyu skirt steak with cheese and herb fries and roasted market vegetables on the side. Let's pair that with a 2009 Cabernet—"

As she continued, moving on to Bentley's meal, Pixie leaned back in her chair—on the other side of Caitlin—and whispered, "Is she actually ordering for *all* of us?"

"Yes. Yes, she is."

Pixie arched an eyebrow. "Why?"

"Because she can," I whispered back.

"I kinda had my meal picked out already."

"My best advice," I told her, "is to just surrender and let this happen."

Not much later, Pixie stared wide-eyed at her fork, chewing slowly.

"What is this, again?"

"Hamachi crudo," Caitlin said. "It's essentially an Italian take on sushi. Clean and simple. Fresh sliced yellow tail, a sprinkling of cracked black pepper and sea salt, a dash of lime juice, drizzle on some extra-virgin olive oil, and there you go. A delicate dish for a refined palate."

"I *love* it. I mean, I never would have thought to even try this, but I love it."

"I knew you would." Caitlin patted her napkin to her lips, looking smug.

I craned my neck, making sure we had privacy before getting down to business.

"Okay, so the key to this grift is playing on Royce's paranoia. He has to believe that it isn't safe to keep the Judas Coin at the club. That if he *doesn't* move it, we'll snatch it out from under him."

"Start simple," Bentley said, lifting a forkful of salad. "A whisper campaign. We can 'accidentally' let it slip that you're in town to steal the coin, not to win it. You'll deny everything, of course. Which, if you do it properly, will only make him more certain of your guilt."

"Dumb question," Pixie said, "but do demons, um, go online at all? I could whip up some anonymous deep-web traffic mentioning the coin and pretend to be a buyer offering a bounty for it."

Caitlin wagged her fork at her. "Excellent idea. Royce has an affection for technology. If he doesn't hear about it himself, one of his worker bees will report it to him."

"Can you backdate the post so it looks like the bounty went up a few days ago?" I asked.

Pixie gave me a look. "Have you *met* me?"

"If you really want to spook him," Margaux said, "he needs to hear the story from inside his own house, from someone he trusts."

"Naavarasi is a Flowers noblewoman, but she's in Denver," Caitlin mused. "Wouldn't want to use her for this, regardless. She's too valuable an asset. Still, *she* might know someone local who she wouldn't mind putting to good use...I'll call her after dinner."

"At least the knife is secure," I said. "We're halfway to setting Coop free."

Pixie raised her fork. "About that."

"Yeah?"

"You're trading the knife and the coin to this Ecko guy to get Coop back, right?" she asked.

"That's right."

"So," she said slowly, "how are you going to get the money to his widow from *selling* the knife?"

I shrugged. "The cash will have to come from someplace else. Least of my concerns right now."

"What if we just kill Ecko?"

I didn't respond, not right away.

"Think about it," Pixie said. "If I can locate this place of his with the geotags from the phone, why bother with the coin at all? It can't be that hard to scrounge up some guns in this city. Let's go kill him, kill Stanwyck, free Coop, you sell the knife to your original client, and we all go home."

I tugged the cloth napkin off my lap, loosely folded it, and dropped it next to my plate.

"Pix, may I have a word with you? In private?"

I led her away from the table, over to a vacant corner near the kitchen doors.

"Okay," I said, standing close and looking her in the eyes. "Out with it."

"Out with what?"

"Out with the reason why Pixie, radical anarcho-progressive hacktivist for peace, is eagerly calling for the heads of two men she's never met." I put my hands on my hips. "This isn't you. This isn't the woman who nearly refused to ever speak to me again, after the fallout with Ben and the Redemption Choir, because you were *that* adamant about not letting anyone get killed."

"People change."

"In my experience," I said, "no, they really don't. Little bits, maybe, superficial things, but Gandhi doesn't pick up an AK-47, and Pixie doesn't volunteer to splash blood on her hands. What's gotten into you?"

She looked away. Her breathing went shallow. I could sense

her trying to piece the words together, but she needed a little time. I waited until she was ready.

"Before we came downstairs," she eventually said, her voice soft, "remember I used your bathroom?"

"Yeah?"

She turned to face me. "While I was in there...I watched the video."

The video Ecko had sent me. The video of Coop, undead, chained to the floor, tortured. My heart sank.

"Pix...I told you that was nothing you wanted to see."

Her brow furrowed. "Well, maybe I needed to see it. I just can't understand...who does something like that, Faust? Why? Coop was a good guy. He didn't deserve this, any of this."

"Stanwyck is a gambling addict. He shot Coop and Augie because he needed the money. Ecko...for him, what he's doing to Coop, it's leverage to get what he wants. It's just business, Pix. That's all."

"And the fact that you can say that," Pixie told me with a tremor in her voice, "just that you can *say* it, that something that fucking evil is 'just business'—"

"I know," I said.

Her eyes glistened. "No. You don't. You don't get it. I'm—I'm in this world now, *your* world, whether I like it or not. But I'm not *in* it, not like you and Caitlin and everybody else. Which means I could be the next one to end up just like Coop. I thought if I—if I toughened up, if I was more like *you*, if I could kill someone and not have it tear me up inside, maybe I'd stand a chance of *surviving* all this."

Sometimes the consequences of your actions were immediate and obvious. Other times they lurked in the shadows, waiting for the chance to jump out and punch you square in the gut.

"Pix, you actually thought..." I shook my head. "You want to know the reason I can pull a trigger on somebody without flinching? Because I've done it too many times. Way too many times. And for some shitty reasons. Hurting people, it...it doesn't toughen you up. It makes *less* of you. You can't take a life—good or bad, whether they've got it coming or not—you can't take a life without burning out a little of the light in your heart. And you've only got so much light."

I reached out and took hold of her shoulder. Then I tried to pull her into a hug. She let me. Stiff-armed, quavering, but she let me. I bowed my head so I could whisper in her ear as I stroked her hair.

"I'm too far gone to save," I told her, "but you've still got some light. Cling to it. Cling to it with everything you've got, because the last thing you *ever* want to be...is me."

"I'm just scared," she whispered back.

"Don't be. Because you're family. And every single person at that table would jump in front of a gun to keep you safe. That's what family is."

She pulled away slowly and tugged her glasses down. She rubbed the back of her hand over her eyes, smearing her tears.

"And to answer your question back there," I told her, "we're not going after Damien Ecko because we don't even know what he *is*. I'm pretty sure he's not a demon, but beyond that, your guess is as good as mine. He might just be a skilled necromancer—which is all kinds of trouble in and of itself—but I've got a bad feeling there's more to him than that. In my line of work, you don't go gunning for somebody unless you *know* you can kill him."

"I know what he is. He's a monster."

I shrugged. "No argument here."

"If you *can* kill him," she said, "will you?"

"Only if you promise me something," I said.

"What's that?"

"Promise me that when I tell you it's time to go home, you go home, and you leave the rough stuff to me."

"Okay," she said. I wasn't sure I believed her.

"You promise?"

She gave me the ghost of a smile. "I promise."

"Good." I rubbed her shoulder. "There are too many monsters as it is."

We got back to the table in time for the main course. My steak was served up exactly the way I like it: warm, dripping red, and bought with somebody else's money. When dessert and coffee rolled around—Irish coffee, in Bentley and Corman's case—Caitlin excused herself to make a phone call.

"Mama," I said, "how's Jennifer holding up?"

Margaux wagged her hand from side to side. "You ever throw two strange cats into a room together? Know how they snarl and hiss and circle around, waiting for the other one to bite? That's her and Nicky right now. You ask me, *one* of them is gonna bite, and soon."

I sighed. "I already told Bentley, the night I get back in town, we're squashing this beef. Jen and Nicky *are* going to sit down at a table together, whether they like it or not, and neither one of them leaves the room until they come to terms."

Margaux raised her eyebrows at me and sipped her coffee.

"You'd have better luck with cats."

Caitlin strolled back to the table, casually running her fingertips across the back of my neck as she sat down. They left a warm tingle in their wake.

"We're in luck," she said. "Naavarasi had the perfect candidate. There's a local, going by the name Scudder, who fancies himself an information broker. He's on the outs with the Flowers, and with Royce in particular. *Very* eager to earn his way back into his masters' good graces."

"Which means if I go to him for intel," I said, "and let it slip about a plan to steal the coin..."

"He'll be on his phone to the boss two seconds after you leave." Corman lifted his mug to me. "From your lips to Royce's ears. Play it smooth, kiddo."

I took a sip of water and pushed back my chair, turning to pass my envelope of cash over to Caitlin.

"This should cover the tab and get everybody rooms for the

night. If you'll all excuse me, I have to go spread some nasty rumors about myself."

25.

I stood on the edge of a streetlamp's glow, a silent shadow outside the reach of the light. If Naavarasi's intel was good, this Scudder guy could be my best way to shake Royce up a little.

If being the operative word when it came to Naavarasi. The rakshasi queen had a penchant for steering me into traps—half to get what she wanted, and half to satisfy her sick sense of humor. Still, things were a little different now. Caitlin had some things Naavarasi wanted: a potential place at Prince Sitri's table, the respect that the Court of Night-Blooming Flowers refused to give her, and payback against Prince Malphas for conquering Naavarasi's little kingdom in hell's name.

Naavarasi hadn't crossed the line into open rebellion against Malphas quite yet—she was as cagey as she was smart, biding her time and weighing her options—but I figured it was only a matter of time before she hopped fences and joined the Court of Jade Tears.

Which would basically make her my next-door neighbor, magically speaking. I wasn't sure if I was happy about that, but at least she'd be someplace we could keep an eye on her.

An "L" train rattled by overhead, showering pumpkin-orange sparks onto the black pavement below. Scudder's place stood across the street, a hole in the wall with a flickering neon sign in the window that read "Small Appliance Outlet and Repair." It stood shoulder to shoulder with a Chinese takeout place and a mattress store, both of them already closed for the night.

Tarnished bells hung over the grimy front door, but they didn't jingle. The only welcome I got was a dry-throated croak from the back of the cluttered shop. "We're closing in five minutes."

The store was already the size of a shoebox, and the tightly packed floor-to-ceiling shelves turned Scudder's place into an experiment in claustrophobia. *So this is where appliances go to die*, I thought, my shoes sticking to linoleum that hadn't been mopped in at least a decade. Rusted junk packed the shelves, from vivisected vacuum cleaners to microwave ovens with their guts spilling out. It was the crime scene of a mechanical massacre.

I found the perpetrator in back, perched on a stool and taking a screwdriver to the corpse of an innocent toaster. He was old, with thick white whiskers and skin like beef jerky. He looked up at me, scowling, eyes bulbous behind oversized glasses.

"If it's a repair, I'm backlogged 'til next Thursday. Drop it off and I'll write you a claim ticket. Gotta pay half up front."

I got a good look at him, his outline glowing cold and dark in my second sight, and swallowed my anger. Scudder was a hijacker, walking around in skin that didn't belong to him. I wondered how many years he'd been squatting inside his current victim, keeping the real man locked away in a dark corner of his own mind. I knew exactly what that felt like. It took all my effort to remember I had a role to play and not blast him back to hell as a matter of principle.

Never did meet a hijacker I could stand, with the sole exception of Emma Loomis, one of Caitlin's coworkers. Even then, I could only tolerate her because Caitlin privately filled me in on where Emma got her human puppet. Let's just say that the next time you hear about a brain-dead and comatose hospital patient making a "miraculous overnight recovery"...it might not be all that miraculous.

"I'm in the market for something a little more abstract," I told him. "Information. I hear you're the man to see."

He put down the toaster, but he kept the screwdriver handy.

"Yeah? Who told you that?"

"Satisfied customer of yours."

"This satisfied customer got a name?"

I shook my head. "Not one that I'm comfortable saying out loud."

"Then you're not someone I'm comfortable doing business with." He glanced at the bulky Timex on his wrist. "And your five minutes are up. We're closed. Goodnight."

"C'mon," I said, trying to put a little pleading into my voice, "do you have any idea how hard it is for an out-of-towner to get a leg up around here? The second people find out I'm from out west, they clam up."

Scudder's eyebrow twitched.

"How far west?"

"Las Vegas," I said. "The name's Faust. Daniel Faust. You might have heard of me."

"Doesn't ring a bell," he said, but his hunched-up shoulders told me he was lying.

"Suits me better if it doesn't. I'm in town for a job, an in-and-out kinda deal. I hear you've got your finger on the pulse of this town."

He put the screwdriver down and folded his hands.

"Some people say that."

"Then you're the man I need to talk to. My curiosity's been tickled."

"Sounds like a personal problem."

"It is," I told him. "See, once I get curious about something, I just can't rest until I've found a little satisfaction."

"And what has you all curious?"

"The Bast Club. Ever been there?"

Scudder's eyes squinted, just a bit.

"Now and then," he said.

"Big place. Almost a maze, with lots of unmarked rooms and twisty little passages. Makes me wonder if anyone's ever mapped the place. The *whole* place."

Scudder twisted his lips into a lopsided smile. "What, you

looking for official blueprints? You must not have heard: Management didn't exactly build the place the old-fashioned way. The club just sort of *happened.*"

"Sure, sure, but that doesn't mean some daring Theseus hasn't wandered that labyrinth with a ball of thread."

Scudder frowned. "What's a Theseus?"

"Never mind. Let me bottom-line this for you: I'm in the market for a full dossier on the Bast Club. I want to know about the employees, human and otherwise, with as much documentation on their personal lives as you can piece together. Floor plans. All the ways in, and all the ways out. Can you handle that?"

"I know this town like the back of my hand," Scudder said, getting up from his stool. He shuffled over to a battered filing cabinet, its dented sidewalls looking like someone had taken a baseball bat to it. "The question is, can you afford..."

He paused, looking back at me, one hand frozen on a drawer handle. I could hear the gears grinding inside his skull as he tried to sniff out an advantage.

He pulled his hand away from the drawer, leaving it closed.

"I mean, I don't have everything you need here, but I could *get* it, if you can handle my going rate."

"Money isn't an issue," I told him.

Normally, that'd make someone's eyes light up, but his expression didn't budge. He'd already realized something better than money was up for grabs.

"How soon would you need this information?"

"Tomorrow," I said. "Noon at the latest. I'm on a strict timetable. That's nonnegotiable. In two days, my window of opportunity closes for good."

Not coincidentally, in two days, whoever won Royce's poker tournament would walk away with their new prize. I could tell the timing wasn't lost on Scudder.

It wouldn't be lost on Royce either.

"Mind if I ask what you're trying to accomplish? It would help me tailor the package to your specific—"

“I do mind,” I said. “Just give me all the intel you have, and let me worry about sorting it out.”

He held up his withered hands. “Fine, fine, the customer is always right. For a full dossier like this, I’d say…two thousand dollars. Cash.”

“For that much money, this had better be worth it,” I said, knowing he’d never deliver. “Call me tomorrow when it’s ready, and I’ll swing by with your payment.”

He passed me a whittled-down nub of a golf pencil and a greasy receipt for a pepperoni pizza. I flipped the receipt over and scribbled my cell number on the back, holding it out to him between two fingers.

“Pleasure doing business,” he said. “Now, unless I can interest you in a slightly used toaster…”

I glanced down at the pile of mangled parts.

“I’m good,” I said. “Trying to cut down on carbs. Call me tomorrow.”

I let myself out. A light mist hung in the air, making the streetlights glisten. I was sure Scudder wouldn’t wait to make a phone call, not to me, but to Royce, trying to worm his way back into the hound’s good graces with a gift of information.

What Royce did with it, of course, was up to him. That was the tricky part.

I strolled down the quiet sidewalk, thinking, not in any particular hurry. My thoughts kept drifting back to the airport and what Royce said about Caitlin. Every time they did I kicked them, hard, to the task at hand.

The timetable couldn’t be tighter. The tournament was the day after tomorrow, which gave us about twenty-four hours to pull this off. I didn’t like short cons: you had to put on the pressure, hard and fast, and people under that kind of stress could get unpredictable. Unpredictable in bad, bloody ways.

No other option, though. Slow and steady was usually the right play, but not in a race like this one. I couldn’t go to bed without doing a little more to ramp up Royce's paranoia, making sure I had him where I wanted him. I called Caitlin.

"Hey," I said, "so far, so good. Scudder took the bait. Think I'm going to stop by the Bast Club and find out if anybody looks nervous to see me. Care to scope out the local wildlife?"

"I bought a new dress for the occasion," she said.

Caitlin met me at our hotel room door, wearing something short, black, and vaguely scandalous with her red-bottomed Louboutin heels. We almost didn't make it off the elevator. To our credit, we disentangled before the doors chimed open, but it was a close call.

I called Halima from the vinyl backseat of a cab, and she gave me instructions to relay to the driver.

"Have him drop you off at that corner," she told me. "Wait until he leaves, then walk half a block east. That will take you to the parking lot. Management frowns on bringing cab drivers any closer than that."

"Got it," I said. "Anything else Management frowns on that we should know about?"

She let out a long-suffering sigh. "Yes. Probably anything and everything you're planning on doing in Chicago."

"Well, good," I said. "He can get in line with everybody else."

26.

"Corman was right," Caitlin said, standing beside me in the Bast Club's sprawling lounge. A veil of burgundy light washed over us, carried on a lilting serenade from a quartet that played over unseen speakers from every corner of the room.

"About what?" I asked.

"It looks like Jules Verne built a brothel."

"It's a little excessive, huh?"

Caitlin blinked, looking around wide-eyed.

"What? No, I *love* it," she said. "They just need to fix the music. The ambiance is screaming for some OMD or Depeche Mode."

I didn't see Trevor Manderley anywhere, and that suited me just fine. Amy was in full effect, though, holding court for a small gaggle of human and cambion onlookers as she demonstrated a ragged-looking poppet from her seemingly bottomless briefcase.

"That's Amy Xun," I said to Caitlin, nodding her way. "Local black marketeer. She wants the Judas Coin, bad, and I gather she's not confident of her chances in the tournament. She's looking to buy it outright from whoever wins."

"Could be useful," Caitlin murmured. "Anyone else I should know about?"

There was, and she was coming our way holding a tall carrot-tinged Bloody Mary that matched her hair dye.

"Mr. Vegas," Freddie said, flashing a smile. "You out-of-towners are multiplying like rabbits. Who's your lady friend?"

"Freddie, Caitlin. Caitlin, this is Fredrika Vinter."

Caitlin's eyes got even bigger.

"As in, *House* of Vinter?" she asked.

Freddie beamed. "The one and only, *dahling*. You've heard of me?"

"Heard of you? Half the clothes in my wardrobe have your label. I stumbled across your work two years ago, when Pierre Foss did that Fashion Week profile on you for *Vogue*, and I've been a fan ever since."

"Foss?" Freddie waved her hand in dismissal. "That was a hatchet job. He said I was terminally trapped in the eighties."

That, I thought as I looked between them, *explains everything*.

Caitlin nodded. "I see you as more...influenced by a keen grasp of important historical trends, yet finding your own aesthetic voice."

"Something tells me you two have a lot to talk about," I said. "Why don't I leave you to it? I'm going to grab a drink at the bar and poke around a little."

Freddie locked her arm around Caitlin's. "Come right this way. Let's find someplace to talk where everyone can see how *amazing* we are, while you tell me which of my designs you like the most and why."

I squeezed in at the crowded bar, shoulder to shoulder with a yellow-eyed cambion biker and a rail-thin woman with short-cropped hair and a silver ankh pendant at her throat. I waited to catch the bartender's attention, lost in a sea of swirling psychic currents. The Tiger's Garden back home could get loud, on a magical level, but nothing like this place. I suppose it helped when you *knew* all the minds you were brushing up against.

Maybe that was why I was taken by surprise when a slender hand clamped down on my forearm like a drowning victim grabbing for a life preserver. I turned to find a goddess at my shoulder. Delicate cheekbones and a curling bob of golden hair, lush lips painted cherry red, and eyes so pale blue they made me think of stained glass. I knew I hadn't seen her before. A face like that, you don't forget.

"You have to help me," the woman said in a breathless whisper.

"I'm sorry," I started to say, "I don't think we've—"

Her hand squeezed harder. "*Please.* He's going to kill me if you don't do something!"

I didn't like the sound of that. She tugged my arm, pulling me away from the bar. The woman looked like she was around twenty-one, but that was only skin deep. Now I could see the black-diamond aura pulsing in my second sight. The mark of an incarnate demon.

Not a cold aura, though. A warm one. Like Caitlin's.

"Who?" I said. "Who's going to kill you?"

She shot a glance over her shoulder then looked back to me, her eyes wide with terror. "*Royce.* I shouldn't even be talking to you, but you have a reputation for being able to help people and I'm just so *scared*—"

I took her hand. "It's all right. Deep breaths, okay? Nobody's going to hurt you, not while I'm here. Just take some deep breaths, calm down, and tell me everything."

She pulled me across the room, leading me to one of the empty conversation nooks. We sat side by side on the plush red velvet divan, and she clung to my hand as she talked.

"My use-name is Nadine. I'm with the Flowers. I mean, I'm nobody in the court, but...Royce has a human spy, who's *obsessed* with me. I rejected his advances, and I just found out he's, he's—"

Her voice hitched. I gently squeezed her hand, trying to reassure her. "It's okay. Nadine, listen, it's going to be okay. I'll protect you."

"He's fabricated evidence," she told me, her eyes glistening, "tons of it, 'proving' I'm a traitor. He's here, tonight, and he's given me an hour to change my mind. If I don't do what he wants, *anything* he wants, he'll go straight to Royce, and Royce will believe him. He'll *kill* me! Y-you believe me, don't you?"

Of course I did. The question was how to stop him? No violence inside the club. I could lure him out, come up with some pretense, then what? Drop him fast, drag the body to one of those Dumpsters around the corner—

"Now that must be a world record," Royce said, dropping into the chair beside us. "You've known that woman for all of three minutes, and unless I'm mistaken, you're strongly considering murdering someone to protect her. For hell's sake, man, get ahold of yourself. Or *can* you?"

I blinked. Jarred from my thoughts, I tried to pull my hand away, but Nadine held it in an iron grip. She stroked my wrist with her other hand, her fingers sliding under the sleeve of my shirt, gently massaging. It felt good. Too good.

"Don't pull away," she whispered. Her aura of fear dissipated, replaced with a soothing gentleness reflected in her voice. "You don't want me to stop touching you. You *like* this."

I did.

"Introductions are in order," Royce said. "Daniel, please meet Mistress Nadine, Grand Matriarch of the House of Dead Roses, the eldest daughter of Lust in the Court of Night-Blooming Flowers. Nadine, why don't you tell our human friend what you're doing to him right now?"

She had the softest, saddest smile I'd ever seen.

"Right now," she said, "your hypothalamus is flooding your brain with a chemical called oxytocin. It works to promote feelings of bonding with your mate, as well as trust and contentment. The dose is far, far higher than what your brain could produce on its own. Your body is telling you that you can trust me. That you are safe to trust me. That you are right to trust me, because you want to be with me. Isn't that so?"

Her voice took on a lulling cadence, a hypnotic rhythm that pulled my legs out from under me.

"I'm also dosing you with a flood of endorphins. Endorphins are a natural morphine created by your body, and they can have all kinds of fascinating effects when properly put to use. Given enough time, I could train you to associate fear and pain with the heights of pleasure. But I would never do that, of course. I care about you. I'm only doing this because Royce ordered me to. You believe me, don't you?"

I did. I believed every word she said, even though I knew she was lying.

"I'll level with you," Royce told me. "Nadine, here? She scares *me* a little. She's really a nasty piece of work. You should see what she likes to do with a pair of scissors. Now, she's got this pet theory that your species—who she normally refers to as 'filth-eating monkeys,' by the way—was created by Lucifer to serve the Choir of Lust. It's why she can tinker with your nervous system just by touching your skin. Me, I think that's a bunch of hokum."

"That's not true at all," Nadine cooed. "I care about humanity. We all do. I care about *you*. More than anyone in the Court of Jade Tears does. We cherish our human subjects. You should come and work for Prince Malphas. You should pledge yourself to *me*."

Royce crossed his legs and leaned back in his chair, enjoying every second of this.

"Bad idea, sport," he said amiably. "I mean, you *could* do that, if you fancy being dragged down to Nadine's tower in hell and suffering a few hundred years of unimaginable torture and degradation until she gets sick of you and finds another victim to play with. Or, now here's a great idea I just had, you could open your eyes and grasp the point of this little exercise."

I couldn't move. Couldn't think. I knew he was telling the truth. I knew she was telling the truth, too. I sat there, impaled on the paradox, turned to stone by Nadine's kindly gaze.

"What," I said through gritted teeth, "is the point?"

"That all she had to do," Royce said, holding up a finger, "is touch you. Everybody knows a succubus's *kiss* can be more addictive than heroin, if she wants it to be. *That's* no secret. That's the crude magic, the battering ram at the doors of your soul. But the elders of the Choir of Lust, the truly skilled ones...they can be subtle. Out of idle curiosity, when you first met Caitlin, how many times did she casually touch you?"

I stood in my circle of salt, drenched in gore, while Caitlin slowly tore

Artie Kaufman to pieces in front of me. My heart pounded as she stepped into the circle and pressed one bloody fingertip to my lips.

Shh.

She curled her fingers in my hair, stroking the back of my neck, as she pulled me in for a kiss.

And I wanted her. Amid all the carnage and horror, I wanted her.

Nadine leaned close and whispered. "I don't like saying nice things about my enemies, but Caitlin's better at this than I am."

27.

"We're trying to help you," Royce told me. "Scout's honor, sport. You're fighting for the wrong team. This is your official wake-up call."

"The truth is," Nadine purred into my ear, "since the moment we met, all I've been thinking about is you, me, and my favorite pair of scissors. I think I'd start by gelding you, like the vile animal you are. And despite knowing this? Despite hearing me tell you exactly what I think of you and how much I'd enjoy making you suffer? You still don't want me to stop touching you. You still *like* me."

I did. I hated myself for it, but I did. *I'm just misunderstanding her*, I thought. *She's not really like that. She's just saying that because Royce told her to. If the two of us went somewhere alone together, away from him, I bet we could sort this all out.*

Nadine cupped her free hand around the back of my neck, massaging gently, like Caitlin had a few hours before.

"You look so confused," she said, sympathetic. "I could fix that. One kiss, and you'll never be confused again. Wouldn't that be nice? A life of absolute clarity, of purpose."

"Ooh," Royce said with a grin. "I really wouldn't do that, sport. That would be a bad, bad life decision."

"He knows that," Nadine snapped at Royce, frowning. Then she turned back to me, her expression softening, and took her hand off my neck. Now she stroked her nails under my chin, batting her eyelashes at me. "Doesn't he? Oh, he *knows* how unwise it would be, but he still wants to say yes."

"Let go of me," I croaked, no will behind the words. It wasn't what I wanted to say. Wasn't what she wanted me to say. Same thing.

Nadine whispered in my ear, "Beg me for a kiss." Her voice was a gust of silky smoke, slithering into my ear, coiling around my brain. "*Beg* me, you filthy little worm."

I bit down on my tongue until I tasted blood.

A shadow loomed over us. Freddie, cradling a freshly poured martini. From the flush on her cheeks, it wasn't the second or the third drink she'd had tonight.

"And who exactly," she asked, loudly enough to draw glances from across the room, "is the skank holding hands with my new BFF's boyfriend?"

Nadine let go of me, standing up like a shot. "*What* did you call me?"

Freddie looked her up and down, gesticulating with her glass as she spoke. "On further reflection, I'm downgrading your rating to 'Gucci-drone tacky-ass bitch.' You may resubmit your application for evaluation in six months."

That got Royce on his feet, too. "Mind your tongue while you still have one, Vinter. This woman is an esteemed noble—"

"Who, her?" Freddie said, jerking her glass in Nadine's direction. Her martini sloshed over the rim, splashing Nadine's dress.

A strangled yowl rose from the depths of Nadine's throat, a sound like a dozen tortured cats in a burlap sack, as her eyes turned to swirls of molten copper.

"*You*," she hissed, flashing a mouth lined with shark's teeth. Around us, the shadows responded. Congealing on the walls, growing thick and furry, sprouting legs as they skittered across the ceiling.

Royce saw them too. He grabbed Nadine's arm, yanking her back a step.

"Not *here*," he said, giving her arm a shake. "No fighting in the club."

"Do you have any idea," Nadine growled, "who I *am*?"

Freddie rolled her eyes. "I just told you who you are. You know, you can get some help for that attention-deficit problem. While you're at the clinic, see if they can get you a personality transplant."

Nadine flexed her hand. Bones cracked and elongated, fingers curling as her nails became claws of black iron. The shadows on the wall bulged and took on three dimensions, a curtain of hairy fist-sized spiders with legs bent to pounce.

"*Nadine*," Royce snapped. "*Not here*. That's an order."

Nadine took a deep, shuddering breath. She looked down at her drenched dress, then back at us.

"Later then," she hissed as she stormed off, "for *both* of you."

"You'd best mind yourself," Royce told Freddie. "Don't forget who I am and who I serve. I represent hell's law in—"

Freddie's index finger shot up. She wagged it at him. "I'm not a demon, don't answer to you, don't care, buh-bye."

Royce gritted his teeth and looked my way.

"I hope you take my little demonstration to heart, Daniel. Your 'lover' is using you. Playing your heart like an instrument, like my Nadine did, just now. When you grow tired of being an abused pawn, remember: you would find yourself welcome in *my* court as an honored guest."

Freddie snorted and tossed back what little remained in her glass. "Buh-*bye*, Royce. Don't make me say it a third time."

"Oh? And what if I do?"

I felt change in the air, even before the light around us shifted to faded blues and blacks. Not the club's shadows now. Hers. Chill washed over me, the chill of a famine winter, and my breath puffed out on a curlicue of frost. Even though I'd eaten a full meal a few hours ago, my stomach growled and knitted itself in knots of hunger as if I'd been starving for days.

"I've always wondered," Freddie said, her voice slow and soft, "what the flesh of an incarnate demon tastes like. Maybe I'll get to find out."

Royce's eyebrow twitched. His lips curled in a defiant sneer, but he still took a step backward.

"I have a tournament to prepare for," he said. "No time for this nonsense."

As soon as he left, the light returned and the warmth flooded back. Freddie stood over me, her bubbly boozy mask firmly back in place.

"I am surrounded," she proclaimed, "by tacky-ass bitches. They're all around us, and they don't even know they're tacky. Hey, are you okay? You look sick."

I shook my head, slow. "I'm not okay."

"I'll go get Caitlin," she said but stopped when I held up one empty hand.

"No. Don't do that. I need to be alone right now."

* * *

Alone didn't last. I suppose, on some level, I didn't want it to. Alone meant time to think. Time to think too much.

Caitlin found me in the gaming parlor, eyeing the Judas Coin as I circled the glass display case. I recognized the sound of her high heels, clicking their way toward me from the door.

"Any luck?" she asked.

"Ran into Royce."

"And?"

I turned and shrugged. "Not sure. He didn't ask me about the coin, or let on that he knew about my talk with Scudder, but he did try to mess with my head a little."

She frowned. "What did he say to you?"

I waved off the question and started walking to the door. Caitlin fell into step with me.

"I think he wants to recruit me," I said, opting for half the truth instead of a whole lie. "Or make me think he does, anyway."

"Either is possible. The Flowers have had you on their radar ever since that whole mess with the Redemption Choir. Winning you to Prince Malphas's side—or taking you off the board—would make up for the embarrassment they suffered."

"Yeah, well, I wouldn't care for my coworkers." I paused, a question on my lips, not sure if I should give it voice.

What's the problem? I asked myself. *Are you afraid of what she'll say? Or afraid of what she won't?*

"Royce had a buddy with him. Woman calling herself Nadine. Does that ring any—"

Caitlin grabbed my arm. Hard. She stopped in her tracks at the parlor door and turned me to face her.

"Nadine is *here?*"

"Yeah," I said. "Pretty, blond, has a Taylor Swift thing going on? Hobbies include moonlight walks on the beach and cutting people up?"

She didn't say another word—and didn't let go of my arm—until she'd hustled me out of the building and into the parking lot. A damp chill hung in the air, the kind of cold that seeps into your bones. We walked through the lot, past the odd assortment of old junkers and high-end sports cars, and toward the sounds of traffic one block over.

"Did she touch you?"

"Caitlin, what are you so upset about—"

Her fingers clenched hard enough to leave a bruise.

"*Did she touch you?*"

I didn't want to lie. And in that moment, hearing the growl at the edge of her voice, I realized something that chilled me deeper than the weather.

I didn't want to lie, but I was afraid to tell the truth.

Now it was my turn to stand my ground. I stopped walking and looked her in the eye.

"What's going on, Caitlin? I'm not moving until I get a straight answer."

She let go of me, her hands falling limp to her sides. She sighed.

"What's going on," she said, "is that this situation just became exponentially more dangerous. Nadine leads the Dead Roses. They're a sect, I suppose you could say, inside the Court of Night-Blooming Flowers. Half monastic order, half training academy."

"What kind of training?"

"Spies. Assassins. Seducers and killers. Nadine's agents are the backbone of Prince Malphas's intelligence service. Few in number, but bloody near unstoppable. The Roses' regimen, you see, is...beyond cruel. For every fifty aspirants, only one survives to graduation—and usually with the blood of the other forty-nine staining her claws and teeth. In Nadine's house, you're either the best and brightest, or you're meat for their table."

"So what does this have to do with her touching me?"

Caitlin bit her bottom lip.

"Certain members of my choir," she said slowly, choosing her words one by one, "the eldest, and most skilled, can manipulate natural energies in ways that others can only dream of. Nadine is arguably the greatest daughter of lust alive, and she's earned her reputation. She's been known to...subvert people with nothing more than a gentle caress. I was concerned that Royce might have used her to get at you."

I stood in the heart of a verbal minefield.

"I always thought," I said, stepping lightly, "you had to kiss someone to get into their heads. You, collectively, I mean."

"Most do, yes."

Ask her what SHE can do. Go on, ask her.

"So," I said, "Nadine...she's extraordinary?"

"Let me put it this way: you know the myth of Helen of Troy? The woman so desired she launched a thousand ships and brought a nation to war?"

"Sure," I said.

Caitlin gave me a wistful half smile. "Though it's never been proven, rumor has it, that was Nadine in disguise. She cared nothing for the love of Menelaus or Paris. She just started a war to see if she *could*. Some say she's even older, that she was one of the original daughters of Lilith. Suffice to say you'll rarely meet a more dangerous member of my choir."

"Rarely," I echoed. *But you didn't say never.*

"Rarely," she said.

28.

Back at the Four Seasons, our room was dark and warm, with the faint humming of a heater the only sound. We hadn't talked much in the cab on our way to the hotel. Not much we could say with the cabbie listening in, and besides, I needed time to think. Caitlin did too, I supposed.

I just wasn't sure what she was thinking about.

I felt confused. I felt anxious. More than anything, though, I felt guilty as hell.

Caitlin had risked her job for me, risked her *life* for me more than once. And here I was, putting her on trial without even telling her.

Sure, Nadine had made me feel things with her powers, things like what I felt for Caitlin. Sure, she and Royce could be telling the truth, and sure, maybe I'd been Caitlin's sucker since day one.

But who had more motivation to lie?

And the worst part is, I thought, *just the fact that I'm asking these questions means I don't trust her as much as I should. It's like I'm betraying her just by wondering.*

That was how love was supposed to be, right? Absolute trust? Hell if I knew. I was never much good at relationships. I had a lot of whiskey-fueled one-night stands in my rearview mirror, along with a scrapbook filled with affairs that had gone off the tracks as soon as they started. Lovers flitting in and out of my life, here one week and gone the next.

Jennifer and I had been doomed from the start, but at least it was over fast and our friendship came out stronger than before. Roxy? I'd thought Roxy was the one, but I managed to torpedo that relationship until there was nothing left but driftwood and sinking rubble. Some part of me knew, I think, that I didn't deserve something that good in my life. So I ruined it, to save her from me.

And now here I was, with the woman I loved, and getting ready to wreck things all over again.

Caitlin closed the door behind us and latched the dead bolt. I reached for the light switch, but she caught my hand, cradling it gently.

"No light," she said.

"What is it?"

She moved close to me in the dark. I could smell her musk perfume, feel the warmth of her breath on my cheek.

"She touched you. Didn't she." It wasn't a question.

"Yeah," I said. "She did."

"I imagine she told you things about me. Ugly little lies."

"I didn't listen."

"But you *heard*." She took a deep breath, held it, and let it out slowly. "My kind are not jealous creatures, Daniel. It isn't in our nature. But we are territorial."

"Caitlin, I don't know what you think happened—"

She pressed her finger to my lips. *Shh*. Just like she did in Artie Kaufman's kitchen. No blood this time, only perfume.

"I need two things tonight. I need to feed, to replenish my energy. And I need to examine you. To make sure Nadine didn't slip a spider into the back of your mind. Will you allow me to?"

"What, you think she hypnotized me or something, like some kind of Manchurian Candidate deal?"

"I think," she started to say, then fell silent. Her shadow hovered before me, barely breathing.

I put it together. I just had to look at it from Caitlin's perspective. She knew that an older, far more powerful rival (*Nadine says Caitlin is more skilled than she is*, argued the voice in the back of my head) had cornered her lover tonight. She knew that Nadine could mess with people's heads just by touching them (*except Nadine says Caitlin can do it too*). And she knew that Royce would benefit in all kinds of ways by stealing me from her.

I've been feeling insecure since we left the club, I thought.

And so has Caitlin.

"Will you allow me to?" she asked.

That voice in the back of my head asked what she would do if I said no. The rest of me already knew my answer.

"Do what you have to."

She took my shoulders and turned me around, facing the bed.

"I'll just be a minute," she said. "Be in bed when I return. Be naked."

She stepped into the bathroom. I undressed and slipped beneath the covers, sinking into the soft mattress. She returned a few minutes later. Her silhouette paused by the pile of my discarded clothes, crouching. I heard the whispering slither of my belt, pulling free from my trousers, before she stood up again.

"Daniel," she asked, "do you trust me?"

Don't trust her, said the traitor in the back of my head.

"Yes," I told her.

She held my belt loosely, looped between her hands. Then she yanked one end, hard, making the leather *snap* as it drew taut.

"Put your hands over your head."

I slid down on the mattress a little, crossing my wrists above my head on the pillow. Watching her as she slipped out of her dress, a sinuous shadow, the belt dangling in her grip.

"Caitlin, what are you—"

"Do you trust me?"

The traitorous voice in my head was quieter. "I trust you," I said.

She pulled back the sheets and straddled my waist, trailing the tongue of the belt across my bare chest. Then she leaned in and twisted the leather around my wrists, tethering them to a spoke on the headboard. At first slow, gentle—then she gave the belt a sudden, vicious yank to draw the leather tight. She knotted it.

"Pull on that," she said.

I tugged at my wrists, but she'd knotted the belt too expertly, too tight. My hands weren't going anywhere. Caitlin sat up and rested her fingernails on my chest, over my heart.

"Helpless," she said.

I gave the belt another tug.

She leaned in, her hair falling across my face, and kissed the curve of my neck. My skin tingled in the wake of her lips, kindling a fire in the pit of my stomach.

"You know I enjoy hurting people," she said, as if she were commenting on the weather.

"You might have, ah, mentioned that before, yeah."

Another tug. My wrists started to ache. Like she said, helpless.

"It's not an uncommon delight among my kind." She punctuated her words with a flick of her tongue against my earlobe. "*Obviously*, but I consider myself something of a gourmet when it comes to pain. Much like Nadine, really. I'm simply more...discreet."

I took a deep breath and tried to keep my voice from quavering.

"You've never hurt me."

"No. Not yet, I haven't."

"Do you...think you're going to?"

She chuckled, low and throaty.

"I'm saying," she whispered, "that I could if I wanted to. And you couldn't stop me. The belt is just to drive the point home. I don't need you in bonds to do as I please with you."

She sat up, took hold of my chin, and turned my head to look up at her. Her eyes glowed in the dark, faint orbs of swirling copper.

"So all that being said, I have one question for you, Daniel. Just one, and I expect a truthful answer. I'll know if you lie."

I believed her.

"What's the question?"

She studied me in silence, then finally spoke.

"Daniel, are you afraid of me?"

Her question hit me like the tip of a spear. It drove through my shield of self-loathing, my armor of doubt, cracked the bars of the cage Nadine and Royce had tried to put me in, and thrust right into my heart.

Because I knew the answer without thinking.

"No," I said.

"No?"

"No. Because I know you won't hurt me. Because I do trust you. I've trusted you with my life before. I've made that gamble and won, and you've done the same for me. I'm not afraid of you, Caitlin, because I'm in love with you. And I believe that you love me too."

Caitlin slumped against me, the tension draining out of her body as she coiled her arms around me and clung tight.

"Thank you," she whispered.

I let out an uneasy laugh and wriggled my fingers. "Good. So can you untie me? I think my hands are falling asleep."

"No." She straightened up, straddling me. "Not yet."

"Not yet?"

"I like looking at you like this." She reached down. Her slender fingers curled around me, gently squeezing and stroking. "And as I said, I do need to replenish my energy. Here you are, all tied up and nowhere to run. Can't move, no way to release all that pent-up energy...hmm. Now I'm wondering. Think I can make you cry out so loudly that someone calls hotel security?"

"I...I don't think that's entirely necessar—" My words shattered into a groan of pleasure as she guided me inside her.

"Oh," Caitlin said, rising up and then easing down again, agonizingly slow, "it is *entirely* necessary."

* * *

I lost track of time. Caitlin had that effect on me. I just remembered snuggling in a happy haze, my freed arms wrapped around her shoulders, our sweat-drenched bodies entwined on the king-sized bed.

"There's just one thing I have to do," Caitlin murmured. "I hope you'll forgive me, but I have to send a very pointed message to Nadine."

"Huh? Sure, but why would I need to forgive—"

Her teeth clamped down on the side of my neck, biting hard enough to make my eyes water, her mouth suckling as I cried out. It felt like minutes passed before she let me go, taking hold of my chin and tilting my head to one side.

"There," she said, sounding satisfied. "That'll bruise nicely."

"*Ow*. What the *hell*, Caitlin?"

"You will wear an open-collared shirt to the tournament, no tie. I want her to see that. I want all of her people to see that, too."

I stared at her in the dark.

"I'm gonna have a massive hickey." I winced as I rubbed my neck. "What, are we in high school now?"

"It's a *love bite*, not a hickey. Daniel, humans who...belong to members of the courts are customarily given identifiers of various sorts. A tattoo, a brand, perhaps a soul-mark. It's territorial."

"This," I said, "is a hickey."

"You don't...'belong' to me the way that most humans belong to one of my kind. So certain traditional marks of owne—of *companionship* would be considered gauche. Like wearing a wedding ring when you're only dating. So, in the meantime, one makes do with what one has. Nadine will understand the message."

"That message being?"

"Hands off," Caitlin purred, pulling me into a kiss. "You belong to *me*."

And as I slowly tumbled into a dreamless sleep, the darkened hotel room giving way to the darkness behind my eyelids, the traitorous voice in the back of my mind finally fell silent.

For now.

29.

Sunrise came like a stampede of bulls, kicking me out of bed and into the shower as my mind lurched into high gear. We had one day. Royce's tournament was almost here, and at the end of the game, the Judas Coin would most likely slip out of our grasp—and our best hope for saving Coop would vanish along with it.

That gave us one day. One day to manipulate Royce into handing us an edge we could use.

The curtain parted and Caitlin stepped into the shower with me, stifling a yawn behind her hand. "I just called the others. Everyone's up and about, or at least getting there slowly. We're all meeting in Bentley and Corman's room."

As we stepped into their suite, the smell of fresh-brewed coffee wafted out to greet us, steaming from a six-pack of cardboard cups beside a mixed box of donuts. Corman had already gotten started on the donuts, judging from the dusting of powdered sugar on his golf shirt.

"And this is why I love you," I said, scooping up one of the cups. The coffee was hot in my hands and hotter going down, bitter and black. Margaux and Pixie weren't far behind us.

"Did some digging on your client," Pixie said, "and found something weird."

I knew it. Cameron Drake and his "employees" were too fishy to be real. "What'd you find?" I asked her.

"Nothing. That's the weird part. Drake is one-hundred-percent legit."

My momentary excitement deflated like a punctured balloon. "You're kidding me."

"Nope." She stepped around me and squinted at the box, plucking out a chocolate glazed donut. "He won the lottery, went from roofing contractor to *nouveau riche* overnight, and started spending money like it was going out of style. Nothing shady in his background, nothing questionable about the lottery itself. He's just really, really lucky. Like, struck-by-lightning-five-times-in-the-same-day-and-lived lucky."

"What about the ranch? Find anything on that?"

"Eastern Pines belonged to an investment company, and it'd been sitting on the market for years. Drake bought it for twelve-point-six million, sight unseen. Guess the guy really wants to play J.R. Ewing."

"Seems to me we should focus on the task at hand," Margaux said, picking up a coffee cup and prying off the plastic lid. "That coin ain't gonna steal itself. Where's the sugar and cream?"

Corman arched a bushy eyebrow at her. "Don't ruin a perfectly good cup of coffee. Drink it black, like nature and God intended."

"Comin' from a man who puts ketchup on scrambled eggs," Margaux snorted.

"All right," I said, "let's get to it. Most of today is on my shoulders. If Scudder did his job and ratted me out, then right about now Royce is expecting me to make a move on the coin. That means he'll have eyes on me the second I go downstairs. If there's not somebody waiting for me in that lobby right now, I'll be sorely disappointed."

Bentley put his hands behind his back and paced the room, thinking. "Assuming he won't be shadowing you personally, given that you know his face, do we know how large a team he can field?"

"Not large," Caitlin said. "That's the good news. The bad news is he has the aid of an organization called the Dead Roses. Stealth and subterfuge is their specialty, and they are highly skilled."

Bentley tilted his head. "Humans, or...?"

"A little of both. The Roses will take anyone except for cambion. Expect a mixture of humans and demons wearing human skin. The humans will wear heavy clothing to conceal extensive bodily scarring and surgical modification. If male, they've generally been castrated, though you're not likely to get close enough to tell."

"Excuse me." Pixie held up one hand, looking queasy. "Did you say 'castrated'?"

"The Roses will take anyone," Caitlin said, "but you have to prove that you *want* it. I'm told that the knife they're given is rusted. And blunt."

I clapped my hands together. "So with that cheerful news, here's how we'll play it: Caitlin's going to arrange rental cars for herself and Mama Margaux. Margaux, you're going to be my second shadow. I want you on my tail all day, trying to spot who *else* is following me. We don't know if Royce is going to put a tail on Caitlin or not, but it's a safe bet that everybody in the Court of Night-Blooming Flowers has her face memorized, so she's going to drive around the city and waste their time."

"What about us?" Corman nodded to Bentley. "Want us to keep our peepers on Royce?"

"I want you on the Bast Club. Astral overwatch, but *don't* try to go inside. Lots of weird energy and weirder security in there. Just watch the door, and let us know if you spot Royce coming or going. If we can get him to move the coin, we'll need to know the second it happens. Pixie, I need you to set up a secure conference call for us, a line we can all listen in on, all day if we have to. And did you get that web post up about the bounty on the coin?"

Pixie swallowed a mouthful of donut. "Yep. Seeing a few ripples of activity, too. It's got some eyeballs on it."

"Good. Put up a response. Make it look like it's coming from me, and I'm doing a lousy job of covering my tracks. Just don't make it *too* easy for them."

"You got it. What should it say?"

"That I'm on the move," I said. "And I expect to have the coin in my hands before sundown."

* * *

Alone in the elevator down, I slipped my Bluetooth earpiece on snugly, hearing a soft hiss of static in my eardrum.

"Okay, ladies and gents," I whispered, "it's showtime. Mama, you on deck?"

"Mm-hmm," Margaux murmured back.

"Good. Caitlin, you're up at bat."

Right about then, Caitlin would be strolling through the lobby, taking her time on the way to the hotel's front doors. Right past Margaux, who'd have a prime seat in the lobby, watching the room while she pretended to play with her phone. As the elevator touched down and the doors chimed, Margaux spoke softly.

"Caitlin, you've got two on your tail. Those yuppie-looking boys who were standing by the window, braggin' about their stock options. They're stuck to you like white on rice."

"Two just for me? Mm, I'm flattered."

I strode off the elevator and headed straight for the concierge desk, not giving anyone in the lobby a passing glance. The concierge stood up sharply at my arrival, back straight and shoulders square.

"Mr. Greyson," he said, "good morning! Is everything to your liking?"

Hotels where they remember my name were *always* to my liking. Even if it was a fake name.

"Absolutely," I told him. "Just one question. I'm going to need to rent a car, just for today. Can you direct me to the closest rental place?"

"I can do better than that. We'd be happy to arrange it for you and have a car brought around front. It won't take any time at all."

I took out my wallet and peeled off a couple of twenties.

"Fantastic," I said a little louder than I needed to, matching his glowing smile watt for watt. "Something with a hatchback would be perfect. I'm doing a *lot* of shopping today."

"Don't look left," Margaux whispered. "Stocky man with a rolling suitcase perked up once you started talking, and now he's texting somebody."

While I waited for the car, loitering by the big glass sliding doors, I dug up a phone number for Scudder's repair shop. I disconnected from the conference call and gave him a ring.

"We still on for today?" I heard him clear his throat on the other end. Nervous.

"Yeah, no, turns out I can't help ya."

I smiled with relief.

Scudder could only fall two ways: either he'd take my offer and play it straight, or he'd sell me out to Royce in order to bolster his rep with the Flowers. Obviously, he'd chosen the prize behind curtain number two. Just like I wanted him to.

"You can't, or you *won't?*" I demanded, doing my best to sound angry.

"Means the same thing far as you're concerned, right? Look, I don't have the intel you want. I can't deliver, and I'm not in the business of rippin' people off."

The hell you aren't, I thought. *I've seen your shop.*

"I'm very disappointed, Scudder. Fine, I'll go with my backup option. They've got what I need, and they'll be *happy* to take my money."

"Wait," he said. "Wait, who? What backup option?"

"Oh, nothing. Just found somebody with an inside connection at the Bast Club. Heavily inside. They're more expensive than *your* services, but y'know, you get what you pay for. See you around, Scudder."

"Wait, wait. Hold on just a—"

I hung up on him and got back on the conference call. I figured he'd be falling all over himself to warn Royce. Good.

A valet brought my rental around front. A silver Chrysler 300 with a hatchback. Perfect. As I slipped behind the steering wheel, Margaux's warning crackled over my earpiece.

"Careful, Danny. Three men just got off the elevator, walking in step with each other and moving fast. All three wearing long coats and leather gloves, and they're not even outside yet."

"I'll drive slow," I said, "and make sure they catch up with me. Bentley, is Corman ready?"

Up in their room, Corman would be sitting cross-legged, breathing shallow, deep in a trance. Astral projection was his specialty. Bentley babysat Corman's body while he wasn't inside it and translated his faint whispers for us.

"Cormie says he's floating about ten feet above your car."

"Okay, let's leapfrog. Have him follow me while Margaux gets her own rental car. Mama, as soon as you catch up with me, trade off. You tail me from there, and Corman can watch the Bast Club. Cait, how are you doing?"

"Leading my pursuers on a merry little chase. No worries. You just focus on the ones dogging *your* heels."

Part one, complete. I needed to show Royce that I intended to steal the Judas Coin right out of the hallowed confines of the Bast Club. By now, he had to believe it.

Now the tricky part: making him think I could actually pull it off.

30.

My first jaunt was to the suburbs, stopping at a hardware store at the end of a strip mall. My purchases were as random as they were ominous: two pickaxes, three shovels, five orange hard hats, and a hundred-foot coil of stout rope. I also grabbed twelve cans of WD-40 and a carton of galvanized steel nails.

Have fun figuring out what I'm doing with all this junk, I thought, humming a happy tune as I loaded my cartload of supplies into the back of the Chrysler. Sure enough, as I pulled out of the parking lot, I heard Bentley's voice on the conference line.

"Cormie says one of the men from the hotel just gave the cashier twenty dollars for a copy of your receipt. He also asked her to repeat everything you said to her, word for word."

"Good. Mama, where you at?"

"Close now," Margaux said. "I can see you up ahead. I'm holding about two hundred feet back."

"Excellent. Switch off. Bentley, tell Corman to start watching the club."

"He says he can hear you, Daniel."

"Corman," I said, "start watching the club."

"Now he says," Bentley replied, then paused. "I'm not translating that. It would be rude."

My next stop was back in the city, pushing my way through a molasses snarl of traffic on my way to Wicker Park.

"Oh, no," Trevor Manderley said as I strode in through the

front door of the Hermetic Inquiry. "No, no, no. You can*not* be in here. I did everything you wanted, damn it."

"Relax," I said, surveying the empty shop as I strolled toward the register. "I'm here to give you some free money."

He scrunched up his forehead. "Why would you do that?"

"Because a couple of minutes after I walk out of here, a guy is gonna come in and offer you a bribe to tell me what I bought. He gave a hardware-store cashier twenty bucks. I imagine the great Trevor Manderley could talk him out of a Benjamin, at least."

He sniffed at the bait, looking for a hook. "And what is it you're buying?"

"A story." I counted out five twenties and laid them on the counter between us, side by side. "A two-hundred-dollar story. I'll pay for half now, and the rest later."

"What's this story about?"

"It's a story about a book that you sniffed out for me on the black market, rush-ordered, and that I paid you *very* handsomely for. Do you know anything about ancient Taoist sorcery?"

"Not my field," he said.

"Good. Then it was a book about ancient Taoist sorcery. Do you speak Cantonese?"

"No, but—"

"Good," I said. "Then it was written in Cantonese. What you do know is that it was the real deal, a genuine magical grimoire, and I was absolutely insistent that I had to have it *today*. I even said, explicitly, that I needed it before the poker tournament at the Bast Club."

Trevor's gaze shifted between me and the money on the counter.

"And this won't blow back on me?"

"Zero chance."

"And," he said slowly, eyeing the cash, "what if I tell them the truth?"

I shrugged. "Well, you don't get the other hundred bucks. Oh, also, I'll kill you. Any more easy questions?"

He shook his head.

"Good. Just think of it like this: you've got two options, and you have to pick one." I held out my hands, palms upward, juggling them up and down like the arms of a scale. "Free money? Bullet in the head? Free money? Bullet in the head? Now, I'm no professional merchant such as yourself, but if it was up to me? I'd take the free money."

He pocketed the cash as I walked out the door.

Now I'd thrown magic in the mix, as unpredictable as a revolver with one loaded chamber. Royce would know that I had something exotic cooked up, but that was as far as it went. With no details and no idea exactly how I would be coming for the coin, he couldn't devise a plan to stop me.

My final destination waited down in the Chicago Loop, on a side street off a boulevard lined with high-end boutiques and electronics stores. "KM Film Supply" read the sign out front, painted to look like a torn-off movie ticket. "Rental and Leasing Options Available!"

More of a warehouse than a store. I stood amid racks and racks of cameras, lights, and gadgets. The counter clerk, wearing a name tag that read "Hi! I'm Dell!", was a college-age hipster in skinny jeans and a loud plaid shirt.

"Hey," I said. "I'm doing a small local production, and I need to get my hands on some lighting equipment."

He lit up, closing his dog-eared *Cineaste* magazine and standing straight.

"Sure, we can hook you up! What kind of production is it? Are you shooting exteriors, interiors...?"

"Interiors," I told him. "But I need something bright. Really bright. The brightest lights you have."

He rubbed the back of his neck, looking dubious. "Huh. Well, I assume you'll want multiple intensities, or at least variable settings, right?"

"Nope. Just very, very bright. So bright that there isn't a single shadow in the shot."

Dell looked back toward the steel shelves. "Uh, you know that'll like, wash out *everything*, right? I mean that's not really how it's done—"

"Listen to me." I moved closer, leaning against the counter. "Our needs are very specific. We want to *kill shadows*. Got it?"

"Kill shadows," he repeated, blinking. "Okay. Hey, sure, you're the customer, whatever. Let me guess...this is an art film, isn't it?"

"I do like to think of myself as an artist, yes."

Dell shrugged. "Okay, well, if you really want to go all-out, we've got an open-face HMI that runs as hot as eighteen kilowatts."

I had no idea what that was, but it sounded good to me. I was never going to use it anyway.

"Fine. How much does that cost?"

"Twenty-four thousand dollars," Dell said. "Or we can talk about our daily rental rates?"

I took out Peter Greyson's credit card.

"Yeah," I said, "rental sounds good. Definitely rental."

I idly wondered, as I lugged a heavy clamshell case made of rough black plastic out to the hatchback, if a powerful enough spotlight *could* kill the Bast Club's guardian shadows. It was definitely an idea to file for future consideration. For now, all I needed was word of my latest acquisitions to get back to Royce.

I gave it ten minutes.

I knew that instead of moving the coin, it'd be a lot easier for Royce to have his agents take me out. So for the final trick of the day, I had to perform a disappearing act.

"How's it look, Mama?" I asked as I rode up an expressway on-ramp. I couldn't see her in the snarl of traffic behind me, but I knew she wasn't far.

"They're good, Danny. Too good. You've got three cars on you, at least, and they keep swapping places and changing their distance."

A professional tail, then. I'd expected nothing less. "At least? You spotted others you're not sure about?"

"I just can't tell. Maybe four. There's only two on you right now, but the third was just—*guete!*"

"That sounded like a bad word," I said.

"Those other two? They're on *me*."

I craned my neck, watching for road signs. "Break off, right now. Hopefully if you do, they'll all follow me. Cait? We're on the Eisenhower Expressway, heading west. Are you anywhere close?"

"My GPS says I can't be. However, I'm inclined to disagree." Given Caitlin's penchant for fast driving, I didn't doubt her.

"Okay," I said, thinking fast. "Mama, you get off at the next exit and coordinate with Caitlin. Meet up, someplace public. If they do follow you, they won't start shit in front of Cait."

"What about you?" Margaux asked.

"Don't worry about me. I'll improvise."

Easier said than done, stuck in a clump of traffic on an endless expressway. The speedometer said forty miles an hour, but it felt like an endless crawl. I had no idea how many goons Royce had put on my tail, but one thing was certain: I had to lose all of them, all at once.

Concrete barriers lined the middle of the expressway, dividing the east- and west-bound traffic. No easy way to pull a U-turn. I spotted small openings every quarter mile or so, for emergency vehicles, but I'd have to telegraph my move and slow down so much that it'd be easy for at least one of Royce's men to follow me.

So maybe I do more than slow down, I thought, easing into the far right lane. A forest-green sign announced another exit, two miles up ahead.

I took a deep breath, then swerved the wheel right and slammed on my brakes. The Chrysler skidded to a jolting stop on the shoulder and all at once, I spotted brake lights flickering in the passing stream of cars. A dirty pickup truck veered out of his lane, earning a screaming horn and nearly causing a pileup, and just as quickly swung back in line.

You've all got two choices, I thought. *Either pull over and give yourself away, or keep going with the traffic and hope you can double back fast enough to catch me.*

I counted off thirty seconds, slow, making sure that anyone on my tail had to have overshot my impromptu parking spot. Then I stepped on the gas, tires rumbling as I rode along the shoulder, making a beeline for the off-ramp ahead.

And you won't catch me.

I swung off the expressway, caught a green light at the bottom of the ramp, and drove fast toward nowhere in particular. All that mattered was putting as much distance between me and the chase cars as I could, and not leaving any breadcrumbs for them to follow. I threaded through the streets, coasting on autopilot, choosing my direction on a whim and going anywhere but back.

Half an hour later, I started feeling safe. I'd swung through the backstreets of a north-side suburb, passing a dozen look-alike townhouses with white vinyl siding and perfect lawns. When I checked my rearview mirror, there wasn't a car in sight. Either Royce's agents could turn invisible, or I'd lost them.

What came next sealed the deal. Bentley's voice echoed across the conference line, the first comment he'd made in an hour.

"Everyone. Cormie says that Royce just showed up at the Bast Club with a...very angry-looking blond woman in tow. They left their car running in the parking lot and stormed into the building."

"Now that's more like it," I said. "Okay, let's get ready to improvise."

31.

I pulled over to the side of the road long enough to fumble with the GPS on my phone and figure out where I was. Plotting a route to the Bast Club seemed my best bet, hopefully putting me on a collision course with the Judas Coin.

"Someone's coming out," Bentley said. "It's those two men we saw you with at the airport, Daniel, the ones with Royce."

"Mack and Zeke? Interesting. Anything look different about them?"

"Cormie says, one moment—yes. The big one has a metal briefcase handcuffed to his right wrist. They're getting into a sedan. Should he follow them?"

"Hold on," I said. "Let me think."

Caitlin cleared her throat, chiming in on the conference call. "If the coin is in that case, Corman *needs* to follow them."

And if it weren't, he'd be off on a wild goose chase. Corman's astral eyes were our only vantage point on the club. The one bullet in my gun. If I pulled the trigger now, I'd better be right.

"The car is pulling out of the lot," Bentley said.

"Daniel." Caitlin's voice was strained. "Need a decision. Now, please."

I squeezed the steering wheel until my knuckles turned white.

"No," I said. "No, it's a diversion. Bentley, tell Corman to stay put. Let them leave."

The line fell silent. I got back on the road.

"He says they just turned out of sight," Bentley told us. "I hope you were right."

"I am."

"How do you know?" Margaux asked.

"Playing the odds. Look, Royce thinks there's a serious, viable plot to raid the club and steal the Judas Coin. He's got to take action, and fast. Given the scale of what he *thinks* we're plotting, and the number of unknowns he has to deal with, it's reasonable for him to suspect we might have eyes on the building."

"So you think they were a decoy to draw off anyone watching before they move the coin for real," Caitlin said.

"Royce has Nadine with him and access to her elite operatives," I said. "Taking that into account, if you were in his shoes...would you trust *Mack and Zeke* to get the coin to safety? I wouldn't trust those idiots to walk and chew gum at the same time."

"And given," Caitlin said, "that Royce knows this, mightn't he have used them with the *expectation* you'd let them slip right through your fingers?"

Suburbia rolled by outside my window, trimmed lawns glistening under a cold autumn sun.

"Maybe," I said, suddenly unsure. "Yeah, maybe. Guess we'll find out."

Twelve minutes ticked by in silence.

"Daniel," Bentley said, hesitant, "Cormie's getting tired. It's been years since he's spent this much time out of his body in one stretch. Do you think...?"

His voice trailed off, but I knew what he was asking.

"Five minutes," I said. "Can he give us five more minutes?"

I kept half an eye on the dashboard as I drove, watching the digital clock. The minutes drifted away, counting down, five, four, three—

"Someone's coming out," Bentley said urgently. "It's her, the woman who arrived with Royce. She's got another metal briefcase."

I slapped my steering wheel and grinned. "Nadine. Okay, she's got the real deal. Have Corman follow her, but keep his distance. She's an incarnate, she's old, and she's tricky. Everybody else, get ready to converge wherever she ends up. We're going to start our very own coin collection."

* * *

Nadine's trail took us forty minutes west of Chicago, to a suburb called Naperville. "The Golden City" read the sign on the way into town, and the main avenue looked like Norman Rockwell had a head-on collision with new money. Colonial buildings with historic plaques rubbed shoulders with expensive-looking boutiques and fusion-cuisine restaurants.

According to Corman, Nadine's final destination was a little florist's shop by the commuter rail station. She'd gone in with the metal briefcase and came out empty-handed five minutes later. I met up with Caitlin and Margaux, the three of us parking side by side at the edge of the railway parking lot, while Bentley helped Corman recover back at the hotel.

"Okay," I said, getting out of the Chrysler, "why a florist?"

Caitlin leaned back against the hood of her car, an anonymous blue rental sedan, and stretched.

"It's what passes for humor among that crowd. The Court of Night-Blooming Flowers has a shell company, just like my court uses the Southern Tropics Import-Export Company back home. There's a Harvest Bloom Florist in every county under their influence, all over the Midwest. They act as outposts, listening stations, meeting spots. They also sell flowers."

I could see the shop from where we parked, a brick building with a bright purple awning and shiny plate-glass windows. A chain-link fence ringed the back of the building, topped with a coil of concertina wire.

"That many stores?" Margaux asked. "They can't all be staffed by demons...can they?"

"No," Caitlin said. "Unless our intelligence is severely flawed, few of them are. Most have a staff of four or five people, all humans, and they may or may not be aware of who they really work for. More often than not, it's only the manager who's in the know. The shop is completely legitimate during daylight hours. All the fun happens at night, when the innocents go home. That's...the usual arrangement."

"And the unusual arrangement?" I said.

Caitlin shrugged. "Well, those locations deemed critical—for example, fronts used to store contraband—have a fully educated staff, sometimes with a competent magician or two, and a demonic overseer. They're drilled in crisis response and small-arms combat."

"Would you say, given Nadine drove forty minutes to get here, that this is one of those places?"

"Oh," Caitlin said agreeably, "more likely than not."

"Any chance they'll all go home when the store closes?" Margaux asked.

Caitlin shook her head. "None. I know Nadine—and so do they. If she ordered them to guard that briefcase until the tournament tomorrow, they will *guard* that briefcase. It's worth more than their lives. If anything, security will increase after dark. No customers around, no need to conceal the firepower."

This was no good. For one thing, I had no intention of getting into a brawl in the middle of Wonder Bread, Illinois, where I suspected the police response time would be approximately two seconds flat. Then there were the tracks to consider: namely, that we couldn't leave *any*. If there were any way to tie the Judas Coin's disappearance to us, it'd be tantamount to picking a fight with the entire Court of Night-Blooming Flowers. Considering Caitlin's involvement, I had to imagine that'd be considered an act of war.

No, that was no good for anybody.

"Let's move up," I said. "I want a closer look."

No cameras alongside the shop, but no windows or access points there either. I peeked around the corner. The back was better protected. A security camera angled down from the eaves, keeping watch over the back door and the trash cans, and a length of thick chain and a heavy-duty padlock kept the gate latch secure. Camera or not, the back door was a no-go: with no windows, we could be walking into anything. I had to assume that everybody on site was armed, with bullets, sorcery, or both.

I looked up to the eaves. "Got an idea. Mama, can you go in and scope out the shop? Buy some flowers for your boyfriend or something."

"Antoine? I broke up with that no-good lazy bum last Monday. Thinks he's too *good* to get a job. Well, I told him exactly what I thought about—"

"Yes," I said quickly, "but that's the third time you've broken up with him this month. So maybe buy some flowers for when you inevitably get back together?"

Margaux *hmph*ed, but she couldn't argue my logic. I turned to Caitlin.

"Cait, think you can boost me up? I want to check out the roof."

"You sometimes forget," she said, moving behind me and clasping her hands around my waist, "that I'm a *tiny* bit stronger than you, love."

To drive the point home, she hoisted me up like I was a feather pillow. I grabbed the edge of the roof, fingers straining on the hot, rough stone, and hauled myself up and over.

The flat roof, coated in white pebbles, sported a stovepipe vent, a satellite TV dish...and a skylight, cracked to let a fresh breeze in. I trench-crawled on my belly, easing up to the edge of the skylight, and took a look.

The skylight overlooked the shop's back room, a dingy, concrete-floored stockroom cluttered with cardboard boxes and floral supplies. Pretty mundane, if you overlooked the wall rack lined with shiny, well-maintained assault rifles and two suits of heavy riot gear.

At a table in the corner of the room, a demon in a man's stolen flesh chowed down on a meatball sandwich, licking driblets of marinara sauce from his fingers while he watched a football game on a grainy portable TV. Nadine's briefcase sat on the table, inches from the hijacker's hand.

I inched away from the skylight and took out my phone.

"Bentley," I whispered. "How's Corman?"

"Fine, fine, he's just napping before dinner. That astral jaunt took a lot out of him. Why are you whispering?"

"I'm on the roof of an evil flower shop, and I don't want to get shot."

"That sort of answer," he said, "really shouldn't surprise me anymore."

"Feel like doing a little acting gig?"

"I'm always fond of the limelight. Shakespeare in the park?"

"Something like that," I said. "Need you to bring some supplies, too. Need at least fifty feet of rope with a good carry-weight, a can of spray-on lubricant for hinges, and a shabby bouquet of flowers. Actually, scratch that, I've got rope and a lifetime supply of WD-40 in my car. Just bring flowers."

"Can't you get flowers from the evil flower shop?"

"Yes," I whispered, "but then they'd be *evil* flowers. C'mon, Bentley, try to keep up."

"You know that charming tic, Daniel, where you start making jokes in a dangerous situation, and we all pretend we don't know you're doing it in order to cover up how nervous you are?"

"What about it?" I asked.

"I was just asking if you were aware of it."

"Nope," I said. "Come as soon as you can, okay? This is *really* uncomfortable."

32.

A little over an hour later, I crouched silently on the flower shop roof with Caitlin at my side. We'd texted the details back and forth, to keep from being overheard through the open skylight, and she wordlessly knotted a strand of rope around me. The stout yellow coils slid under and around my thighs, circled my waist, and looped at my shoulders, forming a makeshift harness.

It wasn't exactly *Mission: Impossible* levels of technology, but we made do with what we had. I crawled back to the edge of the skylight, carefully oiling the hinges. I didn't know if they were squeaky, but we couldn't afford a single stray sound.

I gave Caitlin a thumbs-up. She looked back over the edge of the roof and waved. Down below, that would be Bentley's signal to start the show. I imagined him marching into the flower shop, cradling the shabbiest thing he could find on short notice: a wilting *Happy Graduation* wreath lined with half-deflated balloons.

A door between the front of the shop and the back room hung halfway open, and I could hear Bentley's voice below as he boomed, "This is grotesquely unacceptable, and I demand to speak to your manager *at once!*"

I couldn't hear the response, but an enraged Bentley was a rare thing to behold.

"*Unacceptable!* I have been sorely aggrieved by your company's heinous disregard for basic competence, and I shall not waste my time dealing with some malodorous peon! Perhaps I need to escalate this to the legal authorities and encourage them to search the premises? I'm quite certain you youngsters are injecting the marijuana, or whatever it is you people do instead of an honest day's work. Why, when I was your age—"

It was at about this point in the monologue that the demon tossed down his meatball sub, grunted, and shambled out of the back room.

I ratcheted open the skylight and looked back at Caitlin. She held the rest of the rope in her hands, hooked to the back of my harness, and made a shooing motion. I swung my legs over the edge of the opening and slipped through.

Caitlin lowered me, one shuddering two-foot drop at a time, down to the concrete floor. I could see the two clerks through the half-open door, now both of them arguing with Bentley.

And if one of them turns around, even for a heartbeat, I thought, *I'm a dead man.*

No pressure or anything.

I padded over to the table as quietly as I could. The aluminum Samsonite case had a three-digit combination wheel with the numbers scrambled. I could work with that.

The first combination I tried was 666. You know how some people always set their passwords to "password" or "secret" even though those are terrible choices? In my experience, ask a demon to pick a three-digit number and nine times out of ten, they go with 666. They just can't help themselves.

Nadine was smarter than that. The latch didn't budge. I'd need to crack her code the hard way. And to be fair, given how flimsy most briefcase locks were, it wouldn't be that difficult—but time wasn't on my side.

"Sir," the hijacker-demon drawled at Bentley, waving a sauce-stained hand, "if you'll just calm down, we'll try to resolve your grievance—"

"Calm down?" Bentley sputtered. "*Calm down?* Look at this wreath. Look at this writing. Can you read? What does it say?"

"Happy...graduation, sir?"

"*It was for a funeral!* Happy graduation? What's he graduated to? Worm food?"

I let them go at it and focused my attention on the case. Coop had taught me this technique a while back. While safes and strongboxes had upgraded over the years, your average briefcase today wasn't any different from the ones people carried to work in the 1940s. The method for getting one open hadn't changed either. It was a rare bit of old-school cracksmanship, and all it took was a light touch and a steady nerve.

At least I could manage the light touch.

I slid the latch and held it in place with one hand, as my other slowly tested each of the three combination-lock wheels. I needed to find the one with the least give. The middle wheel was tighter than the others, and I set it to 0. The other two wheels still moved easily, so I bumped it up to 1.

Once I hit 4, the other wheels suddenly felt stiffer. That was it, the rotary lock finding a groove. One number of the combination down, two to go.

"I'll tell you what, sir, let me just go into the back and I'll—"

"Absolutely not!" Bentley shouted. "You're going to stand right there until you explain yourself."

I glanced at the door as the left-hand wheel clicked under my fingertips. *Come on, come on...*

"Wait a second," the clerk was saying, "this is a receipt from Floral Creations."

"And? What of it?"

"Sir, this is Harvest Bloom. You're in the wrong store."

The latch flicked open. The Judas Coin rested on a bed of gray felt. I let my eyes slip out of focus, sensing something off, and spotted the problem instantly: a baleful witch-eye with a bloody red iris clung to the coin, mucous tendrils wrapped around the ancient silver like some magical parasite.

Like the one Harmony Black had left on my car bumper, its creator could know where the coin was just by thinking about it.

And like the one on my bumper, if I made one mistake trying to detach it, Nadine would know that too.

Still, it had to go. I took a deep breath, trying to ignore that Bentley was running out of options fast. I focused my power like a white-hot scalpel at the tip of my finger, slowly slicing through the tendrils, cauterizing as I cut one slender strand at a time.

"Morty, get this guy out of here. I've got work to do in back."

"Hold on, now," Bentley stammered. "I know perfectly well where I ordered this wreath. You're reading the receipt wrong."

"What? Sir, look at this line, *right here*. It couldn't be any clearer—"

The witch-eye slid free with a wet *plop*. It happily tethered itself to the inside of the briefcase, lolling this way and that as I pocketed the Judas Coin. I shut the case, scrambled the combination wheel, and gave three hard tugs on the rope.

I swung off my feet as Caitlin started hoisting me up, one heave at a time, inching my way toward the waiting skylight. Through the half-open door, Bentley's glance flicked toward me. I gave him a thumbs-up.

"I'll tell you one thing," he roared before he stormed out the front door, "you will never get my business again!"

"We never had your business in the first place, you crazy old bastard," the manager shouted back, then looked to his underling. "Seriously, Morty, don't bother me again today. My damn lunch is probably cold now."

He walked right under my dangling feet, headed straight for the bathroom door. As soon as I was clear, Caitlin and I lowered the skylight back to its original gap and hustled to the edge of the roof.

Back on the ground, we met up with Bentley and Margaux. I showed them my stolen prize.

"They won't know the coin is missing until they open the briefcase," I said. "So probably not until tomorrow morning, maybe not even until the end of the tournament."

"So we have the knife and the coin," Bentley mused. "Mr. Ecko's blood price. Shall we go trade them for Coop?"

I'd been thinking about that.

Obviously, setting Coop's soul free and ending his torment was priority one. Had to be. We could fix that right now, assuming Ecko didn't stab us in the back (and that was a huge *if*). Odds were good that the necromancer had no intention of following through on his end of the trade. On top of that, I had other commitments.

I'd promised Coop two things. One, I'd get his share of the score to his widow. Two, I'd put Stanwyck in the ground where he belonged. Neither job was done, and giving up the dagger to Ecko meant giving up the cash Cameron Drake would pay me for it.

"There's no way to say this that doesn't sound cold," I said, "but I think Coop needs to wait one more day before we set him free."

"Danny," Margaux said, "I know about zombies, all right? You don't understand the kind of suffering he's going through—"

"I understand. Just like I understand it's my fault he's suffering, because I couldn't stop Stanwyck from gunning him and his nephew down. So believe me when I say that *nobody* here wants this less than I do, but he's got to hang on for just one more day."

Caitlin furrowed her brow. "Why? What's the plan?"

"Besides setting Coop free, we need to get the cash for his widow, ensure Ecko doesn't come after us *or* rat us out to Royce, and we need to send Stanwyck straight to hell. I've got an idea, and if we play it right, we can do all four things at once."

"And if we play it wrong?" Bentley asked.

"Then hopefully, it'll only be me who gets killed."

* * *

Back at the Four Seasons, we gathered the crew in my and Caitlin's room, and I walked them through the plan. Pixie was the hard sell, demanding we go charging to the rescue before the sun went down, but she came around to my way of thinking once I spelled out what the final act meant for Stanwyck. She tried to hide it, but her taste for payback was as bloody-minded as the rest of us. That's exactly why I needed to send her home.

"Taking some big risks, kiddo." Corman leaned back in his chair, nursing a glass of scotch. "Bentley and me, we'll do our best when it comes to our parts, but there aren't any sure things when it comes to poker. There's a reason it's called *gambling*."

"What is it you taught me?" I asked. "Poker isn't about playing the cards. It's about playing your opponent. Well, right now, I'm playing Royce. I've got a pretty good idea of how he'll react if I show up for the tournament tomorrow, and I think he'll make all the right mistakes."

Caitlin sat on the bed, her legs crossed. "The Bast Club may be neutral territory, Daniel, but tomorrow it's Royce's house. He'll use every trick in the book to keep the tournament under control."

"I'll be counting on it." I got up and stretched. "We'll reconvene in the morning, to go over the plan one last time. Right now I need to go meet up with one of our friendly local black-marketeers. I think I've got the proverbial deal she can't refuse."

33.

Amy Xun's eyes seemed to glitter in the shadows, her glossy lips parted as she stared at the Judas Coin.

"Can I hold it?"

I closed my hand, making it disappear.

"We'll talk about that," I told her.

Her shop was a hole-in-the-wall in Chicago's Chinatown, a stone's throw from the bronze and red pagoda-topped gate that straddled Wentworth Avenue. I'd been in bigger walk-in closets, and the precarious piles of clutter on every shelf—most of it porcelain, teak, and old jade—warned me that the slightest misstep could lead to an expensive accident.

Amy Xun could be an expensive accident, too.

She watched me in the washed-out, cherry-colored light glowing from an electric candelabra on the counter, right next to a big-bellied laughing Buddha with a bowl of cheap incense cradled in his lap. The glass case between us was stocked with waving-cat statuettes, plastic tourist trinkets, and packs of dubious-looking gum.

"The coin. How did you get it?"

"Magic." I took a look around. "I don't get this place. You've got genuine Chinese antiques sitting next to garage-sale crap. Who's your target audience?"

"I have something for everyone who walks through my door. If they leave without making a purchase, I'm very disappointed in myself. What can I sell you today, Mr. Faust?"

"Call me Daniel. And it's more about what I'm here to sell you."

Amy put her hand to her chin, tapping her cheek with a fingertip, deep in thought.

"The coin, yes, but it doesn't belong to you, and I normally avoid dealing in stolen goods. At least, traceable stolen goods."

"What if I could make it *not* stolen?"

"And how would you do that?" she asked.

"By winning it fair and square."

"You aim to win it," she said, "even though you've already stolen it."

I rested the coin on the display case, balanced on its edge. She watched hungrily as I rolled it from side to side with my fingertips.

"Something along those lines. If you could have the Judas Coin, free and clear, one-hundred-percent legit, would you be interested?"

"'Have'? Nothing is free."

"Nope," I said, "and neither is this. I'll need your help. It's low risk—for you, that is."

"Low risk is still a risk, and the Court of Night-Blooming Flowers is not an enemy I can afford to make. *No* risk, on the other hand, would be calling Royce to report the theft. He'll punish you and reward me. A superior risk-to-reward ratio."

I waved my palm over the coin. Now she looked down at an empty counter.

"Sure," I said, "he'll reward you with a handshake and a cash envelope, maybe, but not with *this*. You know your odds of winning the tournament are lousy. If you didn't, you wouldn't have been offering to buy the prize outright from everyone at the Bast Club. More likely than not, come tomorrow night, the coin slips out of your grasp forever. My offer is better. Play the odds."

She thought about it, still staring down at the smudged glass where the coin had just sat. I gave her all the time she needed.

"What would I have to do?" she asked.

I walked her through the plan.

"All right." Her jaw moved silently, like she was chewing her words before she spoke them. "We have a deal. I'll see you tomorrow at the tournament."

"Pleasure doing business," I said and turned toward the door. She cleared her throat. I glanced back and she gave me an expectant look, her fingers gliding to rest on the curve of her cash register.

"Fine," I said, digging out my wallet. "How much for a pack of gum?"

* * *

I left Amy's store toting a glossy plastic bag with four packs of gum, a painted ceramic waving-cat statuette, an antique wooden teacup, and a pamphlet explaining how to pronounce two dozen essential tourist phrases in Cantonese.

I had no idea how that happened.

I was standing on a corner, trying to figure out the best place to look for a cab, when a sleek black limousine pulled up to the curb. The back door opened and a smiling man in a cheap polyester jacket clambered out. He was big, with a belly that protruded against his tucked-in polo shirt, and a nose that had been broken one too many times.

"Hey, pal," he said, "your ride's here. Get in."

"Think you've got me confused with someone else," I said. The look on his face told me he hadn't. His smile stayed plastered on, but his eyes were cold enough to put a chill into a polar bear's spine.

"Hey," he said, leaning close. "Let's not make a scene, okay? My boss wants a word with you. Just a word. So please, get in the fuckin' car."

I saw a few ways this situation could go, and most of them ended badly for me. I got in the car.

I recognized one of the two men inside, sitting on the opposite-facing bench in the back of the plush limo. The one I didn't recognize had a face like a ferret and a five-hundred-dollar haircut. He stank of unearned money and frat-boy arrogance.

The other was the short Indian man I'd seen coming out of Nicky Agnelli's office back in Vegas. The "liquor distributor" who had all the markings of a rakshasa. Rakshasi? As far as I knew, the right word depended on their sex—but how can you tell, with a shapeshifter?

The big guy got in beside me and slammed the door shut. Frat boy gave him a gracious nod. "Thanks, Sal."

Sal crowded me on the backseat. As he nudged in, I could feel the hard edge of the gun under his jacket.

"All right," the frat boy said, looking through the open window into the driver compartment. "Get rolling. Just cruise around a little while we have our conversation."

The chauffeur inclined his head, wordless, as the limo pulled away from the curb.

"Daniel Faust," Sal said with an air of exaggerated formality, "please allow me to introduce Mr. Angelo Mancuso."

"How polite. How about this one, he got a name?" I asked, looking over at the rakshasa.

"Who, him?" Sal said. "That's Tony."

"My name," the Indian said in a somber voice, "is Kirmira."

"He still don't get the joke," Sal said, grinning at Angelo.

"No," Angelo said, "no, he does not. Dan—can I call you Dan? My father is a very important man in this town."

"Great. Throw a parade."

"We do, every year around Columbus Day. Goes with the whole philanthropy thing. You know how it is. Or maybe you don't. Whatever. More to the point, my father also leads a very important organization, a pillar of the community, with roots deep in Chicago's history."

I laid my head back against the seat, stifling a groan as the pieces clicked together. "You're Outfit men. Wonderful."

Sal snickered. "Winner, winner, chicken dinner."

"We've got a lot in common, you know," Angelo said. "Chicago *built* Las Vegas. Sure, the New York families had their hand in, but Vegas wasn't Vegas 'til the Outfit took charge."

"There a point behind that history lesson?" I asked.

"Only to establish a certain level of, shall we call it, prior claim?"

"I'm not positive," I said, "but I think after sixty or seventy years it becomes more of a finders, keepers sort of situation."

Angelo slapped his knee. "Now, you see? That's almost exactly what Nicky Agnelli said when Tony here went to extend the hand of friendship. The way we hear it, things aren't going too well out there. Federal sharks are circling, and there's plenty of chum in the water. Dangerous times."

"Let me save you some time here," I said. "I don't work for Nicky anymore, and I don't have one ounce of pull when it comes to how he runs his business. Whatever you want from him, I can't help you get it."

"See, that's where you're wrong. And yeah, we know you two are quits. That's why we're having this conversation. Nicky's on his way out. Fact. Maybe the feds take him down, maybe he eats a bullet, but the 'King of Las Vegas' is yesterday's news."

"We wanted to help the guy out," Sal said. "Set him up someplace cushy and far away, with beaches and tropical drinks, y'know? In exchange for facilitating a, uh, what do ya call it? Regime change."

Angelo pointed at Sal. "Regime change. Very good. Classy way of putting it."

Sal tipped an imaginary hat in Angelo's direction.

"But Nicky's got these delusions of grandeur," Angelo added.

"Can't argue that," I said.

"Power abhors a vacuum," Angelo said. "And there's gonna be one hell of a vacuum, any day now."

I stretched out my legs as the limo made a slow left turn.

"Maybe, maybe not," I said, "but nobody ever got rich underestimating Nicky Agnelli. Still don't see what any of this has to do with me."

"We understand you're highly placed in a certain…community. Now, my father, he's averse to working with, ah, what's the word—"

"Freaks," Sal said, grinning at me. Kirmira gave him a murderous stare but kept his mouth shut.

"Freaks," Angelo said, "for lack of a better word, and no insult to current company intended. As you can probably guess, I don't share my old man's point of view. Frankly, *I'm* the traditionalist here. My grandfather, he had a *strega* from the Old Country, and so did his old man before him. It's just how business gets done."

Now it made sense. "And you want our help with this 'regime change.'"

"Hey, it's a matter of lead, follow, or get out of the way. Mostly the second two, because the leader job is already taken. Once the Outfit is running things, you and your people are gonna have two choices: you can toe the line and share the wealth, or things can get ugly. It'll be good times for everybody, Dan. Boom times. Lots of work, lots of money to go around."

"That's for the good little freaks who do what they're told," Sal chimed in. "Otherwise, y'know, let's just say we're not big fans of competition."

"I don't know how things are done in Chicago," I said, "but you wanna know why Nicky Agnelli has held on to power as long as he has?"

Angelo spread his hands. "Enlighten me."

"We *let* him. See, we had some friction in the early years, and ultimately it came down to a simple rule of live and let live. We, by which I mean the Vegas occult underground, don't hit anything or anyone Nicky owns. It's a strict policy of keeping our hands off Nicky's toys. In return, he leaves us alone to do our thing."

I left Jennifer unmentioned. The Jennifer situation was messy, and it stood to get messier with the Chicago mob in the picture. Maybe she'd get a better deal with them than with Nicky, or maybe it'd get a whole lot worse. I wasn't feeling too optimistic.

"Nicky leaves us alone," I went on, "because he's a smart guy. Smart enough to know that he could take *one* of us out. Any one of us. And then the rest of the underground would crash down on his head like the hammer of God. That's our style. We're slow to anger, but very quick to smite. You think you can break Nicky's throne? Take his place? Fine. Go for it. But expect the same arrangement he had, nothing more."

"Yeah, see, we've got a problem with that," Angelo said. "Like Sal said, we're not big fans of competition. You wanna work in one of our towns, you work *for* us, or you don't work at all. No rogues, no loose cannons, and everybody pays to play. Oh, and you're wrong about one more thing."

"I am? What about?"

"We're not gonna take Nicky out," he told me. "You are."

34.

"Come again?" I said, wobbling a little as the limousine rumbled over a pothole. "I must be going deaf, since I *thought* I just heard you say something about me taking out Nicky. And that's crazy talk."

"Think about it." Angelo sounded like a used-car salesman. "He trusts you. Not a lot of people get one-on-one face time with the man these days. You could get nice and close, maybe without those fucking creepy bodyguards of his hanging around. Tough guy like you, yeah, you could bring him down."

"That's the means and the opportunity," I said. "I'm waiting to hear my motive."

"Learn from history. Regime change is a messy thing. If we have to go to the mattresses with Nicky and his crew, it might be over quick but it won't be clean. And you and your fellow freaks might wanna play Switzerland and stand on the sidelines, but do you *really* think that's gonna be an option?"

"Collateral damage is a bitch," Sal said.

"People get hurt in the crossfire." Angelo shrugged. "People die. Maybe innocent people. Or hey, maybe people you know."

Sal dug in his jacket pocket and pulled out a crumpled photograph. He shoved it in my face, giving me a good look: me and Jennifer, walking out of some taco joint on Charleston Boulevard, taken from a long-range lens.

"Like this broad," Sal said. "Jennifer Juniper? Now what kind of fuckin' name is that? She ain't gonna be no Switzerland, will she?"

"No, hey, good point." Angelo got wide-eyed, pretending he was just figuring this out. "Yeah, this lady right here, she's one of Nicky's top earners. Now, if we have to play this the hard way and muscle our way into Vegas, I'd say it's more likely than not that some of Nicky's people are gonna get hurt. Wouldn't you agree, Sal?"

"Inevitable," he repeated, resting the photograph on my lap. "I mean, we try to be reasonable guys, but accidents do happen."

I took the photograph. Gave it a long, hard look.

"There's something else," I said softly, "something that Nicky understands and you don't."

Angelo tilted his head. "Yeah? What's that?"

I locked eyes with him. I spoke slowly, making sure he heard every word.

"You don't ever threaten one of my friends."

Angelo let out a surprised laugh and held up his open palms. "Hey, don't put words in my mouth, now! I'm not threatening anybody. I'm not a threatening kind of guy. Ask anybody."

"He's a teddy bear," Sal said.

"I'm just talking about actions and consequences," Angelo explained. "We *are* taking Vegas, Dan. This is as inevitable as time and tide. And it can happen one of two ways: with a long, drawn-out war and blood on the streets, or with a single bullet at close range. You're the one man who can fire that bullet. Only you. So if you care about that lady, and all the other people who might end up hurt in the fallout, I think you know what you've gotta do."

"We just wanna be friendly," Sal said. "And if you don't wanna be friendly with us, well...we ain't got much use for you either, do we?"

My deck of cards grew hot in my hip pocket, responding to the anger roiling the pit of my stomach. No fucking way was I playing the triggerman for these scumbags. Nicky and I had bad history, but he'd been a stand-up guy when it came to taking down Lauren Carmichael, and more importantly—with the exception of his little feud with Jennifer—he left my family alone. Angelo had just guaranteed the Outfit *wouldn't*. I wasn't having that.

That said, I didn't think Angelo would take my refusal kindly. I needed an exit strategy.

I had to figure he was strapped. I knew Sal had a gun—I could feel it bumping up against me, under his jacket, but at this angle there was no chance I could grab it without giving Angelo a shot at me. Then there was sullen Kirmira, looking at all three of us like he was picturing our heads on stakes. If my hunch was right and he was a rakshasa like Naavarasi...well, I'd seen Naavarasi transform into a five-hundred-pound Bengal tiger in the space of a breath. I didn't want to think about what kind of damage Kirmira could do inside the back of a limousine.

I glanced toward the driver's compartment. The chauffeur held the wheel steady, rolling up on a big four-way intersection.

"There's two other ways this could end," I said casually. Half my mind focused on tapping the threads of my power, stroking the cards in my pocket to eager life.

"How do you figure?" Angelo asked.

"Third option is you back off, forget all about Las Vegas, and learn to be happy with what you have. Personally, I find that focusing on the good things in life is an important part of being a healthy person."

"That ain't gonna happen. What else ya got?"

"Well, I could always kill you and your buddies here as an object lesson, along with any member of the Outfit who sets foot in Vegas, along with anyone who even thinks about looking cross-eyed at one of my people. Is your dad a reasonable man, Angelo? I mean, give me a rough estimate. How many bodies will I have to drop before he backs off? Or should I just go straight to the top?"

Sal's hand eased into his jacket. Angelo's lips curled as he straightened in his seat. Kirmira didn't move. He didn't even breathe.

"You leave my old man out of this," Angelo whispered.

"Just you, then," I said. "Fine. Let me bottom-line this for you, Angelo. Chicago is yours. Don't be greedy. Stay the fuck out of Las Vegas, or I *will* kill you. There's not going to be a war. There isn't even going to be a discussion."

"Damn right there isn't," Angelo snarled. "Sal, shoot this piece of—"

I triggered my spell, a crackle of force lancing down my spine and out across my arm as I flung my hand upward, curling my fingers in a C-shape. The playing cards leaped from my pocket, riffling toward my hand in a steady stream. Instead of catching them, though, I angled my cupped hand and sent them flying. A whirlwind of cards whipped through the limousine, diamonds and spades lashing in all directions, bouncing off the windows, swarming in the men's faces like clouds of stinging gnats.

Kirmira threw himself over Angelo, pushing him to the floor of the limo and shielding him with his body, while Sal batted at his face and howled as a card winged past and sliced open his cheek. The chauffeur, blinded in the sudden storm, slammed on the brakes and yanked the wheel hard to the right.

I tumbled from the bench seat as the limousine crashed into a parked car, a car alarm shrieking over the sound of crumpling metal and breaking glass. I hurled myself against the door, shouldered it open, and rolled out onto the cold, hard street. I clambered to my feet and ran, hearing shouts at my back, bracing for a gunshot.

The bullet never came, though—Sal was smart enough not to open fire on a crowded street, at least not from inside his boss's car. I veered left, heading up a residential road where old two-story brownstones stood shoulder to shoulder, and ducked down a long side alley.

I ran until my lungs burned and my legs felt like aching jelly, steadying myself with one hand against a cold stone wall while I tried to catch my breath. I was pretty sure I'd lost them, but all the same, I figured I should stay out of sight.

Once I could breathe again, I took out my phone.

"Hey," I said, panting, "next time you find out that a major crime syndicate wants to take over Vegas, maybe let me know *before I go to the city where they live?* Send me a letter, maybe? Send up some smoke signals?"

"Wait, what?" Nicky said. "The Outfit came after you in Texas?"

"In *Chicago*, Nicky. Where the *job* is. The job you set me up for."

"Hey, I didn't know that! How could I know that? All I knew was Cameron Drake had a thing, and Drake lives in Texas."

"Fair enough." I took a deep gulp of breath, leaning hard against the wall. "But you're still an asshole. Chicago wants to make a play for our town, and you didn't think that might be useful information?"

"I'm handling it."

"Oh, yeah, you're handling it. You're handling it so good that the don's kid just tried hiring me to kill you."

"Yeah?" Nicky hesitated. "How'd that work out?"

"They didn't like my counteroffer."

The line went silent for a moment.

"Gotta ask you something," he said.

"Is the question 'Are you really pissed off right now, Dan?' Because yes. The answer is yes."

"No, I mean," he said, hedging, "if they asked you to take me out, they might be asking other people. Locals. Do you think, maybe..."

He left the question unfinished. I squeezed my eyes shut, feeling a headache coming on.

"Nicky, goddamnit, the *second* I get back to Vegas you, me, and Jennifer are having a sit-down. This paranoid infighting was bad enough when we only had the feds to worry about, but if Chicago's serious about muscling in—and believe me, they looked pretty damn serious—we've *got* to work together."

"She won't even answer my phone calls."

"She will if I ask her to," I said. "I'll be back in town tomorrow night. Until then, sit tight and don't do *anything*."

I hung up and tried calling Jennifer, but it went straight to her voicemail.

"Hey y'all," her voice drawled. "Can't talk now. Leave your digits and I'll call ya back in two shakes of a lamb's tail."

"Hey," I said, "it's me. I'm still on that business trip. Just found out a competing firm is interested in some local Vegas holdings, and they're contemplating a hostile takeover. Their headhunters definitely have your name, so just be aware they might try to contact you. I'll tell you everything in person, tomorrow night. Take care."

I poked my head out of the alley long enough to jump in a taxi, slinking low in the backseat as we headed for the Four Seasons. Back at the hotel, priority one was gathering everyone in one spot so I could fill them in. I barely got started, though, before I realized the whole room was giving me weird looks.

"What?" I asked, looking around.

Margaux looked over at Bentley and Corman. "Really? You're gonna make *me* point it out?"

"I'm just," Bentley said, "I mean, I don't even know what you're—"

"You've got a big ol' hickey on your neck," Corman said.

Caitlin sat primly and smiled, looking pleased with herself.

35.

The next morning, I woke with the dawn. I'd spent the night restless, couldn't quiet my brain enough to sleep, but I knew the airplane-sized liquor bottles in the minibar would only leave me groggy and hung over. I needed to be sharp. Sharper than Royce, Nadine, and anything they could throw at us.

Caitlin drifted into the bathroom as I finished shaving. She stood behind me, one hand gently resting on my shoulder.

I'd started noticing, more than usual, her casual little touches.

"Ready for our big day?" she asked.

I splashed on some aftershave that smelled like fresh cedar, running my thumb over my smooth cheek.

"No. But that's okay. It's the times when I think I've got it made that everything goes sour."

We gathered everyone together for one last run-through. First, though, I took Pixie aside. She handed me a folded slip of hotel-room notepaper embossed with the Four Seasons logo. The only thing written on it, in neat, tight handwriting, was an address.

"This is it?" I asked. "You're sure?"

"Positive. I pulled the geotag from the video Damien Ecko sent you. Then I did some local recon to make sure. That's a warehouse on Printers Row, just off West Harrison Street. That's where the video was recorded. That's where Coop is. I pulled the property records, and Ecko owns it under his own name. He doesn't even try to hide it."

"Until today, he never needed to. You did good, Pix."

She stood there, rocking back and forth on her heels.

"You know what happens now," I said.

"Yeah." Her voice was soft. "This is the part where you send me home."

I reached out and touched her arm. She stared at my hand. I put it down again.

"You promised," I said, "that when the time came to save Coop and settle accounts, you'd leave the rough stuff to me."

"I did. Just don't forget what you promised me."

I looked to the windows. Out on the waters of Lake Michigan, the sun's reflection glittered like a chunk of fool's gold.

"Right about now," I said, "I imagine Stanwyck's sitting down to eat his last meal. Hope he picked a good one."

"I'm counting on you. For Coop."

"We'll make things right," I said.

Pixie bundled her laptop under her arm and walked to the door. She looked back at me, something sad in her eyes.

"You never 'make things right,' Faust. The best you ever do is damage control."

I shrugged. "Sometimes that's the best anyone can do."

As she walked out the door, I wondered if some part of her hated me, just a little, for sending her away. That was okay if she did, if that was the price for keeping her at arm's length. I could have used another pair of hands for this job, and part of me—part of me I didn't like much—said I should have given her what she wanted. Brought her all the way into my life and let her find out exactly how it felt to get bloodstains on your hands.

In the end, though, I'd rather Pixie woke up tomorrow morning hating me instead of hating herself.

* * *

I had one call to make before we left.

"Damien Ecko speaking."

"It's Faust," I said. "One question: are you going to the tournament at the Bast Club today?"

"Ah, Mr. Faust, this is an unexpected pleasure. I was beginning to think I'd never hear from you again. Just as well, I'm starting to enjoy spending quality time with your friend here. I'd hate to lose him."

"Sorry to disappoint, but I'm bringing you the coin and the dagger, tonight. Get ready to hand Coop over."

Ecko chuckled. "Please. You had plenty of time to lay your hands on the coin, while it was barely guarded, and you couldn't do it. Do you honestly think you'll steal it from a crowded room, right from under its owner's nose?"

"My plan *depends* on having a crowd around." I was lying, but it sounded good. "Here's the thing, though: you need to stay away from the club today. If you're here when the theft goes down, there's a good chance you'll be implicated. I can't have that."

"Such concern for my well-being."

"Don't get it wrong. It's concern for *mine*. If Royce thinks you were involved in the theft, don't even pretend you wouldn't give me up to save your own skin. Helping you get away clean is my best chance of survival. Promise me you won't come to the tournament."

"Hmm," Ecko said. "Very well, I wasn't all that keen on the spectacle in the first place. Here's a thought. Perhaps I'll spend the day with your friend. Make no mistake, Mr. Faust, if you don't follow through, and the dagger and the coin aren't in my hands by sunset, he and I will most certainly be having an exciting—and very *long*—night."

"Wait for my call," I said and hung up on him.

One obstacle down. Only a few hundred to go.

When we got to the Bast Club, just shy of ten in the morning, cars already overflowed the parking lot and clogged the curb outside the building. Lots of rental cars and out-of-state plates, cars from New York and Florida, with windows tinted black as obsidian.

From the moment we'd checked out of the Four Seasons, leaving at carefully staggered intervals, our united band had become a handful of splinters. Bentley and Corman went first, fifteen minutes apart, and even they wouldn't say a word to one another until the tournament was over. Then Margaux headed out, leaving Caitlin and me as the only couple in the crew.

"The one thing I'm worried about," I told Caitlin as we crossed the parking lot, "is that Royce saw everyone's faces back at the airport when you first landed. He still might put two and two together, if he's paying attention."

Caitlin smiled. "He'll be a *bit* distracted. And if we play our parts capably, even more so."

"True. So let's go give him something to worry about."

The club's parlor was standing room only, packed with eager spectators and would-be contenders, and my head flooded with psychic chatter. The energy flowing through the room could have powered a small city, and from a quick look around, only half the crowd was identifiably human.

The rest, like Caitlin, had very good disguises on.

I caught frantic waving out of the corner of my eye. Freddie, drink in hand, reclined on one of the plush red divans. Halima sat in the chair beside her, her knees tight together and shoulders tensed.

"Freddie, Halima," I said as we walked over. I nodded at Freddie's glass. "Starting a little early, are we?"

"It's a Bloody Mary," she said, swinging her legs down from the divan and patting the now-vacant seat. "That's *breakfast food*, darling. Look it up."

As Caitlin sat next to Freddie, Halima shook her head. "I really, really don't like crowds. This is not my thing at all."

Freddie sipped her drink. "You just need to loosen up. Caitlin, this is my BFF, Halima. Halima, this is my new BFF, Caitlin."

I stayed on my feet, casually glancing from side to side, giving the room a once-over and watching for familiar faces. Bentley walked by on his way to the bar. We didn't even make eye contact.

"You can't have two best friends," I said, "as implied by the word *best*."

"Hush, you. I can have anything I want...*except* for a lack of utter nausea from watching *that* tawdry display."

I followed her gaze to the doorway, where Nadine—wrapped in a gown of hot-pink silk that clung to her curves like a second skin—strolled into the room. She wasn't alone. Five men, chiseled, pretty enough to be models and dressed in black Armani suits, followed her lead. She talked animatedly as they walked, her hands constantly in motion, brushing a shoulder here, a cheek there.

"Oh, no, she isn't," Caitlin said, her voice hard.

"*You* know what she's doing. I know *you* know," Freddie said to Caitlin.

Caitlin's left eyebrow twitched. "Madonna. The 'Material Girl' video, 1984."

"She'd better not even *pretend* that was accidental," Freddie said.

Halima leaned sideways in her chair, giving me a pained look. "Do *you* know why they're upset?" she whispered.

I shrugged, helpless.

"It's...a territorial thing. I think?"

"Now, a Whitesnake video, that's more her speed," Caitlin muttered.

"More. Like. Motley. Crue," Freddie replied, pronouncing each word like a judge handing down a death sentence.

I felt Royce before I saw him in the crowd, a big bundle of smug headed right for me.

"Surprised to see you here, sport," he said, smiling bright enough to light up the room. "You must be feeling a tad frustrated this morning."

I played dumb, like he'd expect me to. "Meaning?"

"Well, I simply heard that you were quite the busy bee yesterday. Flitting here, flitting there, but not really getting much accomplished, were you?"

"I was practicing my poker skills," I said.

Royce moved close, standing inches away, pitching his voice soft.

"Probably would have been a better use of your time. You see, Daniel, we were onto you from the very start. It was a cute attempt, but understand this, and understand it well: the only way you're *ever* getting your hands on the grand prize...is by winning it fairly."

My hand brushed my hip pocket, feeling the hard contour of the Judas Coin.

"What can I say?" I told him. "You got me."

"Good. As long as we understand each other. Also? Sweet perdition, man, button your shirt all the way up and put a tie on. You've got a hickey on your neck. What are you, twelve?"

"It's a love bite," I said.

Caitlin gave me a thumbs-up.

Royce rolled his eyes, stepped back, and let his voice boom like a carnival barker. "Ladies and gentlemen, welcome! Welcome, one and all. At this time, registrations for the tournament are being held in Parlor B, courtesy of the lovely Nadine. Seats are first-come, first-served if you haven't already paid your buy-in, so I urge you to move with haste."

"Oh joy," Freddie said as she stood up, pausing to drain the last of her Bloody Mary through an oversized straw. "We get to talk to the *lovely* Nadine. Halima, you coming?"

"I think I'll sit this one out," she replied. "Don't worry, I'll be cheering you on when the game starts."

A line stretched down the hall toward the open door of Parlor B. I stood on my toes and craned my neck, checking out the people ahead of us. I saw a few familiar faces—like Stanwyck, gripping a wad of cash in both hands like a chump waiting to get rolled. When he looked to one side, I caught the expression on his face: panicky as a lemming on the edge of a waterfall. By now he had to have figured out that the Bast Club wasn't any ordinary gambling den.

And if you think you're out of your league now, I thought, taking deep breaths to keep my anger in check, *just wait until you see what I've got planned for you.*

36.

Trevor Manderley stood beside Stanwyck, gabbing with someone else in line, not even trying to be comforting. No reason to: he'd already made his money, "sponsoring" the sucker. I didn't pay Manderley any mind. As far as I was concerned, that score was settled, so long as he didn't pull anything stupid today.

We eased forward in line a few feet at a time, eventually stepping though the open doorway of Parlor B. I wasn't sure what the room was normally used for, but today Nadine held court behind a long folding table, a corkboard behind her lined with tacked-up sheets of paper. As a dark-haired woman at the head of the line handed over an envelope of cash, one of Nadine's boy toys wrote out a name in big block letters and added it to the board where Nadine pointed.

H. WEST
A. XUN
E. TALBOT
V. FIERI

"Looks like they're organizing the names by table placement," Freddie said, standing right behind me and Caitlin in line. "Ooh, I hope I get seated with Amy. She's so neurotic it's impossible *not* to have a good time with her."

Joining the tournament had been Amy's idea. She pointed out, back at her shop, that even though she knew the grand prize had already been stolen, it would look strange if she didn't play.

"It's rational," she'd observed. "Besides the coin, there's a fifty-thousand-dollar payout for first place. Personal security plus a remote chance for a ten-to-one return on investment makes my buy-in a snap decision."

I took her word for it.

Another one of the suited men hovered at Nadine's shoulder, standing still as a guard at Buckingham Palace. He clutched the metal briefcase in his right hand with the handle cuffed to his wrist. With the witch-eye undisturbed, as far as Nadine and Royce knew, the coin was still safe and snug inside its case. I just hoped they didn't try to take it out and show it off before the tournament started.

Eventually we made it to the front of the line. Nadine gave Caitlin a sneering smile.

"Well, look what the cat dragged in. Hello, Caitlin. It's been years."

"Nadine," Caitlin said. "Not nearly long enough."

"Agreed." Nadine looked me over, arched an eyebrow, and pointed at my neck. "And...*really?*"

Caitlin pointed at Nadine's dress. "*Really?*"

Nadine touched one hand to the bodice of her gown. "I wear it better than you ever could, *commoner*."

"I am Prince Sitri's hound. Elite of my court. A bit more prestigious a rank than certain other people here could claim."

Nadine curled her lip. "Please. You might have screwed and backstabbed your way into an unearned title, but you were born a commoner, and you'll always be a commoner. You've got dirt under your claws."

"Hey, Nadine?" I said.

She glanced my way.

"I normally have strong objections to hitting a woman," I said, "but if you talk to my girlfriend like that again, I could see myself getting over it real fast."

Nadine flashed a pearly smile. "Please. Do try. I'd love to watch Caitlin's face while my little helpers here use you as a living punching bag. I'll tell them not to mark you up *too* badly."

"Who?" I nodded at her baby-faced helper with the Sharpie and the paper slips, sitting beside her and looking more anxious by the second. "These guys? A powder puff in an Armani suit is still a powder puff."

Nadine reached over and stroked the man's shoulder. His expression changed from fearful to placid in a heartbeat, his eyes vacant as a cow in an open pasture.

"Oh, this is just a batch of new aspirants. They haven't even been blooded yet. I brought them in to help Royce with security. The one who catches you cheating gets a reward."

"Yeah? What do the others get?"

Nadine's expression went from a bright sunny day to black storm clouds instantly. She glared at me like I'd insulted her mother.

"They get *nothing*," she snapped. The man let out a faint gasp as her hand clenched his shoulder, her fingernails digging into the fabric. He stared blankly ahead while his eyes watered, jaw quivering, obviously fighting to keep from crying out. Nadine let go of him and took a deep breath. Then she smiled again, all sweetness.

"The House of Dead Roses is for *winners*, Daniel. We take the best of the best and make them even better. A winner, a true, born winner, has no room in his life for second place." She looked over at Caitlin. "That's something commoners never understand."

"Understand this," Caitlin said, leaning over the table. "Our buy-in has already been paid. The Court of Jade Tears acknowledges Daniel Faust as its champion in this tournament. He, and I, will be given proper respect as visiting emissaries."

"Oh, of course, we'll be utterly respectful. As soon as he loses in the first round and we send you both back home humiliated and penniless, I'll be certain to give you a polite wave goodbye." Nadine looked to the seated man. "Put him on the board. And please, do note under his name that he's Prince Sitri's champion. I want *everyone* to get a good laugh."

I rested my hands on the table and gave Nadine the cockiest smile I could manage.

"Out of curiosity, is Royce playing?"

"Of course he is," she said. "He's always Prince Malphas's champion for these events."

"Good. Then make sure you get a chair really close to our table. I'm gonna make you watch while I kick his ass."

We walked away, leaving Freddie to strut up and take our space at the head of the line. She slapped an envelope down on the table and loudly announced, "Fredrika Vinter, House of Vinter, champion of good taste. If you don't know what that is, I'll buy you a dictionary."

Caitlin and I stepped out into the hall. I couldn't miss the stiffness in her walk, or the thousand-yard stare.

"Well, that should do it," I said softly. "Now Royce pretty much *has* to focus all his attention on me. If he wasn't going to before, I guarantee Nadine will goad him into it."

"Fine," Caitlin snapped.

"Apparently it isn't." I stopped walking. "Hey, what's wrong? I mean, you're *really* upset."

She pursed her lips and waved me off. "It's nothing."

"It's something. C'mon, what's wrong? Talk to me."

Caitlin leaned against the wall. She shook her head, her eyes distant.

"Daniel, I...worked very, very hard to get where I am today. I've proven myself again, and again, and again. I've warred for my court and my prince, and I've honored them with my blood and my sweat. If there's dirt under my nails, it's because I had to claw my way up from *nothing*."

"Hey, I know that. You've earned your job. From what I see, you *keep* earning it."

"And when someone like that, who was handed everything from the moment she hatched, looks down on me because I've got the wrong blood in my veins..." She looked left and right, lowering her voice. "And *you* know that I'm Prince Sitri's adopted daughter, a little fact that would shut Nadine's mouth in a heartbeat, but I'm forbidden to *tell* anyone. 'All in good time,' he says. Another game of his, I assume."

I stroked my fingers across her pale cheek.

"Well, I'll tell you something." I leaned close. "As far as I'm concerned, you're already a princess."

That got a smile. A small one, but it was a start. I took her hand.

"C'mon. Let's show these snobs how we do things in Vegas."

We had one more part of the plan to carry out before the tournament got underway, and not much time. Out in the club's lounge, I hunted for three people in the crowd: Amy Xun, Bentley, and Stanwyck. Amy spotted me, stopped texting, and slipped her phone into her purse. Bentley loitered by the bar. As our eyes locked for an instant, he set down his glass of wine and gave me an almost imperceptible nod.

Then there was Stanwyck, Trevor still at his side and leading him across the lounge toward a couple of open chairs against the opposite wall. I squeezed Caitlin's hand, let go, and prowled toward them.

"I told you," Trevor was saying, "this is a very elite, *very* underground tournament."

"Underground," Stanwyck muttered. "Yeah, see, to me that means Outfit goombahs and not reporting your winnings to the IRS. It does not mean...whatever the hell is happening here. There was a guy back there with his teeth filed to points like a goddamn great white shark, Manderley. *Shark teeth.*"

"Hi there," I said, stepping right into his path.

Stanwyck stopped in his tracks, off-balance, just in time for Amy to collide with him from the side. He then stumbled into Bentley, coming up on his right and pushing him into me. I caught him by the lapels of his jacket, steadying him, while Amy patted his back. Amy and Bentley hurled profuse apologies at him, buffeting Stanwyck from both sides as he yanked away from me in a sudden panic.

"It's fine," he said, holding up his hands. "It's *fine.*"

Bentley and Amy disappeared into the crowd as quickly as they'd appeared. Stanwyck didn't notice, too fixated on me standing in his path.

"You can't hurt me here," he said quickly, looking to Trevor. "That's right, right? He can't even touch me here."

"That's right," Trevor said, studying his fingernails and sounding bored. "No fighting. Club rules."

"Oh, I'm not going to hurt you, Stanwyck. No, I think the word *hurt* is way, *way* too mild for what I'm going to do to you."

A shadow pooled at my feet, murky and darker than it had any right to be. Around us, tiny shadows the size of cockroaches scurried to join the growing puddle. *Easy*, I thought, *I get the message*.

"I didn't mean to hurt anyone," Stanwyck said. "I just wanted the goddamn dagger. You saw what happened. Coop jumped me."

"I saw you shoot him dead. I saw you blast Augie's skull open. And twice now—*twice* now—I've seen you take a shot at *me*."

"That was self-defense. You were sure as hell gonna kill me, so what was I supposed to do? Damn it, what do I have to do to get you off my back?"

"Bring Coop and Augie back to life," I said. "Barring that? I suggest you enjoy your last few hours on Earth. No, he's right, I can't hurt you here. Here. But the second the tournament is over and those doors open, I'll be waiting for you outside. And there's only one way out of this building."

I didn't know if that was true, but he obviously believed me. "You—you couldn't. You wouldn't. There's gotta be a hundred people here. There'll be witnesses—"

"Take a good look around," I told him. "These aren't the kind of people who call the cops. And I don't *care* what they see. Don't you get it, Stanwyck? You don't belong here. You're an outsider. And you smell like an outsider smells, and you walk like an outsider walks, and not a single person in this entire club—including Trevor here—will shed one tear if I gun you down like a dog in the street."

His eyes were wide as his face jerked toward Trevor.

"Is—is that true?"

"Which part?" Trevor said. "That nobody will call the police? Yeah, that's pretty much right."

"Then why did you *bring* me here, you son of a bitch?"

"Whoa, whoa," Trevor said, taking a step back. "Because you needed a chance to win some fast money, and I came through. Hey, I didn't *have* to sponsor your entry. A little gratitude wouldn't hurt."

"I'll leave you two to talk," I said. "See you soon, Stanwyck. I'll be waiting outside."

I had no intention of following through on that threat—and besides, given the high-end sports cars sitting unguarded in the parking lot, I had a hunch Management's protection extended a bit farther than the front door—but from the look on Stanwyck's face he'd bought the lie hook, line, and sinker.

I turned and walked away. My shadow shed roach-sized blobs as I strode across the room, and they wriggled away to the darkest corners of the club.

37.

When I got back to Caitlin, she was having a chat with Royce. They wore nearly identical expressions of strained politeness.

"—of course I'm not saying you had anything to do with the attempted theft," Royce said, "but the human *is* your property, which makes you at least partially—"

"And I told you," Caitlin replied, "that a formal apology will be sent."

I shrugged and held up my open palms. "Aw, there I go, causing trouble again."

"Oh good, you're both here now," Royce said. "I was just explaining to Caitlin that due to...recent events, we've been forced to bulk up security for the tournament, and we strongly recommend not testing us on that. Any attempt to disrupt today's event will be considered an act of grave hostility."

"Security?" I asked. "Like the Chippendales Nadine brought with her? I'm not kidding, Royce, I think those guys are off-duty strippers. I hope you're not paying her a consultation fee."

Royce arched one eyebrow. "Oh, no, I think we can do better than *that*."

He snapped his fingers at one of Nadine's men, who walked over leading a shaggy German shepherd on a long black leash. I caught a crackle of stray magic, and the faint glow behind the dog's sharp eyes told me what we were dealing with. The shepherd had a hijacker.

I'd seen this kind of security before—Lauren Carmichael had guarded her corporate headquarters the same way. Forcing a spirit into a guard dog's body gave you the best of both worlds: a canine's power, speed, and keen senses mixed with the intellect and creativity of a lower demon or a captive soul. The "intellect" part was the challenge. Given the humiliation factor, it was hard to find a skilled entity who would willingly take the job.

"I just wanted to reintroduce you to an old friend," Royce told us. "Say hello, Pinfeather."

The dog pushed its ears back and growled.

"Well hello," Caitlin said, eyeing the shepherd. "The last time I saw you, you were wearing your heart on your sleeve. Because I ripped it out and put it there."

Royce bent down and rubbed behind the dog's ears. "Pinfeather is being given the rare opportunity to make amends for his failures. And if he's a very good boy, in a hundred years or so we *might* give him a human body again."

He nodded to the dog's handler. Pinfeather turned and padded away at a tug of the leash, still growling.

"Now that's arrogant," Caitlin said. "You lecture me about my court's behavior, then bring *him* over here?"

"Anything Pinfeather told you about his mission—before you killed him, let me point out, and you did *not* have to do that—was purely a desperate fantasy. He was a rogue agent, acting without my prince's sanction. Also, we wrote a letter of apology. Don't know what else you want from us."

"That's funny," I said. "I didn't get one. Did you send it to my old apartment? That must be why. See, it *burned down* while I was protecting that asshole from the Redemption Choir."

"I'll see that you get a copy," Royce said. "Just understand that we're watching all of our contestants for any signs of cheating or underhanded behavior. I want a nice, clean tournament."

"Does that go both ways?" I asked.

"Well, of course it does. I pride myself on working at the highest possible level of integrity. Now if you'll excuse me, it's almost time to get underway."

I waited until he walked away before I looked at Caitlin. "That means he's gonna cheat his ass off, doesn't it?"

"That's roughly the highest possible level of integrity for him, yes."

I offered her my arm. "Shall we?"

* * *

The pedestal at the heart of the gaming parlor had been replaced by something new: a human-sized figure standing under a tattered black shroud.

He stood perfectly still in the center of the room, surrounded by a ring of brass-rimmed green felt tables. At first I thought it might be a veiled statue, until I saw the shroud rise and fall with his slow, ragged breath. As Caitlin and I filtered in with the rest of the crowd, the figure turned. Eyes stared out from two uneven slits in the fabric. Wide, mad, and bloodshot eyes, one hazel and one blue.

"Cait," I murmured, "what the hell is that?"

"A conduit. They must have brought it here so Prince Malphas can watch the tournament through its eyes."

Caitlin's people had a conduit too, back in Vegas, living in filth and darkness in the sub-sub-basement of a nightclub. Conduits existed in two realms at once, a living bridge between Earth and hell.

I'd been told they were human, once. I didn't know how they were created, and I didn't want to.

"It's staring at us," I said. The figure turned to follow our movements as we circled the room.

"Well, Malphas knows who we are."

I paused. "So he's watching us, right this second?"

"Most likely." Caitlin folded her arms. "And you will remember that we are diplomatic guests here and not commit whatever petty mischief you were just thinking of."

"How do you know I was—"

"You get a certain look."

"Fine, fine." I sighed. "You never let me have any fun."

Caitlin gave me a mock glare. "He said to the woman who just put up five thousand dollars so he could play a card game."

"Ouch. Touché."

She squeezed my shoulder and smiled. "Fight well. I'll be watching."

I didn't have to wait long for the shenanigans to start. I'd just found my table and gotten comfortable when Nadine swooped in.

"I'm so sorry," she said, "but we have a last-minute table change. Come with me, please?"

"I thought the table assignments were random?"

"They are." Her smile lit up the room. "We've just made it *more* random. We're all about fairness here."

As soon as she walked me to my new table, I figured out the scam. Royce waited for me, already seated and with a glass of mineral water in his hand, eager for a showdown. I knew he couldn't risk one of us getting knocked out of the tournament before we had a chance to play against each other. *He* wanted to be the one to send me home.

When I saw who was with him, though, I knew the fix was in.

"Calypso," I said, "funny meeting you here."

The lean, dark man in the cream-colored suit chuckled as he lit a thin cigarette. I'd last encountered the bargaining demon in Reno, where we'd done a little gambling ourselves. We'd both walked away a winner and a loser that night.

"Daniel Faust," he said, his voice a honeyed rumble. "You know me. I go where the fun is. And I've been known to do a *tiny* bit of card-playing in my day."

Nadine pulled out a chair for me. I sat down, surveying the competition, and gave Royce a tight, humorless smile.

"Let me guess," I said, "the 'totally random' seating method just happened to put the best players in the tournament at this table."

Royce sipped his water. "Are you familiar with the word

apothecia? It's the state of finding significance in random, meaningless data. It's a very common flaw in the human brain."

The meaning was loud and clear: he'd stacked the decks to make absolutely certain I went down hard, pitting me against the best of the best. If he couldn't beat me, he'd at least guarantee that Prince Sitri's champion went home in defeat.

The tables at the Bast Club were smaller than what I was used to in the casinos back home. Thirty-six players spread across six tables, all aiming for one grand prize. I didn't recognize the other three contenders at my table, but the closest, a spectacled man with thinning blond hair and a bulky turtleneck sweater, reached over and offered me his hand. He had a shaky grip, and his skin had a waxy, cheesecloth feel that reminded me of Halima.

"I'm Herbert," he said. "You're not a local, are you?"

"Daniel, and no, I'm from out of town."

He smiled. I thought his cheeks were unusually ruddy until I realized they didn't have any natural color—he was wearing a light shade of blush.

"I knew it. I know all the locals. I'm a doctor. Well, a mortician these days, but I *am* medically trained. If you ever need a little off-the-books patching up while you're in town, come see me."

"Oh, he'll need it," said the player on Herbert's left, a lanky kid with moon-crater acne. He couldn't have been more than twenty-two, dressed in ripped jeans and a concert T-shirt for a band I'd never heard of. "You are *all* getting your asses kicked."

"You know," I said, settling back in my chair, "most of the people who threaten me are old enough to shave. You might wanna wait a few years."

"No threat, just math. Name's Orville. Josh Orville. You might have heard of me."

He said it like there wasn't a speck of doubt in his mind. I took a little pleasure in deflating him. "Nope. Should I have?"

"*Hello?*" He looked like I'd kicked him in the teeth. He wagged his wrist at me, showing off a white-gold bracelet studded with a glittering constellation of diamonds. "*Josh Orville?* MIT prodigy?

Sole inventor of the Orville Matrix Gambling Strategy? Youngest player to ever win the World Series of Poker? Yeah. You've heard of me."

"I don't get out much," I told him.

"So sorry," Calypso said, waving his cigarette in a slow circle. "I should have asked before I lit up. Does anyone mind if I smoke?"

"Duh, *yes*," Josh snapped at him. "It's a filthy habit. And it's making my eyes water. I have very sensitive—"

"But I don't like you," Calypso said. "Does anyone *else* mind, or are we all copacetic?"

The last player, sitting back with mirrored glasses and a broad-brimmed hat slung low over his face, held up a cigar wrapped in yellowed parchment. "I don't mind if you don't," he said in a thick Oklahoma drawl. "So we gonna play some cards or what?"

Royce rose to his feet, taking another sip of water before setting his glass down.

"Absolutely," he said, "just let me make a few opening remarks. I think the room's ready."

Nadine strolled over and ran her fingertips along Josh's shoulder. She leaned in to whisper in his ear.

"Oh, hey," I said. "Kid. Seriously, you're playing with fire there. Whatever she's telling you, it's nothing you want to hear."

The kid was obnoxious, but that didn't mean I wanted him dead—or worse. I wasn't prepared for the smirk on his face when he looked over at me, mirroring Nadine's expression.

"What, are you stupid? Mistress Nadine *brought* me here."

"We're quite proud of Joshua's exploits," Nadine said. "He plays an almost perfect game of poker. Almost perfect. And he hungers for greater things. He's ideal Roses material."

Josh rapped his knuckles on the table. "I win this tournament? I'm in. They're gonna make me the best in the *world*. The best poker player in *history*."

I started to say something but fell silent when I caught the look on Calypso's face. Wistful amusement gleamed in his eyes as he took a drag on his cigarette, shaking his head at me.

"Sometimes," he rumbled, "people have to be dragged kicking and screaming to the edge of perdition. And sometimes...they jump right in. Like they wouldn't have it any other way."

With the tables full—and Prince Malphas's shrouded conduit watching the room in slow shuffling circles, as if it were standing on a turntable—spectators packed the parlor and lined the walls. I looked back to see Caitlin, about ten feet behind me. She winked and blew me an air-kiss. I snatched it out of the air and pressed it to my heart.

Then I took a longer look around, spotting Margaux, Bentley, and Corman in the crowd. Everybody was exactly where they needed to be.

38.

The room fell into a hush as Royce raised his hands. He strode in a slow circle around the shrouded conduit and grinned like a rock star.

"Friends. Visitors. Honored guests. Welcome. These annual games are a time-honored tradition, as established by my predecessor so long ago—both as a tribute to our benevolent Prince Malphas and to the entire Choir of Greed. After all, what better way to promote the virtue? We charge you to attend, then set you at each other's throats as you try to win your money back."

That got a laugh from the crowd. He paused, waiting for the ripple to subside.

"The original games were gladiatorial fights to the death. We had to revise that after a few years because, well, people stopped signing up. Now our bouts are bloodless, but no less exciting."

Herbert leaned my way and murmured, "Not always true. In '08, that was the first and only year we played Monopoly. Four people died."

I blinked at him. "How do people die playing Monopoly?"

"House rules."

"This year's grand prize," Royce said, "in addition to a cash pot of fifty thousand dollars, is a rare treat. A Tyrian shekel from our prince's private art gallery, formerly owned by Judas Iscariot. A piece of living history—and who knows what dark powers it might possess?"

"Ain't got none," the man with the Okie accent drawled in a

low voice as he unwrapped his cigar. "Had my lab rats check it out while it was on display. Just a fancy coin is all. I'm here for the *paper* money. You got a light, mister?"

Calypso turned his empty hand in a flourish, and a silver lighter sat nestled between his fingertips. He slid it across the table.

Royce clapped his hands sharply. "And now, the rules. The game is Texas Hold'em, no limit. You will each be issued ten thousand dollars worth of chips, and there will be no rebuys. When you're out of chips, you're out of the game. The ante will start low and steadily increase over the course of the tournament. As we begin, the small blind is one hundred dollars, big blind is two hundred.

"Games will last until we've lost enough players to consolidate tables, at which point we'll resume after a brief intermission. Now, I shouldn't have to say this, but we expect a clean tournament. Any cheating, be it through sleight of hand, chicanery, or the magical arts, will be punished by torture and death. Torture which, I assure you, will only be the beginning of your eternal misery once our people catch up with you in hell. I do hope we're all on the same page here."

While Royce aimed that barb straight at me, I was entertaining myself watching Stanwyck at the next table over. I'd seen literal ghosts that weren't as pale as his face.

"To the victor the spoils," Royce announced, holding his arms high, "and to Prince Malphas the glory. Let's play."

One of Nadine's boys circled our table, laying out stacks of colored chips. Royce sat back down and cracked his knuckles.

"I hope no one minds if I deal first? Host's prerogative."

Texas Hold'em is arguably the trickiest poker variant, not the least because it seems—at first glance—incredibly simple. You get two cards. Just two, facedown, and three turned faceup in the middle of the table for all the players to share. As the betting goes on, round by round, two more faceup cards are eventually added to the table for a total of five. If you're still in the game at that point, you put together your final five-card hand between the five communal cards and your two facedown ones.

Of course, nothing's that simple. The longer you stay in the game, and the more cards you get to choose from, the more chips you need to risk. If you don't have a strong hand, but your cards have potential, do you bail early or push your luck? A skilled Hold'em player has just the right mix of aggression and caution.

Two hands in, and I had all the confirmation I needed that Royce had stacked our table: these players, even Herbert, were pros. No carelessness, no easy mistakes to punish. I folded every hand, bowing out fast and letting them fight it out.

The fourth time I folded in a row, Royce clicked his tongue. "Are you here to play cards?"

"Sure," I said. "I'm here to play *good* cards. As soon as I'm dealt a couple, we'll talk."

You can't stay out of the game forever. Two rotating positions—the blinds—*have* to bet at the start of each new hand. Sooner than I expected, I heard Nadine shout out, "Blinds have now increased. Two hundred for the small blind, four hundred for the big blind."

Double what they started at, and we were barely twenty minutes into the tournament. Making sure nobody sat on the sidelines for too long.

The dealer position rotated along with the blinds. Once the deck sat nestled in my hands, I heard a faint growl. Pinfeather sat on his haunches next to my chair, the German shepherd glaring at me with too-human eyes.

"Really?" I asked Royce.

Royce shrugged eloquently. "He doesn't trust you. Can't imagine why."

I was tempted to bottom-deal myself a good card or two, just on general principle, but I played it fair. Honesty paid off for a change: my cards were a king and an eight, with two kings faceup on the table. If another king came up—or if the cards kicked me a second eight, building a full house—I'd finally have a solid hand.

I got my eight in the next round of bets and rode it all the way to the showdown.

"Kings full of eights," I said, showing my cards. Calypso, the only player who hadn't already folded, only had two pair. Somehow, I wasn't surprised he was the biggest bluffer at the table.

I raked in my chips, passed the deck of cards to Herbert, and looked down at Pinfeather. "Also, your breath is *terrible.*"

The dog whined and trotted away.

My luck didn't hold for long, but that was the nature of the game. The stacks of chips ebbed and flowed between us. It was easy to see Josh taking an early lead—the kid was a mathematical machine with a face of stone, and his plays were impossible to predict. The Okie, Royce, and I took the worst beatings, but we all hung in and kept playing.

An hour into the tournament, I saw open chairs at every table but ours. The fast and the reckless dropped in no time, weeded out by their more conservative rivals. I kept folding early, saving my chips, waiting for the perfect hand. When Nadine raised the blinds to one thousand and two thousand, I knew I couldn't keep turtling for long.

One of her boy toys set a glass snifter by my hand. Three big rocks of ice bathing in three fingers of whiskey.

"I didn't order this," I said.

"Compliments of the house."

It didn't smell right. The whiskey had all the hallmarks of age—a genuine clear, dark color from doing hard time in an oak barrel, not the artificial caramel coloring they put in the cheap stuff—but when I lifted the snifter to my nose, I caught an alkaline edge to the liquor.

I didn't set the glass down, though. Not right away.

This is crazy, I thought. *It's a setup. It's the most obvious setup in the world. I'd have to be beyond stupid to take a single sip of this.*

But it's just one sip.

This close to my face, I spotted something at the bottom of the snifter. The faintest traces of a sigil, sketched on the underbelly of the glass in cherry-red lipstick.

A desire spell. I'd used them myself, once or twice. *You want this*, it said as it fired off, *you need this*, and whispered sweet nothings into your limbic system. The problem with desire spells was that even when you knew one had been cast on you, it didn't stop working. Right about then I was more parched than a man crossing the Mojave on foot, and that whiskey looked like the last drink on Earth.

I forced my arm down, setting the snifter aside, and focused on the game. That was the plan, anyway. With the enchanted glass sitting there, screaming for my attention, my carefully constructed house of cards turned into a condemned tenement. I let Calypso bluff me, giving up the biggest pot of the tournament so far, and then I threw away a hand that could have turned into a queen-high flush.

Damned if I do, damned if I don't. As long as the glass is there, I'm thinking more about the whiskey than the cards. It doesn't matter what they actually laced the drink with.

Maybe I imagined the smell. One sip wouldn't hurt. Then I'd know. Maybe that's the whole trick—that there's nothing wrong with it and I'm fighting for no reason.

It was junkie logic, twisting and rationalizing a lousy decision until it seemed like a good one. It felt like scratching a bad itch as I lifted the snifter—quick, before I could talk myself out of it—and took a sip.

The drink hit me with a chemical fist and burned down my throat like napalm. Whatever they'd done to it, the whiskey was stronger than it had any right to be; one tiny sip and I felt as lightheaded as I normally would after two shots and a chaser. If I could down the whole glass without passing out dead drunk—and I gave it even odds—I'd be worse than useless.

Can't drink it, can't not drink it. That only left me one option. I folded on a decent pair, buying me a minute to focus while the others played. The amplified liquor buzzing around in my head made it even harder to resist drinking more, and I snatched up the snifter again. *Just one sip. Already had one. Two won't hurt.*

We lie to ourselves for all kinds of reasons. Usually, like the first time I put the snifter to my mouth, it's to justify making a lousy choice. Sometimes, though—just sometimes—you can make that lie work in your favor. Wreathed by the desire spell, that glass could have been made from gold and diamonds. It was a priceless gift, something to covet and protect. Moving my hand to knock it off the table, or throwing it at Royce's head for that matter, would have been unthinkable.

With it already cradled in my hand, though, all I had to do was open my fingers and let it fall.

It still took every ounce of effort to make my muscles obey, pouring my willpower into the fight until beadlets of cold sweat broke out on my forehead. One by one, my fingers wrenched back, loosening their grip. I felt like I'd thrown away a fortune when the snifter tumbled to the floor.

Then the glass shattered, a crash that echoed throughout the room and killed the buzz of conversation, and the spell shattered with it.

Everyone looked my way. It was my turn to deal. I shuffled overhand and locked eyes with Royce.

"You should call somebody to clean that up," I told him. "Now let's play some cards."

39.

Players dropped like flies all around us. I saw Stanwyck get up from his table, shaking his head, going home a loser. He spotted me watching him and hustled out of the parlor.

That's right, I thought, *run for it. Just like I want you to.*

Amy Xun had already been knocked out of the game. She sat on the sidelines, watching intently. We made eye contact, and I flicked my gaze toward Stanwyck's retreating back. Amy nodded. Message received.

There was a lull in the action while Nadine reshuffled the seats, cutting six tables down to three. Our table was the only one that hadn't suffered a casualty yet, but the time wasn't far off. Herbert was the first to fall, going all in on his last hand and running out of chips when Josh beat his full house with four of a kind.

"Been a pleasure," Herbert said as he pushed his chair back. He slipped me his business card and added, "Hopefully you remain hale and hearty, but just in case, my clinic is always open."

"You work in the city morgue," Royce said.

Herbert shrugged. "Sometimes it's a morgue, sometimes it's a clinic. I *am* a man of science."

The Okie was next to go. He'd been playing as conservatively as me, folding on four hands out of five, but then Nadine raised the blinds again—setting the minimum ante to four thousand and eight thousand a hand—and three lousy plays in a row ran his stakes down to nothing.

"Aw, hell," he sighed, snuffing the stub of his cigar. "Maybe next year, huh? Good luck, fellas."

Now it was down to Royce, Josh, Calypso, and me, and Royce and I were the low men on the totem pole. With the mandatory antes this big, and one of the two blinds hitting me every other hand, I had to make every play count. I figured it was time for my next move.

"How about a side bet?" I asked Royce.

He met Josh's raise, tossing a handful of chips into the pot, and looked my way. "What do you have in mind?"

"We're both representing rival courts. Let's face it, regardless of who wins the tournament, what people really want to see is which one of us comes out on top."

"Fair enough," he agreed.

"If you get knocked out of the tournament before I do, you have to announce in front of everyone," I said with a nod toward the shrouded conduit, "*and* your boss, that the Jade Tears beat the Night-Blooming Flowers fair and square."

Royce gave me a cocky smile. "Now that's the kind of side bet I enjoy. A little danger to spice things up. But what do I get if you're eliminated before me?"

I pretended to think about it, rapping my fingers against my cards, even though I already knew what I'd say.

"You know what I was after, coming here."

Royce looked across the room, where one of Nadine's men stood watch with the metal briefcase cuffed to his wrist. He chuckled.

"Have to honestly say, sport, for someone who's supposedly a skilled thief, you weren't exactly difficult to see coming. No hard feelings. Caitlin got a black eye by association, and her prince will have to make a public apology to mine. I call that a good day. And we really do want you on our team. I can be forgiving about minor sins."

"I'll tell you who isn't on your team: the person who hired me to rip you off."

His eyes went a little wider. I had his attention. "And that would be whom, exactly?"

I smiled. "Knock me out of the tournament first, and I'll tell you. How's that sound?"

He extended his hand across the table. "It sounds like we have a bet."

What came next was the easiest part of the plan: I just had to lose convincingly. Beyond folding a couple of decent hands instead of letting them play, that barely took any doing at all. Josh and Calypso made sure of it. I wiped out on a garbage hand and tried to look disappointed.

"Well, look at *that*," Nadine said behind me, loud enough for her voice to carry across the parlor. "The champion of the Jade Tears, going home in utter defeat. Vanquished at the hands of Prince Malphas's hound, no less."

"Don't rub it in," Caitlin snapped at her, walking over to meet me as I rose from the table.

Nadine rubbed her hands together gleefully. "I think someone needs to take out the trash around here. Oh, wait, Royce just *did*."

I rapped my knuckles on the table and inclined my head to Royce. "Good game. Once you're done, we'll talk about the side bet."

Caitlin put her arm around me. I let her lead me away, not too far from the table, and leaned my head against her shoulder.

"This had better work," she murmured, "or I'm going to have a lot to explain to my prince."

"So far, so good," I told her. "Now we just have to wait for—oops, there he goes."

Royce threw up his hands, watching the last of his chips disappear. All the same, he strolled toward us with a sunny smile.

"Bad break," I said.

"I didn't have to win the tournament, sport. I just had to beat *you*. That's all anyone's going to be talking about tonight. So ready to give me a name?"

I jerked my head toward the door. "Out in the lounge, not here. This is for your ears only."

"Fine, fine." He snapped his fingers at Nadine. "Time for the final round, love. Consolidate the tables and keep an eye on things, would you kindly? I shan't be long."

I left Caitlin there, walking alone with Royce to the outer lounge. With all the action happening in the gambling parlor, the bar was a ghost town. I took a seat and waved over the bored-looking bartender.

"After all that action, I could use a drink," I said to Royce. "A *legitimate* one."

"Don't know what you're talking about," he said, eyes twinkling.

"Maybe not. Maybe that was Nadine's game. Tell you what, just to show there's no hard feelings, I'll buy for both of us." I looked to the bartender. "Crown and Coke. Two, please."

"Appreciated," Royce said, "but there's still a tournament in swing, and I shouldn't be gone for—"

"Relax. Something I learned a long time ago: when a man has a story to tell, you let him tell it in his own time. You get all the important details that way."

Royce grumbled, but he ended up on the barstool next to me, patient as he could manage while I waited for our drinks to arrive. I raised my glass before taking a swig.

"To your health. All right. So. I first became aware of the Judas Coin thanks to a post on the deep web."

"Right," Royce said. "Believe it or not, we're already aware of that part. Could we speed this along?"

I walked him through it anyway, spinning out the lie nice and slow. How I'd made contact online with a local who wanted the coin. How I'd flown to Chicago and spent a couple of nights scoping out the Bast Club. How I'd come up with a plan for the big heist. None of the details were anywhere close to the truth, but they matched the story he'd already been sold.

"—and then Mack and Zeke gave us the slip when I tried to tail them in my car, so I knew finding wherever you stashed the coin was a lost cause. We abandoned the entire plan."

Royce pinched the bridge of his nose. "Like I've said ten times now, we already *know* all that. I just want the name of the person who hired you. That's it. *Please*."

"Oh," I said, snapping my fingers. "All right, you won the bet fair and square. Just keep my name out of it when you go after him, okay? It was Damien Ecko."

He leaned a little closer on his stool. "Damien Ecko? The jeweler?"

"Yeah, you know him?"

Royce shook his head. "By reputation, that's all. He doesn't really have any dealings with my court. Did he say why he wanted the coin?"

"No, but he doesn't play cards, so he knew he didn't have a chance of winning it fairly."

"Hmm. Well. I imagine he's covered his tracks, but I'll have my people question him regardless. Thank you for that."

"Hey," I said, frowning like I'd just realized something. "I haven't seen him here today. Have you? I'm wondering if he skipped town, thinking you were onto him."

Royce shrugged and slid off the stool, brushing off one sleeve of his jacket. "If he did, he did. He won't cause any more trouble regardless. Oh bother, it's been a while, hasn't it? I really need to get back to the game."

"Right," I said. "I'll join you."

We came back to a dead-silent parlor, all eyes on the showdown at the final table. Even Calypso had been knocked out of the fight, and only two players remained.

"Oh, no," Royce breathed, his face falling.

"Oh, yes," I said with a smile, standing beside him.

Josh flipped over his cards, looking cocky as ever, but his pile of chips was half what it used to be.

Across the table, Corman did the same.

"*Nadine*," Royce hissed, grabbing her by the arm as she strolled by. "How could you let this happen?"

"What?" Her eyes went wide. "Let what happen?"

"That." He pointed at Corman, then at me. "*He's* with *him*."

"And how would I know that? It's not my fault!"

"Never mind, just, just—" He pinched the bridge of his nose again, took a deep breath, and lowered his voice. "Mix him one of your special drinks. Fast."

Nadine put her hands on her hips. "I can't *do* it 'fast.' It's a complicated spell. If you'd asked me twenty, even ten minutes ago—"

"Oops," I said lightly. "Almost like somebody distracted you at a crucial moment, to keep you from cheating. Funny how that worked out, huh? Of course, you helped."

"Helped?" Royce spun on his heel. "What do you mean, *helped?*"

"Everything we did—the whole 'champion of the Jade Tears' thing, the rivalry—had one purpose: to make you fixate on *me*. All I had to do was keep you distracted and stay in the game as long as I possibly could. See, I knew you'd stack the deck, so to speak, and put all the heavyweight players at our table. You couldn't risk the chance that I might win the tournament and make Prince Malphas look like a chump."

"Alas," Caitlin said, sauntering up and slipping her arm around mine, "I didn't just bankroll one player. I bankrolled *four*."

"How'd Margaux and Bentley do, anyway?" I asked her.

"Bentley made it to the final round, you should have seen it. Margaux...eh, I think we've agreed that poker isn't her game."

"Know what happens when you pit the big guys against each other, right out of the starting gate?" I said to Royce. "They whittle each other down. Meanwhile, that left all the fish at the other tables, waiting to get gobbled up. Corman used to play poker for a living. Just guessing, but I'd say he hasn't lost his edge."

Corman slid a stack of chips across the felt. He wore a lazy grin.

"Raise," he said. "I'm feeling lucky."

40.

Josh's left eyelid twitched. Just a little.

"You've got nothing."

"Got enough to beat your punk ass," Corman said amiably.

"You've got *nothing*, old man," Josh snapped. "You won a few lucky hands, but I've got your number now. I've clocked your body language, your tells, all of it. You're keeping no secrets from me. And I'm telling you, you've got nothing."

Corman shrugged and leaned back in his chair. "If you say so."

"Fine." Josh put both hands on the green felt and shoved his stacks of chips, sending the neat columns spilling over. "Fine, you want to play? Let's get it over with. All in."

"Kid, if you wanna gamble like a pro, there's some important skills you need under your belt. Lemme tell you the most important—"

"Oh God," Josh said, rolling his eyes as he flipped his cards. "Spare me the wisdom-of-your-elders bullshit. Just spare me. Here, see? Full house, queens in kings. Beat *that*."

Corman turned his cards. The Queen of Hearts sat face-up on the felt, right under his fingertips. The room fell into a graveyard hush.

"Four of a kind." He held up one of his chips. "The skill in question was how to be a graceful loser. Also, you should learn to figure out when somebody's hustling you. That nervous thing I did with my fingers every time I had a garbage hand? Not an actual tell. Okay, now who do I have to bribe to get a cold beer around here?"

Applause exploded around us, thundering as Nadine's jaw dropped and Royce, wide-eyed and on the edge of panic, shook his head at me.

"Why? Why would you *do* that?"

Caitlin held up her phone. It strobed with a sharp white flash as she snapped a photo of Royce and Nadine.

"Just so I could get a picture of the looks on your faces." She checked the phone and nodded her approval. "Oh, this is going on *all* our holiday cards."

"Peasants," Nadine said, looking like she'd been hit by a bus. "Our tournament was won by *peasants*."

Caitlin smiled pleasantly. "Don't feel too badly about it. Corman's not mine. So you still beat my champion—at *poker*—and your court still gets to puff its chest about it. I think I'll ease the pain of the loss with...what was the grand prize? Fifty thousand dollars? And the Judas Coin, of course. It'll look lovely in Prince Sitri's trophy room. I think he might already have the other twenty-nine. He's *so* hard to shop for."

I strolled over to the table, where Bentley and Corman were wrapped up in each other's arms. Corman normally didn't go for public displays of affection, but sometimes you had to make an exception to the rule. I squeezed their shoulders and walked on by, sidling up to Josh. The kid looked shell-shocked, just sitting there staring at his cards.

"I'm gonna give you a piece of free advice," I told him, "and I really hope you take it. Right now."

He gave me a hangdog look. "What?"

Nadine was coming our way, her hands curled into claws at her sides, and her eyes were molten swirls of copper.

"*Run*," I said and got between them.

"Out of my way," she snapped.

"No." I crossed my arms and stood my ground. "I'm not letting you hurt that kid. He's an asshole, but he doesn't deserve...whatever it is you've got planned. Not happening, not on my watch."

"Daniel," she said through a mouthful of shark teeth, struggling to sound calm. "He lost. He needs to be punished. Which means you need to get out of my way, right now, please."

I looked back. Josh sat frozen in his chair, petrified.

"Not happening," I repeated.

That was when she reached for me.

Caitlin's hand shot out faster than a bullwhip and seized Nadine by the wrist.

"We're here as visitors, under diplomatic protocol," Caitlin said, "so I have to be forgiving of certain transgressions. That said? If you *ever* touch my man again, I start tearing off body parts."

Nadine's men circled us, four of them, and shadows swirled on the floor as their hands eased under their jackets. Freddie loomed over one of the men, coming up from behind, and I felt the heat in the room draining away like somebody had opened a walk-in freezer.

"If I see a gun," Freddie snapped at Nadine, "your gigolo here sees *teeth. Believe* that."

I glanced upward. Centipedes of shadow, ten feet long with wavering, clutching arms, squirmed on the ceiling. Ready to drop.

"Stop!" Royce shouted, his arms flailing. "Everybody, please, just—just stop. Let's be reasonable about this."

"You're not leaving with the kid," I told Nadine. "Not without a fight. And in case you haven't noticed, we've got Management's attention. If you feel like taking your chances, step on up."

Nadine closed her eyes, her features softening, and Caitlin released her wrist. In a breath Nadine was fully human again and spoke with a voice smoother and softer than silk.

"Joshua," she said, "you understand that sacrifices have to be made on the road to greatness. You know that pain makes us strong."

His answer was a muffled, almost inaudible, "Yes."

"And you understand that you failed today. Which means you

need to be corrected to encourage you to do better next time. Joshua...do you still *want* to be the best? Because if I was wrong about you, if you've lost your ambition, you'll just break my heart, but I hope you'll tell me—"

"I want it," he said. My heart sank. "I want to be the best."

"Very well." Nadine turned to two of her men. "Take him. Prepare him for me. I won't be long."

They took Josh by the arms, hustling him toward the door. I felt sick. Nadine flashed a cruel smile.

"He's leaving of his own free will. Which means if you try to stop him, *you'll* be the one starting a fight."

"You sick, sadistic—"

"*Winner*," she said.

Corman cleared his throat.

"Actually," he said, "*I'm* the winner. So I think there's a prize or something? And I'm still waiting on that beer."

Royce hung his head. The shrouded conduit watched impassively from the heart of the room, eye slits slowly turning to follow the metal briefcase as Royce brought it over.

"Right," he said in a flat, drained voice. "It is my...great honor to announce that we have a victor, and the annual tournament is complete. All hail Prince Malphas, glory to his name, etcetera."

The spectators broke out in a round of nervous, scattered applause as Management's shadows slowly faded away. Royce flipped the dials on the briefcase, opened it wide, and froze.

"Er, Nadine? Where's the coin?"

She touched her hand to her forehead, eyelids fluttering.

"In the case, of course. Why?"

He spun it around to show her the empty compartment.

"No," he said, "your witch-eye is in the case. *Not* attached to the coin."

Nadine thrust her finger at me. "*You!* You stole it!"

I rolled my eyes. "Yes. After failing to steal it, somehow I stole it anyway. Then we paid thousands of dollars in buy-ins and hatched an elaborate scheme to win it legitimately. After I already had it. Come on, Nadine, that doesn't even make *sense*. What do you think, I walked in here with the coin in my pocket?"

"He has a point," Royce observed.

"Fortunately," I said, "I can help. When I was scoping out the coin a couple of nights ago, I put my own tracking spell on it. Apparently a subtler one than yours. Somebody bring me a map of Chicago and something to divine with. Does anybody here have a Ouija board?"

I was somehow not surprised that in the hushed mass of spectators, at least eight hands went up.

* * *

Ten minutes later, a big map of Chicago's streets and suburbs lay unfolded on the poker table. I sat beside Royce, shoulder to shoulder, as we each laid two fingertips on a tiny planchette. The heart-shaped wedge of oak had a felt bottom, gliding smoothly over the map as our hands went around in languid circles.

"All right," I said, feeling every eye in the room on my back, "I just need to reestablish a link with my spell. If this is working right, the planchette should orient itself at the coin's starting point: right here."

Slowly, tugging along, the planchette pulled our fingertips along a maze of streets and came to a dead stop with the pointer aimed directly at the Bast Club's street.

"Feel that?" I asked Royce. He nodded, eyes wide.

Of course he did. The ideomotor effect—where you attributed your own unconscious muscle movements to an outside force, like a spell or a guiding spirit—could fool just about anybody, especially if you dressed it up with theatrics.

It was even easier if you cheated and gently moved the planchette yourself. I pulled lightly, careful not to give my movements away, pretending to be guided along with Royce as the wedge crawled across the map.

"Here," I said, standing up sharply and pointing to where the planchette stopped. "That's where the coin is, right now. If we get close, I'll be able to sense the exact spot."

We took two cars. I brought Margaux and Caitlin, Royce brought Nadine and two of her thugs, and we converged on an old brick warehouse down on Printers Row.

"It's here, I know it," I said, jogging across a strip of asphalt outside a shuttered loading bay. Royce charged up the back steps, took the measure of a windowless steel door, and spun into a brutal roundhouse kick that buckled metal and tore hinges. A second kick sent the door tumbling with a *slam* as loud as cannon fire, and I followed close behind as he strode over the wreckage.

"And I'm telling you," Damien Ecko said, "I don't have a clue what you're—"

He froze. So did Stanwyck.

They stood in the heart of a cavernous warehouse, shelves laden with coffin-sized packing crates and dusty antiques. Ecko wore latex gloves and a bloodstained butcher's apron over his shirt and tie, but he wasn't carving up a roast: a desiccated corpse lay in a shallow standing tub, resting on a bed of glittering salt. A scattering of tools on a nearby tray looked like a cross between a modern surgical suite and a collection of archaeological relics.

"What is the meaning of this?" Ecko demanded, his gaze flitting from me to Royce.

"I would ask you the same thing," Royce said.

I put my hand to my temple, eyes squeezed shut and brow furrowed, then pointed at Stanwyck.

"There! He has the coin. It's in his left pants pocket."

Stanwyck slowly dipped his hand into his pocket. It came back out with the Judas Coin, the tarnished metal clutched like a proclamation of doom between his trembling fingers.

"This isn't what it looks like," he said, sounding like he didn't even believe himself.

41.

He was right, though. It wasn't what it looked like.

For that, we had to go back earlier in the day, just before we faced off in the Bast Club. Amy and Bentley's double collision, knocking Stanwyck into me, was a classic pickpocket-gang move. Your brain could only process so many inputs at once, so when you were suddenly startled and had people pawing at you from all directions, it was easy for a skilled hand to slip something out of your pocket.

Or slip something into it.

Then I just needed to scare Stanwyck into leaving the tournament early, giving us plenty of time to set him up for the kill. That honor went to Amy, who waited until he left and then phoned him from the club. She'd given him a fake name and said she was calling with an important wheelman job for a heist to go down in a couple of hours. Very urgent, very high-end, very risky. Could she pay three times his usual rate? Of *course* she could.

Given Stanwyck had just lost his shirt and still owed enough gambling debts to get his kneecaps broken twenty times over, he jumped on her offer like a starving man going after a twenty-ounce steak. So she called him back just as we were leaving the club, with the directions to meet his new boss, directions we'd gotten courtesy of Pixie decoding Ecko's location. I figured Stanwyck must have arrived a couple of minutes before we did.

As for my "tracking spell," same deal, thanks to Pixie. It's easy to use magic to find a place when you already have a street address.

"I get it now," I said to Ecko. "I couldn't get my hands on the coin, so you hired this guy to do the job instead. Pretty clever."

"No," Ecko said, glowering as he figured it out. "*No.* You arranged this. You're setting me up."

"Have some dignity," Royce said. He seemed to get bigger as he moved closer, his form subtly shifting in the dimly lit warehouse. "And spare me the protestations. Now, neither of you gentlemen are under my court's authority, so I can't *technically* pass my formal judgment upon you. I think...we'll just call this a double homicide."

"I'm afraid you've forgotten an important rule of magic," Ecko said. He looked angry but not worried, and that worried *me*. Doubly when his lips curled into a smug smile.

"Oh?" Royce asked. "What's that?"

Ecko swept the flat of his hand across the room as an orange, baleful light shone behind his eyes.

"Never strike at a lord of the dead while you stand within his kingdom."

Wood splintered and tore like tissue paper as a leathery fist punched through one of the packing crates by the door. To my left, the lid of a second shipping box fell free, and a corpse wrapped in moldering bandages opened its eyes and pulled itself out. We closed ranks as wood broke and dust flew around us, the air filled with a cacophony of wheezing groans. That and the sound of Ecko's mad laughter as the half-dissected body on his operating table sat up, baring its teeth in a rictus grin.

I couldn't count fast enough. There were fifteen, maybe twenty of the things, trailing ragged strips of linen as they shambled toward us from all sides. Nadine's thugs pulled their guns and moved to defend their mistress, unloading on one of the mummies at point-blank range. The bullets hammered its chest, staggering it backward a step, each impact bursting with puffs of white dust.

Then it grabbed one of the gunmen and tore his jaw off as easily as a child snapping a wishbone, leaving it dangling from raw, red sinew.

As the mutilated man fell to the floor, screeching and clutching his face, Nadine clicked her tongue and snapped her fingers at his partner. "Fail. You. Do better."

He tried, right until a filthy linen-wrapped fist punched straight through his rib cage and tore out his heart.

Caitlin jumped into the fray, flashing a feral grin as she charged one of the risen dead. She spun low, swept its leg out from under it, and stomped her bootheel down on its face with a brittle *crunch*. Royce was right beside her, ducking and weaving like a boxer as he met one of Ecko's creatures punch for bone-snapping punch.

One of the mummies stumbled into Margaux's path, groping for her. I shouted a warning, but she just lashed her hand out and clamped her palm over the creature's face.

"Sit *down!*" she snapped.

The mummy collapsed like a puppet with its strings cut, dead for good. Margaux's hands blazed with hazy, violet-black energy, like a three-dimensional oil slick, as she turned and shot me a look.

"Might have been his kingdom," she said, "but it's *my* house now. This is what I *do*."

"Can you do that to the whole room?"

"Can if"—she paused, stumbling back, ducking as one of the creatures grabbed at her—"if you buy me some breathing room and herd all these things into one spot!"

I looked over at the fallen mummy, lying still in its ragged, ancient linens, and got an idea.

"On it. Cait, Royce, protect Margaux! Nadine, come help me."

While Caitlin and Royce fought through the crowd of animated corpses, getting Margaux between them, I ran over to one of the broken shipping crates. I grabbed the edge of a plank, put my shoe against the side of the crate, and heaved as hard as I could. Slowly, as rusty nails popped and the wood splintered,

I wrenched a sturdy chunk free. The piece was fat and jagged, about as long as a baseball bat and nowhere near as streamlined, but it would have to do.

"Keep 'em off me," I told Nadine and got down on one knee next to the corpse Margaux had taken down. I grabbed the edge of a loose bandage and pulled, peeling it from around the mummy's arm. The linen came away sticky and stiff, clotted with dirt, dead flies, and ancient herbal pastes that smelled like someone had sprinkled incense over a pile of rotting meat.

I wrapped the linen around one end of the plank, tucking it in as best I could. Then, finding a heartbeat of serenity in the midst of madness, I conjured a single, stray spark of magic to my fingertips and flicked it through the air.

The linens ignited like they'd been doused in gasoline, flaring up and leaving a blue spot in my vision as my chunk of wood became a makeshift torch. While Nadine wrestled with one of the mummies, her dress torn at the hem and a cut along one arm oozing black blood, I saw another one closing in behind her. I ran up, waving my torch in its face, and it fell back with a strangled gurgle.

I advanced, relentless, and the mummy lost sight of anything but getting away from me. So did the next one I waved the torch at, slowly herding them toward the far corner of the warehouse. Every muscle in my body wanted to start hitting them with the torch, but I didn't, for the same reason I didn't try to light them up with my magic. In a room filled with old dry wood, linen, and shuffling corpses, the last thing I wanted was to start a full-fledged blaze with all of us trapped inside.

Ecko's creatures didn't know that, though. All they had were animal instincts—and all animals were afraid of fire.

Caitlin got the idea, and she tugged Royce's sleeve. They flanked me, backing my advance and shoving away any stragglers who tried to go around us. As my makeshift torch blazed, the fire devouring the linen and wood, we got the surviving mummies penned in one corner.

A shout in Haitian Creole cracked through the air, carried on a gust of black light. The risen dead collapsed as one, tumbling to the stone floor in a tangle of unmoving limbs and glassy eyes.

I rolled the torch in Ecko's standing tub, snuffing the fire in the mounds of salt. Finally, the warehouse stood in silence.

Margaux, face drenched in sweat, looked like she'd just run a marathon. We all did. Still, she held up her open hand and gave me an expectant look.

"Whose house?"

I slapped my palm against hers, still trying to catch my breath. "Mama's house."

The necromancer was long gone. None of us had seen him slip out in all the chaos. Royce glowered at the carnage and put one hand on his hip.

"Damien Ecko is finished in Chicago. Scratch that—in the Midwest. I'm putting out a kill order to my entire court. Nobody assaults a hound and lives."

"That goes double for us," Caitlin said. "And we'll catch him before you do."

Royce pursed his lips. "That sounds like a wager in the making."

A shrill scream turned our heads. Nadine, pleased as a cat with a cornered mouse, dragged Stanwyck out of hiding by his hair and one bent-back arm. He'd taken refuge behind a jumble of crates during the fight and probably hoped we'd leave without looking for him.

Bad assumption.

"It wasn't me," he cried. "It wasn't me!"

"Do shut up," Royce said as he strode over, digging his hands into Stanwyck's pockets. He plucked out the Judas Coin, holding it up to study it in the dim light.

"I was *cut* in that fight," Nadine said. "Actually *cut*. I want recompense."

"Hmm?" Royce looked over at her. "Such as?"

She gave Stanwyck's hair a vicious tug, making him yelp. "I want this one. I have some aggression to work off."

Royce turned his back on them with a careless shrug. "Fine, fine, long as he suffers, have a ball."

Stanwyck looked my way, tears in his eyes, as Nadine dragged him toward the exit. "Tell them it wasn't me, damn it. I'll do anything you want. Just *tell them it wasn't me!*"

I could hear him screaming as she pulled him out of sight, then suddenly nothing but wet, agonized choking. I didn't know what Nadine had done to shut him up, and I didn't want to.

Bye, Stanwyck, I thought. *I promised Coop I'd send you straight to hell. Looks like you're taking the long, scenic route instead.*

I'd be lying if I said I gave a damn.

Royce flipped the coin through the air. It spun in a glittering arc and landed in my open palm.

"Tournament's over," he said. "Here's your prize. Do me a favor and get out of town before you destroy anything else."

"Always a pleasure," Caitlin said sweetly.

We waited until he and Nadine were long gone. I had one job left, one thing I needed to do before I could put Chicago in the rearview mirror.

It was time to find Coop.

42.

The hallway in the back of the warehouse looked just like it did on the video Ecko had sent me. Cinder-block walls, broken lights, the air cold and thick with the stench of stale piss and decaying flesh. I shone a light into cell after cell, finding nothing but bones and rusted shackles.

Coop was in the one on the end.

He flinched as the light caught his milky-white eyes, throwing up his emaciated arms and scurrying into the corner like a cockroach. I turned off the light and stepped inside.

"Careful," Margaux said. "You never know how they'll react."

"*I* know." I crouched beside him. Touched his arm as gently as I could. "Hey. Hey, Coop. It's okay. I'm here now."

He looked at me. His stitched-together lips twitched, like he was trying to talk, but nothing came out but a faint, ragged whine. It was the sound a beaten dog makes.

"Gonna take you home, buddy. Okay? *Home*."

I wasn't sure, but I thought he was trying to repeat the word. Some part of him still knew what *home* meant.

Caitlin helped me get him on his feet. With a body twisted by rigor mortis and his skin splotched with thick, puddled bruises, he hobbled toward the cell door. We walked him through the warehouse, past the wreckage and the fallen bodies, and out into the light.

Coop stood in the parking lot, his white eyes fixed on the setting sun. Margaux had a brass scalpel in her hand, plucked from Ecko's table on our way out. She had a question in her eyes.

"Do it," I told her.

She murmured something that sounded like a Creole prayer as she stepped in front of Coop, trying not to block his view of the sun. Then she drew the scalpel along his mouth stitches, slicing the surgical thread.

Coop's jaw dropped open and a stream of smoky golden light, like a morning mist, billowed from his throat. It gusted into the air and vanished. His body slumped, nothing left inside to keep it standing. We gently laid it on the asphalt.

I needed to take a walk.

I stood at the edge of the lot, staring up at the cold, cloudy sky. I didn't hear Caitlin coming, but I felt her hand on my back.

"Are you okay?" she asked.

"I'm a long way from okay." I turned to face her. "And right now, the only thing I can think about is tracking down that son of a bitch Ecko and putting a bullet in his head."

Caitlin frowned, imperious. "He assaulted not one, but *two* hounds. A mortal insult twice over. Both our people and Royce's will pursue him relentlessly. On top of that, I'm certain our princes will try to one-up each other in posting a lavish bounty, which the other courts will be eager to claim. It's safe to say that Damien Ecko has just become one of the most wanted men on Earth. All of hell will hunt him."

"Then you get the word out," I told her. "You make sure everybody knows that when they find him, he's *mine*."

She gave me the faintest of smiles.

"I think that can be arranged."

I looked back at Coop's fallen corpse. Margaux crouched over the body, her hand on his chest, giving some kind of last rites.

"Because *that*," I said, the words catching in my throat as my eyes teared up, "that has to be answered for, and, and—"

That was all I had in me. All I could manage as she pulled me into an embrace, letting me bury my face against her breast and holding me tight while my shoulders shook.

* * *

We said our goodbyes in Chicago. Unlike the rest of my crew, I had a detour to make on the way back to Vegas.

I called ahead, getting the names of a few FedEx offices in Austin. I couldn't fly with the Aztec dagger, after all, so I bought a poster tube and filled it with packing peanuts, shrouding the sacrificial knife in bubble wrap and stashing it in the middle. I shipped it next-day air, so it'd be waiting for me to pick it up.

The next flight to Austin wasn't until nearly midnight. I sat in an empty terminal at O'Hare, listening to the droning hum of a floor waxer and watching the occasional bleary-eyed commuter trudge past.

It wasn't right.

The whole situation wasn't right. The job was done, nothing left but to talk to Cameron Drake, hand over the dagger, and collect my money, but it didn't *feel* done. It felt like it was just getting started.

It's Ecko, I told myself. *Loose ends. This isn't over, not by a long shot.*

That wasn't it, though. Maybe it was the Outfit boys and the trouble fixing to land on our doorstep. Or maybe I was just worn out.

I saw Amy coming up the concourse, and I gave her a tired wave. No idea how she'd gotten past security without a ticket, but she'd told me on the phone that it wouldn't be a problem. I dug in my pocket as she approached and held up the Judas Coin.

"Payment for services rendered?" she asked.

I handed her the coin.

She studied it, rubbing her thumb against its face, and nodded curtly. "Transaction complete. A pleasure doing business, Mr. Faust."

"Don't spend it all in one place," I told her.

She'd barely slipped out of sight when a familiar hand brushed my shoulder. I turned in the blue vinyl seat, smiling. "Cait, did you change your fli—"

Nadine dropped into the seat beside me.

"No," she said. "She's already gone back to Nevada. She left you here. With me. You really think she cared enough to ensure you got away safely?"

I didn't have a weapon, didn't even have my deck of cards, thanks to the fight in Angelo Mancuso's limousine. I wondered, as I slid away from her on the seat, how much pull the Night-Blooming Flowers really had over this city. If she murdered a man in a near-empty airport concourse, could they cover it up?

"You're cute when you panic," she said, reading my face. "Don't worry. I'm just here to talk, to give you a present, and to see you on your way. Oh, and I wanted to ask you a question. Did you even notice that you asked me to protect you?"

"What?" I shook my head at her. "When?"

"In Ecko's warehouse. You didn't ask Caitlin to protect you while you made your little torch. You asked me."

"No, you've got that twisted. I wanted Cait to protect *Margaux*, because I didn't trust *you* to do it. I wasn't worried about myself."

"But you did ask. And there you were, a perfect target. In all the confusion, I could have just stepped aside and let the dead men have you. Or killed you myself and blamed it on them."

"Your point being?"

She reached over and took hold of my hand. Her skin was smooth as silk sheets and smelled like jasmine.

"That *I protected you*. Just as you asked."

"So?" I said. "You could have made me ask you, right? Isn't that your whole schtick? Playing with people's heads?"

She chuckled. "Except...I didn't touch you in the warehouse. And no, not just heads. I also play with their bodies. Like Stanwyck's. You know, he told me the most *fascinating* story about a theft gone wrong at Damien Ecko's shop. I started following the evidence, and a very different picture of the last few days' events has begun to emerge."

"Maybe he's lying."

"No one lies in my chambers," she said. "The truth comes out, one drop at a time, in the shape of blood and tears. Do you really think I took him because I wanted someone to play with? I have chattel for that. I wanted to question him personally, away from Royce."

"I thought you two were tight."

"We serve the same prince, but not *all* of our goals coincide," she said. "And it pleases me to protect you still, so I'll not be telling any of this to Prince Malphas's hound. You'll learn to trust me, in time. I'll teach you."

"The only thing I want, right now, is to get on that plane and—what's this?"

She pressed an envelope into my hands. It was small, the size of a wedding invitation, pressed cream paper with a lipstick imprint on the back. Sealed with a kiss.

"My present. See, I know you don't believe Royce when he talks about Caitlin, and you haven't learned to trust me yet, so consider this a bridge between us."

I didn't like the sound of that. My fingers traced the edge of the envelope. I didn't open it.

"Inside," Nadine told me, "you'll find the name and address of a very special person. Caitlin's last lover, *before* she met you. Still alive, if...not doing very well, and more importantly, not connected to our court in any way whatsoever. You'll be able to verify that for yourself. And he will verify the most important fact of all."

Nadine leaned close, her hand squeezing mine as she whispered in my ear.

"Caitlin is using you. She will betray you. And she will most likely murder you. It's only a matter of time."

Her lips brushed my cheek. My skin tingled. Electrified.

Numb. Then she stood up and stretched, stifling a yawn with the back of her hand.

"That's all," she said. "Have a safe flight, lover. And don't worry about Stanwyck. With no tongue and no hands...who's he going to tell?"

I stared at that envelope for a long time. Barely hearing the flight announcements or noticing anyone around me. My whole world fit into a neat rectangle of cream-colored paper and the imprint of Nadine's lipstick.

It wasn't an envelope. It was a hand grenade, primed and ready to explode, and she'd just tossed it into my lap. Should I throw it away? Open it and follow the breadcrumbs, knowing it could be another mind game? Tell Caitlin everything and show it to her to see how she'd react? Three options. Any or all of them could be a trap waiting to close over my head. I couldn't outfox Nadine's game, because I wasn't sure what her game *was*.

Tired, aching from my bruises, and watching the clock on the flight-departures board creep toward midnight, I knew I only had one option. The only choice that wouldn't change everything. The only choice that would let me pretend none of this had ever happened.

I didn't open it.

I didn't throw it away either.

It sat nestled in my hip pocket, a viper sleeping in the dark. It would keep. For now, it would keep.

43.

I slept on the plane, suffering through fitful dreams of storms and turbulence, crashing and burning. I woke up in Texas.

I grabbed some breakfast at a cheap diner and loitered outside the FedEx for a few hours. My package eventually showed up, just in time for Cameron Drake's limousine to meet me at the curb.

"You have the object?" Ms. Fleiss asked through a rolled-down back window, her eyes shaded behind dark glasses.

I tapped the poster tube. "I'll deliver this in person, if you don't mind. And collect my money."

The limo door clicked. She slid over on the backseat.

They'd tightened up security since my last visit. More two-man patrols walked the grounds of Eastern Pines, rifles slung over their uniformed shoulders, and the limo had to wait at the outer gate while security guards checked the car's underbelly with a mirror on a telescoping rod.

"Expecting trouble?" I asked Fleiss.

"Preparing for an arrival. We have a very special guest coming to visit." She paused. "Not you."

"Right," I said, drumming my fingers on the cardboard tube. "I'm just the errand boy."

Pachenko waited for us on the front steps of the plantation house, silent and surly. The building hadn't lost any of its malevolent glow. If anything, it was worse than before—like some tumor in its bowels had swelled from neglect. Then again, I had my senses turned up to eleven, ears perked and watching for trouble.

In my experience, the handoff was the most dangerous part of a deal. If your client decided to pay you in bullets instead of cash, this was where it would go down.

Cameron Drake sat behind his desk, remote control in one hand and a half-drained bottle of Southern Comfort in the other, rocking back and forth in his tall-backed chair as he watched ESPN on all twelve television sets. Pachenko followed Fleiss and me inside, looming in the office doorway. I turned so I could keep all three of them in sight, but Cameron wasn't the one I was worried about.

I uncapped the poster tube and shook it out on his desk, foam peanuts spilling across the polished wood and onto the cash-green carpet. Then the dagger slid free, wrapped in a blanket of pale gauze.

Cameron unwrapped the dagger and held it gingerly, like he was afraid it would bite him. "This is it," he said, then looked at Fleiss. "Right?"

She plucked the blade from his hand and studied it from end to end like an appraiser, though she still hadn't taken off her dark glasses.

"Well done. Mr. Pachenko, please give Mr. Faust his reward."

Pachenko's hand sat on his shoulder holster. Too close. I'd already moved up on Fleiss, making a backup plan in slow motion. *One. Snatch the knife. Two. Stab Fleiss in the throat. Push her toward Pachenko. Three, roll over desk, grab Cameron, use him as a shield—*

Instead of a gun, he whipped out an envelope. A big glossy plastic mailer, half sealed. Rubber-banded stacks of bills peeked out at me through the flap.

"Thirty thousand dollars," Fleiss said. "As agreed."

"You can count it if you want," Cameron said so quickly he stumbled over the words.

I waved a hand, taking in the room.

"That's okay." I finished sealing the envelope and tucked it under my arm. "You wouldn't stiff me. I know where you live."

"I hope we didn't put you to any trouble," Fleiss said.

"Nah. Walk in the park."

Cameron got up, wobbly-legged, and walked around the desk. He thrust out his hand.

"Thanks for coming," he said. His eyes said something different. They darted left and right like a crazed ferret, the alcohol not strong enough to quell his fear.

When I shook his hand, I felt more than skin. A tiny square of folded paper rested in his palm. I snaked it into mine and pinned it with my thumb.

"We'll see that Mr. Faust gets home safely," Fleiss told Cameron.

I wasn't out of the woods yet. Considering Cameron wasn't the shot-caller around here—and didn't know about the first time Fleiss and Pachenko nearly killed me as part of the "job interview"—the payoff could have been a charade to keep him happy. Lead me off the ranch, gun me down, and take the cash back? It wasn't out of the realm of possibility.

Still, once we were back in the limo, the way Fleiss was talking had me thinking I was almost free and clear.

"We expect your continued discretion," she said. "Frankly, we expect you to forget that you ever met Cameron Drake. Given his high profile, any public association with...if you'll forgive me for saying so, common criminals would be ruinous for his reputation."

I wasn't offended. I held the envelope on my lap and rapped it with my knuckles. "This buys you all the discretion in the world. I won't tell any tales if you won't."

Cameron's Gulfstream sat fueled up and ready to fly. Fleiss walked me to the boarding stairs, then paused.

"I won't be accompanying you, but the crew has orders to take you directly to Henderson Executive Airport. Do not return to Eastern Pines. Do not attempt to communicate with Cameron Drake. We will not meet again."

"Pleasure working with you, too," I said, tipping an imaginary hat as I strolled up the stairs and onto the jet.

No painter's tarp or death traps this time, just plush white leather seats and a couple of wall screens with satellite TV. *I could get used to traveling like this*, I thought as I buckled in. The crew didn't waste any time; they closed the hatch behind me and fired up the engines.

As we taxied down the runway, I finally had a moment of privacy. I unfolded the tiny square of torn notebook paper that Cameron had slipped me in our parting handshake. It bore a single line of text in a shaky ballpoint scrawl.

please help i am being held prisoner

The Gulfstream lifted off, roaring into a blue Texas sky.

* * *

I turned on the satellite television, tuning it to a sitcom I could ignore while I planned my next move.

On the surface, this whole thing played like a home-invasion writ large. Cameron hits it big in the lottery; Fleiss and Pachenko show up on his doorstep with a gun. As long as they kept him isolated and afraid, they could live large on his winnings and nobody would be the wiser.

That was the surface level. Scratch a little deeper, and the weirdness set in. Like the raw malevolence in the underbelly of Cameron's house, setting my teeth on edge. Or how my psychic tendrils slid off Fleiss like she was made of glass. I didn't have the whole picture, and if I was going to get Cameron out of there, I needed one.

Was I going to, though? Was it even my problem?

No, I thought, *not my problem. My payday*. Cameron Drake was worth millions. Pulling off a hostage rescue—well, it wasn't my usual line of work, but it had to be good for more than a thank-you.

I figured I'd get the crew together and we could talk it out. This wasn't going to be a one-man job. It could wait until I'd settled the beef between Jennifer and Nicky, though. With the Outfit on our doorstep, keeping our home turf safe had to be my top priority.

The Gulfstream touched down at Henderson Executive an

hour before sunset. I'd never been so happy to feel the arid Nevada heat, wrapping me in its desert embrace as I strolled down the boarding stairs.

I felt like I'd been gone forever, but here I was in Vegas. Home at last. I thought I'd walk the Strip tonight, get lost in the crowds and the neon and the money. My dirty little paradise.

With Caitlin? Yeah. With Caitlin. Nadine's envelope still sat sealed in my pocket, but I didn't have to deal with it tonight. Tonight, I just needed to look in my lover's eyes. Then I'd know everything was all right. Trouble could wait.

Except it wouldn't.

I took a cab to the parking garage at McCarran Airport to pick up my car. We were two minutes away when my phone started to buzz. Jennifer.

"Hey," I said, "I was just about to call you. I'm back in town, heading to—"

"We got a problem, sugar. I need you, *right now*."

I sat forward on the cracked vinyl seat. Jennifer might get furious at the drop of a hat, but she hardly ever got worried. This was worry.

"What's going on?"

"Just got a call from one of my guys. Nicky thinks he's talking to the feds, and he sent the twins after him. One of *my guys*, Danny. He's hiding, but—"

"But the twins are like bloodhounds, I know. Where is he now?"

"At his house, barricaded inside. I'm on my way—will you meet me there?"

The cab pulled up curbside at McCarran. I tossed the driver a twenty and didn't wait for change.

"On my way," I said.

Jennifer gave me an address, and I ran for the parking garage. For one dizzying moment I thought the Barracuda was gone, that Agent Black had used some pretense to have it impounded, but I'd just forgotten what aisle I'd parked in. There it was, sleek and cold, witch-eye still fixed to the back bumper. I tore Black's tracking spell free with a burst of crude magic, tossing the spectral eye to the pavement. I didn't have time for subtlety.

Then I opened the steel lockbox in my trunk and grabbed my Taurus Judge Magnum.

The last thing I wanted was to get into a gunfight with Juliette and Justine. As far as I was concerned, the only way tonight ended with a win was if everybody went home in one piece. That said, twenty-nine ounces of steel in your hand had a way of stopping a fight before it started, if you used it right. At the very least, it commanded attention.

I hit the road with one hand on the wheel and one eye on the speedometer, cruising at a steady nine miles over the speed limit and no higher. Catching police attention right now would steal time I didn't have. The twins weren't just bloodhounds—they were a two-woman wrecking crew when it came to dealing with anyone Nicky perceived as a threat.

Whatever kind of barricade this guy had put up, it wouldn't be enough to save him.

As I swung into the driveway of his seedy tract house, with a rusted-out Nova in the driveway and a yard full of scraggly weeds, I knew I was too late. The front door hung wide open, the lock blown out like someone had shotgunned it. I grabbed my piece and ran for the door, keeping low, watching the curtained windows for movement.

The smell of cannabis almost knocked me flat. The house was a grow op. The living room to my left and the dining room through a big open arch on my right were filled with hydroponic beds and grow lights, shining harsh yellow down on a field of marijuana plants as tall as desert cacti.

I froze in the doorway, ears perked, listening hard. Nothing but the hum of the lights and the soft gurgle of flowing water. Keeping my pistol level, padding across the scuffed-up floorboards and wincing at every stray creak, I eased my way up a stub of a hall and around an open doorway.

The man hadn't been dead long. He sat slumped in a chair, his face a blasted-in ruin.

I touched his neck. Still warm.

That was it then. Up until now, Nicky and Jennifer had just blustered, daring each other to cross the line. Should have known Nicky would pull the trigger first. Taking out one of Jennifer's people was going too far. Even if this guy had really turned rat, he was Jennifer's problem to deal with.

There'd be no sitting them down to talk it out, not now.

Still, the scene didn't sit right with me. This was a blitz hit, in and out with lightning precision. Since when did the twins kill like that? They liked to play with their food, and Nicky had a couple of kill houses set up just for that flavor of fun. They could have grabbed this guy, tossed him in a trunk, driven him to the edge of nowhere, and taken their time doing him in. He hadn't even been handcuffed. It was one shot, one kill, probably taking him by surprise.

Okay, I thought, *call Jennifer and tell her to stand down, then get hold of Nicky, find out exactly what—*

The squawk of a siren made every muscle in my body go tense. Not an approaching siren. One from a car parked right outside.

"*We have the building surrounded,*" shouted a voice through an electronic bullhorn. "*Come out through the front door, slowly, with your hands in clear view.*"

44.

I crouched low, scurrying like a trapped rat to the back of the house. Red and blue lights strobed through the shades of the kitchen window, and silhouettes stood sentry at the backyard fence. Front, same deal. They weren't bluffing.

"*Leave the house now*," the voice on the bullhorn bellowed. "*Or we will be forced to take action*."

No last-minute escape. Not this time.

There were only two ways I could play this: their way, or suicide by cop. I looked down at the gun in my hand and tossed it to the floor.

A couple of uniforms blitzed me before I'd taken two steps out the front door, wrestling me to the pavement and wrenching my hands behind my back. They asked if I was alone in the house. They asked if I had any accomplices. They asked why I did it.

I maintained my right to remain silent.

I ended up in an interrogation room, with my pockets empty and my wrists shackled to a stainless-steel table. I didn't know how long I sat there, waiting in silence. No clocks on the walls. Eventually a couple of plainclothes detectives decided to test my will.

Around the seventy-eighth time in a row I answered their questions with, "I want my lawyer," they gave up and left me alone to stew a little longer.

When they came back, wheeling in a cart with a cheap television set and a DVD player, they had a guest. Harmony Black.

"Congratulations," she said, pulling back a chair and dropping a tan folder onto the table. "You've been upgraded. Now you're a *federal* prisoner."

"Which doesn't change my right to legal representation. Oh, hey fellas, I see you joined the AV Club. That's good, extracurriculars are really important. Maybe you'll get a decent job someday."

Harmony sent the detectives away. It was just me, her, and the evidence.

"Konstantin Floros," she said. "Greek expat, here on an expired work visa. Known associate of your friend Jennifer Juniper. At least, I thought she was your friend. I guess you picked sides, huh?"

"Jennifer called me. She was worried about the guy and asked me to check on him. I saw the door hanging open, went inside, and found his body. Next thing I know, I'm center stage at a police convention."

"You 'found' his body. And it's a sheer coincidence that he was murdered with a single .45 Colt round to the face—the exact kind of ammunition in a Taurus Judge Magnum we found at the scene. A gun with your fingerprints all over it and a registration—a fake one, as it turns out—in your glove compartment."

I snapped my fingers. "There you go. A gun that hadn't been fired. Hell, they gave my hands a GSR test when they ran me in here. Check it out. I'm clean. I *couldn't* have killed the guy."

She opened the folder and spun it around so I could read the top page.

Residue Test Results: Confirmed. 2000+ particle count w/spheroid GSR.

"That's *bullshit*," I snapped, reading it twice. "I haven't fired a gun in weeks."

"Really?" Harmony said, arching an eyebrow. "That's funny, because according to this, you sure did. And your gun *had* been fired. Recently. Just one round. We both know where that round ended up, don't we? Then we checked your trunk. Thirty thousand dollars in cash, in an envelope—"

"I can explain that."

"—and we also found these."

She turned the page and showed me a stack of surveillance photographs. Snaps of Konstantin Floros and his house from all angles.

"Did Nicky Agnelli give you these pictures when he hired you to kill Floros?"

"You found it in my trunk," I echoed flatly. "Goddamnit, Harmony, this is a setup. This whole thing is a setup."

She leaned back and smiled.

"Damn, I *hoped* you'd say that. Because then I'd get to see the look on your face when I show you this."

She turned on the television.

"Floros," she said, fast-forwarding a grainy black-and-white camera feed, "was a little paranoid about security. Happens a lot with these narcotics types. His whole house was wired."

When she hit play, Floros was sitting in the chair he died in, flailing his arms as he begged for his life.

I was the one holding him at gunpoint.

"I didn't *say* anything," Floros whined. "I wouldn't *do* that!"

"Nicky Agnelli says otherwise," I told him. "Know what else he says?"

"Don't, just don—"

"Bye-bye," I said and shot him in the face.

My duplicate paused, just for a heartbeat, and looked toward the camera. Harmony froze the frame.

"Agent Black," I said slowly, "you need to find out if the evidence tech who did my GSR test, and whoever brought my gun in, is still in the building. But I don't think you'll find them, because they're already dead. They've been replaced."

She shook her head at me. "What are you even—"

"Listen. Very. Carefully," I said, leaning close and whispering so the security camera wouldn't pick up my voice. "I'm being framed. There is a rakshasa, a shape-shifting hunger spirit, working for the Chicago mob. The only way this fucking GSR test came back positive is if someone tampered with it. *He* tampered with it, after making it look like I shot Floros. This thing is in the precinct, right here, right now."

Harmony slammed her folder shut and scraped her chair back.

"It's always something, isn't it, Faust? You've always got a story. Well, I've got one for you. It's called 'The Boy Who Cried Wolf.' And I'm done listening."

As she walked to the door, taking my last shred of hope with her, there was only one thing I could do.

Laugh.

Just a giggle, at first, but then I doubled over in my chair, cackling on the edge of hysteria.

"What's so funny?" she said, looking back at me.

I got it under control, but I couldn't wipe the grin from my face.

"All this time," I said, "all this effort...and you finally busted me for the one crime I *didn't* commit. That's...that's some top-notch police work, Agent Black. Kudos, really, kudos."

"A jury will decide what you did or didn't do," she told me. "My job is done here."

I slouched back in my chair. My manacles rattled.

"Not by a long shot, Agent. Not by a long shot. There's a war coming. Right here, in the streets of Las Vegas, and the blood is gonna spill. This wasn't the opening salvo. This was just a hello and a handshake. The Outfit is letting us know they're ready for battle. I hope you're ready, too."

She opened the interrogation-room door, lingering on the threshold. She looked back at me.

"A war, huh? Well, you won't be around to see it. Premeditated murder, conspiracy, racketeering...you're looking at life behind bars. And that's my wish for you, Daniel Faust. A long, *long* healthy life."

The door clicked shut behind her, leaving me alone with my thoughts and my nightmares.

It was funny, though, feeling your back pressed to the wall had a wonderful way of clearing up your priorities. You realized, very fast, what really mattered most in life.

Right now, what mattered most was breathing free air. No matter what I had to do, no matter how many bodies I had to climb over, *nobody* was going to keep me in a cage. One way or another, I was getting out of here.

My second priority? It came to me as I pictured Angelo Mancuso's smirking face. Him, his pet rakshasa, his entire crew of gangsters, and Damien Ecko too. It was so simple I could sum it up in a single word.

Payback.

Epilogue

Back in the late nineties, Eastern Pines Ranch had played host to a country-western star for a few years. He'd made a few renovations throughout the grounds, not the least being the addition of a small recording studio in the basement.

The new owners had made some renovations, too.

In what used to be the old "live room" for the band, behind a wall of glass, Cameron Drake danced barefoot on a sheet of polished metal. It was a strange, shuffling hop, and his brow scrunched in concentration as he mouthed every memorized step. *Left to right to heel to—*

He screamed as a torrent of electricity flooded through the metal sheet, sending him crashing to the ground in a twitching heap. A thin trickle of blood leaked from his nose.

Out in the mixing booth, on the other side of the glass, Fleiss watched impassively behind a bank of modified controls. She clicked on the intercom and leaned toward a standing microphone. Her voice echoed through the studio.

"No. Two steps left, not one. Begin again."

To her side, a fat, leather-bound book lay open on the console, thick with dense calligraphy. She glanced toward it, then again a moment later, as if she expected to see something different.

"Why?" Cameron asked, his voice weak. "Why are you doing this to me?"

"Because you bought the winning ticket."

"You keep saying that, but it's not an *answer*."

"The answer," Fleiss said, "will give you no comfort."

"*Please*."

Fleiss sighed, curling her lip. "*Ordo ad chaos*."

Cameron pushed himself up to his knees, staring through the glass.

"What? I don't even know what that—"

"From order, chaos. The subjugation and corruption of old societal infrastructures in order to further our aims. A work of quantum magic—a Great Work—that has literally never been attempted and never will be again."

"I…I don't understand," he said, shoulders sagging.

"I told you that you wouldn't."

Fleiss glanced over at the book, her exasperation fading into a faint smile. She traced her fingertip over the spidery text.

The Year King: I…I don't understand.

Mater Tantibus: I told you that you wouldn't.

"We must all play our part," Fleiss said into the microphone. "And you must learn your part of the ritual, flawlessly. Now stand up and begin. Or I'll activate the floor again."

As Drake pushed himself to his feet, Fleiss turned the page. A woodcut caught her eye: the image of a blank-faced man, dragged backward in chains by a pair of towering demons.

Her cell phone rang.

"Yes?"

"Dear one," the Smile's syrupy voice oozed over the line. "Was the knife retrieved as I requested?"

Fleiss sat bolt upright, clutching the phone as her eyes went wide.

"Flawlessly, my lord. It is an honor to serve you."

"Yes. I know. And Faust?"

She glanced at the book.

"I'm watching to see. There's always a chance of rejection, but we did our best to contaminate his—"

The breath caught in her throat. A pinpoint of flame rose from the brittle page, tracing its way across the woodcut. It vanished, snuffed out, but now the picture was different.

Now, the man in chains had the face of Daniel Faust.

Act Five, Scene One, read the text beneath the image. *The Thief is taken away to face torment and death at the hands of the False Warden.*

"The Play has spoken, my lord." Fleiss's fingers trembled as she touched the book. "Faust has been absorbed into the pattern. He belongs to us now."

Afterword

There's always more trouble to go around, isn't there? While the Enclave Job storyline wrapped up in *The Living End*, now we stand on the threshold of the Battle of Las Vegas. Daniel will be along shortly, just as soon as he deals with that little incarceration problem. And as for the shadowy man with the Cheshire smile, well...you'll see.

Providing more questions than answers is part and parcel of a new story arc. All I can do is assure you that yes, there is a road map. I have a serious dislike for stories where the creators don't know the answers to any of their own mysteries and make it all up as they go along (looking at *you*, X-Files, Battlestar Galactica and Lost), and honestly one of my biggest kicks is setting up little bits of plot that pay off much further down the line. As a reader, I love that "so *that's* what that was all about!" feeling of revelation when it's done well, so as a writer I try to deliver the same when I can.

Of course, I don't do it alone. Thanks as always to my awesome team: Kira Rubenthaler on editing (any good bits are hers, any lingering mistakes are mine), James T. Egan on cover design (I am not worthy), and Maggie Faid on PR (and keeping me on-task, never an easy feat).

Want to get the advance scoop on new books and projects? Head over to www.craigschaeferbooks.com and hop on my mailing list. You can also reach me on Facebook at facebook.com/CraigSchaeferBooks, on Twitter at @craig_schaefer, or just email me directly at craig@craigschaeferbooks.com. Always happy to hear from my readers. Even if I screwed something up. Which I probably did.

One last thing! If you liked the book (which I hope you did!), would you mind taking a minute and posting a short review wherever you purchased it? Reviews are a huge help in spreading word of mouth and attracting new readers to the series, and the more readers I have, the more books I can write. See? Everybody wins.

Meanwhile, stay braced for the next installment, in which Daniel swears off his criminal ways for good and quietly does his time behind bars, realizing he must pay his debt to society.

Just kidding.

Made in the USA
Lexington, KY
09 November 2015